DIVINE AMBROSIA

A REVERSE HAREM ROMANCE

VIVIENNE SAVAGE

*E*sme had a month of school to endure before the semester let out for winter break. She would have sold her soul to be anywhere else, but fate was the kind of asshole that put a girl in the last remaining open seat of a bustling lecture hall next to her douchebag ex-boyfriend and his side chick.

Fate sucked.

While twirling a lock of black hair around her index finger, Esme forced her gaze forward and tuned them out. Daniel tucked a note into Shelly's second-skin jeans, like he was a twelve-year-old asking his crush to circle "yes" or "no" if she liked him. Who the hell passed notes still in college unless they were trying to cheat on an exam?

People with common sense sent texts written beneath their desk if they didn't want to be seen, but given the way they were behaving, they wanted to be seen. The oblivious art history professor was too preoccupied with gushing about Rembrandt to chide them for immature behavior.

He was way too happy to at least have a few students hanging on to his every word, accustomed to jocks like Daniel and his friends enrolling in the course for an easy A.

Esme rolled her eyes and jumped out of her seat the moment the dismissal bell tolled over the system.

"Esme, wait up!" Marie called out.

Esme glanced over a shoulder, seeing Marie pushing her way through the exodus of students spilling into the dull gray corridor and Daniel not too far from her. He was standing beside the door with an arm around Shelly's waist, his green eyes lit with a mischievous light.

College had changed him from the boy she'd dated since junior year of high school. Hanging out with the cool kids and becoming the star of the football team had enlarged his ego to epic blimp proportions and changed her former sweetheart into... a prime douche nozzle.

Not worth my time.

Marie slipped alongside her and brushed in close, hugging her laptop against her chest with one arm and unfastening her bag with her free hand. She lowered her voice to a low whisper. "Are you okay?"

"Yeah. Fine. Nothing I haven't seen before."

"You should have swapped chairs with me. I swear, I tried to save your usual seat, but this dickhead muscle brain wouldn't move out of it."

When Esme had first entered a couple minutes late for class, she'd been startled to see one of Daniel's football pals occupying her usual seat beside Marie. Then she'd understood what was happening when she realized the only empty space was right beside her ex-boyfriend.

Esme scowled. "That was Chad. He's one of Daniel's buddies. Anyway, taking your seat would have given them the satisfaction of winning. They wanted a reaction from me. I chose not to give them one. I hope they both fail the upcoming test since it didn't look like either of them took a damned note all hour."

Until about a week after the start of semester, Shelly had been part of their close inner circle and a friend they'd known throughout high school. And then she'd been let go from Memory Lane, the antique shop where they both worked as sales associates. The owner, a sweet older lady, hadn't approved of Shelly's tendency to flirt with the customers like she was searching for her next rich sugar daddy—which she was. Shelly had confided in Esme, admitting to going out on dates with two older, *married* clients who often popped in.

Esme had nothing to do with Mrs. Robinson letting her go, but Shelly was positive she'd tattled on her. The truth was that their boss's son saw them out together at a high-class restaurant and put two and two together on his own after speaking to a few of their frequent buyers.

"Man. She needs to get over herself and this vendetta she has against you. If she hadn't been using Memory Lane as her own personal escort service, she'd still have a job. Instead, she has broke-ass Daniel and a bunch of regrets."

A few chortles snuck out of Esme. "Yeah. I guess so."

The world beyond the university's art building spanned before them in shades of dirty gray—a cloudy, sunless sky above miles of snow and filthy slush. Living less than two miles away from campus meant they walked to and from school on most days, braving the snow-encrusted grounds when they could tolerate the unforgiving mountain wind.

Esme shivered when they reached the street corner and a gust of wind cut through her sweatshirt and coat, both garments as useful as tissue paper.

"Why did we have to enroll in a university in the mountains? Isn't perpetual warm weather the whole point of living in California?" Esme demanded.

"*You* enrolled in U of A because your granny taught here and the Internet told you it had one of the most affordable art programs in the state. *I* enrolled in it because I was a dumbass who had to follow you."

"Point."

They made a left turn off Main Street after passing Old Ashfall's village center, the hub of activity where a stretch of cozy hotels placed tourists near the action.

Most of the town's architecture hadn't changed since it was founded in the 1800s. Instead, the greater city of Ashfall Springs had sprung up beside it, though most older residents wanted nothing to do with big box stores and preferred the quaint and cozy feel of their little community.

Neither did Esme. She loved living in Old Ashfall. The whole town reminded her of something designed for a Viking movie or her favorite video game, with a classy veneer of sophistication. Almost every building had been built using heavy lumber and stone, but they had large windows as well, pairing delicacy with strength. During the warmer months, visitors enjoyed carefully tended flower beds and landscaped miniparks. Once November arrived, the entire area of Old Ashfall became a festive wonderland. The air perpetually smelled like Christmas, no matter the season.

A tingle danced over the nape of Esme's neck, and she shivered again before glancing to the left and right, heart slamming in her chest. Her pulse raced without any apparent reason, reminding her of when she'd been ill a year ago and taken a steroid prescription for the sinus infection. This pounded and raised the fine hairs on her arms beneath her jacket and sweatshirt, filling her with unexplainable fear.

She reached out and grasped Marie by the arm, clutching her tight and burying her fingers into her friend's bicep. To her left, at the mouth of a narrow alley between two souvenir shops, a dark shadow flit by and disappeared beyond her sight.

"What's wrong? Girl, you're suddenly gray as a ghost. Are you okay?"

"I don't know. I don't know—it's like, there's something wrong and..."

God, she was shaking so hard concerned pedestrians slowed down to watch them in passing, and a nice old man asked if she was okay. Her whole body was hot, scorching, like she'd been in a sauna, and sweat beaded across her brow despite the icy nineteen degrees.

"Do you need me to get anyone?" Marie asked, gripping her by the shoulders.

"N-no. It's passing, I think."

The sensation cooled, her heart slowed, and the breaths rapidly cycling in and out of her lungs diminished to a peaceful rhythm. She wanted to sag into a recliner and hug her favorite pillow, her legs so weak she could barely stand.

Marie guided her into a chocolatier and settled her at a small table for two before approaching the counter. She returned a few minutes later with a few of Esme's favorite truffles, sweet milk chocolate with an Irish cream center, strawberry cheesecake wrapped in dark chocolate, and turtle fudge.

Esme couldn't savor them. Couldn't really enjoy them. They were unsatisfying, cool and buttery chalk in her mouth. Marie even brought her a tasteless root beer float, and then she crouched beside her and set a hand on Esme's shoulder.

"What happened back there? I thought sugar would help, but you still look *awful*."

Cupping the float between both of her hands, Esme stared at her lap and shook her head. "I don't know. I felt... like something awful was going to happen. Like everything in the world that could ever terrify me was there all at once. Like waking up from a nightmare at three in the morning, your heart about to burst from your chest, but hell if you remember the dream."

Marie nibbled her lower lip. "Maybe it was a panic attack. I mean, those things can happen to anyone. You're under strain, today was a shit day, and you're burning the candle from both ends with preparing for finals on top of putting together this enormous fundraiser. Honestly, you're doing the work of two different people. You're doing decor, notifying the media, *and* contacting an assload of donors."

Esme dragged in a breath, filling her lungs with cold air. "Technically the work of three different people."

"I'll give you a hand, okay? I know I didn't sign up for any preparation stuff, but if it's got you freaking out like this, I'll do whatever I can to take some of the load off."

Esme nodded.

"C'mon, let's get you home. You can tell me about that wild dream you had last night while we walk."

"What makes you think I had one?" Esme asked. She shouldered her bag and followed Marie outside into the cold. The oppressive feeling of terror had lifted.

"Um, 'cause you could have woke the entire neighborhood."

"Ugh, this is embarrassing."

Marie only grinned and nudged her with an elbow. "Hey, they say you're not really besties until you've heard each other's freaky 2 a.m. sex dreams. C'mon, I never have hot dreams anymore, so I gotta live vicariously through yours."

"It was nothing. I don't recall much more than something about missing a shoe. Then a hot guy turned up with it. Funny thing is, I can't recall his face. I just remember dark and curly hair. Brown eyes, I think. Like honey."

"So... Cinderella with a mysterious hottie. That's new."

A soft laugh bubbled up, and she shook her head. "No glass slipper, sorry. But thanks for distracting me."

"Anytime, girl. I still wanna hear about the dream sex, though."

Ten minutes in the blustery cold delivered them to a cozy neighborhood a half mile from the main tourist strip. Most of the brick homes were single-story houses with single-car garages and little fences. Their flirtatious older neighbor to the left was shoveling the sidewalk. He waved, glasses fogged above his rosy cheeks and red nose.

"Hi, girls! Enjoying this weather?"

"Oh yeah, it's just fine, Mr. Keene," Marie said, rolling her eyes.

Esme forced a weak laugh and glanced back at their too-friendly neighbor. She froze.

An enormous man in a gray sweatshirt stood beside one of the houses farther down the road, face concealed in the shadows of his hood though he was staring at her. Had to be staring at *her*. A scream rose in her throat—she grasped Marie, tearing at her hand.

"What? What's wrong? Is it another panic attack?"

"No, there's a—" A nothing. A big nothing. Just a gray trash can beside the same house, nothing ominous about it. "I swear, I thought I saw someone watching us."

"Yeah? Maybe it was one of our crazy neighbors, or a tourist out for a stroll."

"In this weather?" Esme's shoulders sagged.

"Is everything all right, girls?" Mr. Keene called. He leaned against his shovel, exertion moving his chest.

"Everything is fine, Mr. Keene, thank you," Marie called back to him before hustling Esme up the drive and to their porch. In a quieter voice, she murmured, "What won't tourists do in this weather? They wander up and down the streets all day fussing about the architecture and how nice it would be to move here. And don't forget the renters."

Ever since the neighbors to the other side had listed their two-bedroom cottage on a hospitality site for rental, they were flooded by a stream of strangers coming out to visit historic Old Ashfall.

Her parents had wanted to list her grandmother's house in a similar way until Esme had convinced them it would be more trouble than it was worth to have random strangers in and out every other night. They already had enough trouble with the long-term tenants in their other property.

Marie punched in the security code for the doorknob, and Esme's Scentsy warmer greeted them with a rush of cinnamon and apples, the aroma of dessert wafting from her bedroom. They dropped their bags by the door and flicked on the lights, casting a cheery glow over the cobalt carpet and chocolate-brown sofa.

Until about four years ago, the house had belonged to her grandmother, and it still bore traces of her, including an antique mirror on the wall, the old piano Esme couldn't play, but had begged her parents not to sell, and her grandmother's china cabinet, still filled with those beautiful dishes Grandma had protected her entire life but never used except for holidays.

Esme kicked off her winter boots and tossed her coat onto the rack.

"You feeling better, girl?"

"I'm feeling like I can eat a whole pizza by myself."

"Then I'll order pizza and make some boozy hot cocoa, and you lay out this fundraiser stuff. I'm totally down for convincing some rich people to cough up some money."

Every year, the University of Ashfall's art department sponsored a fundraiser for the children's wing at the local hospital. On top of displaying the various projects college students worked on during the year, they also highlighted artwork from the elementary, middle, and high school. Local businesses donated items for the silent auction, but only after someone cajoled them into volunteering.

Esme unpacked her MacBook and removed several folders, some of them filled with flyers she wanted to post around Ashfall and drive out to high-traffic shops in Las Verdes nearby. She flipped open the manila folder containing contact details for previous years' donors and a sheet with suggested individuals for this year. She'd highlighted several, but the name at the top had no e-mail or phone number. Even though he lived in the mountains at the outskirts of town, he was a figurative ghost who no one ever saw. His work sold online for hundreds of thousands, sometimes millions.

Alexander Smith, had become California's wealthiest artist and blacksmith, a billionaire hermit with work frequently showcased in the homes of Hollywood's rich and famous. She'd once watched an episode of some home makeover show where a rich basketball player placed one of the artist's million-dollar sculptures in his living room.

Esme tapped the name and grinned. "If I can get you

to donate, that's medical care for dozens of kids. I just need to figure out how to find you."

———

ALEX HURRIED OUT OF THE MORTAL REALM AND INTO THE In-Between, a foggy zone where time stopped or, at the very least, slowed down for traveling gods and supernatural creatures. If he'd been recognized, it may have put their entire plan in jeopardy.

Though he was positive she had no recollection of him from her past existence, it wasn't worth the risk. He watched her a while longer, standing close enough to the veil to see mortal life unfold at normal speed, but distant enough to go unseen.

The moment Alex turned to go home, Luke appeared in a blur of motion. "Pushing it a little close, aren't you, big guy? I thought we all agreed to keep at a distance, or at the very least, to the In-Between until it's time to start making contact with her."

Alex shook his head. "I'm not breaking my part of the bargain, shrimp. Something was back there in the mortal realm. I crossed over to find it, but it got away from me."

"Ah." The younger god put both hands in his pockets and glanced away. "Anyway, I wasn't trying to chastise. I actually came to find you for a reason."

"What do you want?"

"Other big guy wondered if you wanted to kick back tonight. You know, actually come out of your hidey hole and do some shit besides sculpt titties in your mancave."

Alex scowled. "I do more than that."

"Sure, old man. Sure. Anyway, you coming or not? He's got beers and pizza all set up."

"Yeah, I'm in. Tell him I'm on the way. But I'm bringing my own drinks. That cheap swill you two prefer tastes like watered-down piss."

Luke whisked off. Alex gave a final look toward the house before he turned away and forged down the path.

2

Only the crazy students who loved the snow bothered hanging around outside between classes once winter hit and the campus became an ivory wonderland. Esme had been that student to take an unfortunate spill last winter, feet losing traction on the ice and sending her down four steps to the sidewalk.

Her tailbone had been tender for weeks. Nowadays, she spent as little time outside as possible until the groundskeepers could shovel away the trampled snow. There was a storm going on now, ferocious winds whipping away great white clouds across the school grounds, and while it was beautiful to watch, no one could have paid her to go out there yet.

From the serene study room of the student recreation center, she considered herself safe from the danger of humiliating herself again. It was the closest in proximity to the university's school of arts building.

This was perfect weather for hot cocoa or a creamy

13

mocha caramel coffee from the small cafe nearby. *If* she'd remembered to bring her wallet and student ID card. Her heavy backpack occupied the space beside her feet while she huddled with her sketchbook in a recliner with a window view of the main courtyard.

The area was snug between the campus bookstore and a Feldman's Bakery, like a double whammy temptation urging her to buy this week's new release books or delicious donuts with the credit card she saved for emergencies only.

Her belly rumbled, a plea for her to text Marie and beg for a couple bucks. Using a credit card with zero balance was like breaking a seal, and every purchase thereafter would be easier to make than the last.

Esme resisted and sank into her seat instead, thoughts drifting to her most recent dream. She'd awakened a sweaty mess beneath the tangled sheets after fantasizing all night about a long-haired bearded man on a fierce warhorse, clad in old Greco-Roman armor like a cast member of the movie *Troy*. She'd sketched him in charcoal, but the drawing didn't do him justice.

"Hey. Esme, right?" a warm, masculine voice spoke up from behind her.

Esme snapped the sketchbook shut against her chest. She twisted around and froze, a reply stuck in her throat at the sight standing behind her recliner. How did the school's star athlete even know her name?

"Um, yeah?"

Luke Tempest ran in a different crowd from her, being a popular guy who had somehow become the university heartthrob overnight when he transferred in last year out of the blue. Not that he gave anyone the time of day, no matter how much they flirted or danced around him in their microscopic shorts and miniskirts. The guy was all about his track career and college education when he wasn't chugging drinks with his social circle of groupies.

His widening grin mesmerized her for a second, making it difficult to determine what she liked the most about his handsome face. Was it the smoldering hazel eyes that shone like gold or the dimple in his right cheek? "I heard you're a computer genius. That true?" He stood beside her chair in a casual pose, both hands tucked in to the pockets of a dark umber hooded sweatshirt.

Her mind drew a blank, and she stared at him like a dimwitted child until his motivations finally clicked. Annoyance swept away the starstruck stupor. "I don't know about being a genius, but I do all right. Why? Looking for someone to do your homework for you? Because I don't do that."

"Not even for a hundred bucks per paper?"

She blinked. A dozen ways to spend a hundred dollars flitted through her mind, hot cocoa at the top of the list along with a pair of cute knee-high boots she saw on sale. Meanwhile, Luke grinned and laughed at her before dropping into the adjacent chair with the confidence of a man who had been invited to join her. The husky sound of his warm chuckle sent shivers dancing along her spine.

"I'm kidding," he said. "I don't need you to cheat for me. I was actually hoping you could give me a hand, you know? All that HTML shit makes my brain hurt. So I thought maybe you'd be willing to tutor me."

"Tutor you."

"Yeah. I can still pay for your time. Maybe start with joining me for coffee?"

She pushed her glasses further up her nose and considered the offer. A hundred bucks was a temptation she couldn't easily pass up. But for the resident rich kid, it was chump change. Rumors around campus claimed he had a trust fund. Both of his parents had died at an early age in a mysterious car accident.

"Make it three-hundred and you have a deal." She waited for him to decline and walk away.

Luke's grin widened. "Deal. Now how about that coffee? My treat."

Esme stared. "Wait, you mean right now?"

"Why not? You're not in class. I'm not in class. Seems like a good time for us both."

"Sure, I guess." So much for finishing her novel. She tucked in a bookmark and fought the urge to send an ecstatic text to Marie about her not-date with the school's most coveted hottie.

When she reached for her bag, he beat her to it and plucked the heavy thing off the floor, exposing the image of a shoe with white wings stitched into the back of his jacket. That kind of brag on anyone else would be arrogance. For Luke Tempest, it was absolute honesty. Rumors claimed some guys from the *Book of World Records* had come and scouted him, but he'd shooed them away, claiming he had no interest in holding any titles. Dismissed them in what had to be the greatest show of modesty or stupidity their college had ever seen.

Feldman's and the cafe were tucked beside each other,

practically sharing the same space without a wall separating them. Students frequently went from one register to the other.

Esme and Luke chose a table by the glass wall dividing the cooler study hall from the fragrant aroma of baking pastries and steamy beverages, placing their bags beside chairs opposite one another before moving in line. Around this time of the day, the place was bustling with activity, over half of the three dozen tables occupied.

While they stood in line, Esme eyed an enormous canvas display advertising the season's mint chocolate chip cocoa. "Too late to swap that coffee for a hot cocoa?"

"Nope. Was considering one myself. 'Tis the season, right?" He turned to the clerk behind the counter and made an order for two large cocoas, extra whipped cream, peppermint chips, and chocolate shavings on both, like he'd read her mind. He paid with a crisp twenty and stuffed the change in the tip jar like 100 percent tips were a common thing in university food shops.

People were staring now as they moved off to the side and waited at the pickup counter for their decadent chocolate beverages. A pair of girls at an adjacent table leaned close, dropping their voices to a whisper level. One stole a look at Luke with her phone while pretending to take a selfie that conveniently included him in the photo over her shoulder.

Esme knew all the tricks. She rolled her eyes.

Luke snickered suddenly. Then their drinks arrived, and he passed her one of the creamy delights. "So, what kind of major requires art *and* web design courses?"

"Interior design." She risked scalding her mouth for a

small sip of liquid calories to distract from the occasional curious face glancing their way.

He pulled out her chair. Esme blinked. Compared to other college guys she knew, Luke was a world-class gentleman among oversized children, making their interaction all the more puzzling with every passing second. Who did that anymore under the age of forty? Her dad didn't even pull out chairs for her mother, and they had been married for thirty years.

"The hell does interior design have to do with web design?"

His scrutiny unnerved her, making warmth spread over her face and releasing a swarm of butterflies in her belly. More than anything, she wanted to squirm in her seat, but she refused to give him the satisfaction of seeing her uncomfortable if this was all some sick, immature joke dreamed up by an ex hell-bent on hurting her. "It's an elective for me, but I figured it couldn't hurt to know how to do my own stuff."

"Yeah? That's cool. So you'd be doing that whole decorating thing like MTV Cribs, right?"

"Something like that but less, you know, gaudy."

"Hey, some of those places were a little stylish."

"A few."

"You trying to say a wraparound pool with three golden statue fountains and four burning platforms ain't tasteful? Maybe I want my house to look like a sacred Aztec temple." He sipped his chocolate, straight-faced, while she choked on hers.

"Please tell me you're joking."

"Yeah. If I'm gonna be that extra, I'd rather have

Grecian columns and towering marble statues in my yard. Way classier than South American decor. Naked statues too, because you can't really call it complete without a nude Aphrodite beside the driveway."

"Now I *know* you're messing with me."

"Maybe." He leaned forward, mischief dancing in his honey-colored eyes. "What are you doing to—"

The rapid click of clunky heels clattered to them and stopped beside the table, worn by a blonde in low-rise jeans and a pink top revealing her pierced navel despite the unforgiving weather outside.

"Oh my God. It took me forever to find you. Like I had to go check out the TV room and the video game stations before someone finally said they saw you around here."

Luke's attention darted away to the plastic bimbo. Every break during the semester or in between, Rhonda got something else done to her body on her daddy's dime. Last semester it had been a fresh pair of new tits. This time, she'd gotten her lips botoxed.

As much as Esme tried to hold back her catty criticisms, Rhonda made it impossible when she spent all her time rubbing it in everyone's face, constantly telling them what they should save up to have fixed since they don't have rich daddies to purchase them a nose job or new chin.

Apparently, Esme needed new tits and a little lipo around the hips. At the time, she'd pretended it hadn't stung, but it had.

And judging from Luke's friendly smile, their cafe date was going to come to an abrupt end. Esme sighed. He even twisted around to look up at the intruder, warm smile never wavering. "Rhonda, right? You need something?"

"I totally do. There's going to be a hot tub party at my place this weekend, and I wanted to invite you."

"No thanks."

"Huh?"

"No thanks," he repeated.

"Seriously?" Rhonda's face flushed. "Maybe you don't understand. Everyone who's anyone will be there. Your team captain, Brandon, will be there. I invited *all* the people who matter."

Students en route to their tables slowed down to spectate the train wreck, while Esme slouched down in her seat and tried to become invisible.

Luke raised his brows. "Did you invite Esme?"

"Um, no. Why would I? She isn't anyone important."

"Nah. I'm good. Thanks for the invitation though."

"But why not?"

Luke leaned toward her and lowered his voice. "You really wanna know why?"

"Well, yeah."

"We can start with how your rude ass wandered over and interrupted our conversation. You didn't even acknowledge Esme with a glance. Or the fact that you smell like a chemical reaction between a cheap perfumery and a marijuana dispensary. Try lowering the windows if you're gonna smoke in Daddy's car."

"I—"

"You are trying really hard to rub your last two brain cells together for a witty retort, but it's not happening.

Girl, just go. I don't have time for your entitled ass. I'm not the one."

Lacking any kind of a comeback, Rhonda hurried away and vanished around the corner, out of sight the moment she left the cafe. She'd practically streamed smoke behind her.

"Daaaaamn, son," a kid at an adjacent table said.

"Hashtag savage," another student agreed, giggling. "About time someone let the hot wind out of her. Can't fucking stand her."

Esme let out a quiet breath, under strain from the tremendous effort of keeping her laughter in.

Luke smirked. "Go ahead and laugh if you want. I mean, she kinda had that shit coming. I was going to give her the benefit of the doubt and believe she wasn't going to talk over you the entire damn time she stood there, but..."

"Was all of that because she ignored me?"

He shrugged. "I don't like rude people."

"Just rude?"

"Or petty bitches," he added.

"Well, thanks for that."

"So, are you going to tell me why you keep glancing around this place like the crew from *Candid Camera* is one click away from leaping out to shout 'Surprise!' at us? You got an ex sitting around here somewhere?" Luke twisted in his seat, his bewildered expression appearing genuine despite the raw knot of suspicion twisting in her gut.

"I guess I'm just waiting for the part where you ask me out, I say yes, then you bust out laughing at how stupid I must be to have fallen for it."

"Huh?" The humor faded from his face. "I was planning to ask you out, but I don't know what I've done to make you think I'm that kind of asshole."

Oh shit. Now, more than ever, she wanted to sink into a big, deep, dark pit somewhere and never crawl out again.

"You okay, Esme? You look sick."

"I think I'm just gonna go." She slid from her seat and grabbed her bag. "Sorry."

"Hey, wait." Luke caught up with her before she'd taken three steps. He touched her hand and she froze, startled by the little electric zing that seemed to zip up her arm.

She told herself it was only static, even though she couldn't bear to jerk away.

"Lemme take you out tomorrow night. We can catch a movie."

"Uh—"

"I'll pick you up here after class."

"Um—"

"Great. See you tomorrow, Esme." He grinned then headed off, leaving her to stare at his retreating back and wonder what the hell had just happened.

A moment of silence passed between them, Marie scrutinizing her with a disbelieving stare from the other end of the couch. Or waiting for the punchline to the joke. "You were asked out by the Undateable Hunk?"

Esme snorted at the superheroesque nickname a few irritable girls had attached to the poor guy earlier that year when he received his reputation for refusing to date at the university. "I'm still trying to decide if he was having a laugh at me or something, but the more I dissect his behavior, the more certain I am that he was serious. Or just a nice guy who feels sorry for an awkward girl."

"Isn't he seeing that androgynous supermodel from New York? The one you idolize."

"Dito? I thought so. I should have asked. Ugh."

"There's photos online of them having lunch at some posh place in New York. Okay, well tell me everything! How did he say it? Was he smiling? Like was it a platonic kind of question? I can't believe he walked up to you and asked."

"Don't get your panties in a twist, Marie. He's being nice because he wants me to make sure he passes his finals."

"Milk that shit, girl. This is your opportunity to win him over. Or, if you don't want him, introduce him to me." Marie flashed her an exaggerated smile. "Be your bestie for life if you do."

"If I recall, I already won the Bestie for Life title when I lied to your mother and said you were sleeping over at my place while you were out all night boning Randy Mitchell in a Super 8 motel room after prom."

Marie wrinkled her nose. "Not my finest moment."

"Or your finest lay if I remember your complaints the next morning."

"Smallest dick ever. Lucky for him he had a great tongue." Marie sighed. "Ah, memories."

"Uh-huh."

"Anyway, I expect a full report after your date tomorrow. What movie are you going to see?"

"I have no idea. He just sorta... asked and took my bewildered shock as acceptance. I never actually said yes."

"But you're going to go. Please tell me you're going to go, and you won't leave that hot dude sitting in the cafe alone."

"Yeah, fine, I will."

Marie squealed and clapped her hands. Her excitement was infectious, and Esme smiled herself, suddenly anxious for the date. Luke seemed like a nice guy. Eager maybe, but nice. She couldn't see any harm in a single date.

"I promise to tell you everything, but for right now, we need to focus."

Marie blinked, brows drawing together, and Esme sighed. She reached over and plucked up a flyer from the coffee table, brandishing it at her forgetful friend.

"The fundraiser, remember?"

"Oh, yeah," Marie said. "I got through the first five the other day, but a few are callbacks who had to contact someone above them or a relative before they knew if they could donate."

"Awesome. Now we have like, what? Thirty to go? Oh, oh! Guess what I managed to get?"

"Besides a date? What?"

Esme stuck her tongue out. "I might have managed to catch a glimpse of a certain artist's contact number when I popped into Wōden Gallery on the way here."

"No way. You have the number for Alexander Smith?" Marie practically bounced in her seat. "Are you going to call?"

"Why not? If we managed to get some of his work into the auction, we'd raise a ton of money. People fall over themselves for his sculptures."

"Yeah, but do you think he'll actually offer one up for free?"

"Doesn't hurt to ask. Worst he can do is say no."

Marie drew her knees up and hugged them to her chest while Esme dialed. The phone rang and rang, and just when it seemed no one would pick up, the line connected.

"Smith residence, may I help you?" a cultured British accent said.

"Hi, yes. My name is Esme Caro, and I'm calling on behalf of the University of Ashfall's art department. Is Mr. Smith available?"

"May I ask what this is in regard to, Miss Caro?"

"Yes, of course. The fifteenth Annual Winter Gala and Fundraiser is coming up next month, and I was hoping to speak with Mr. Smith about donating a piece. All proceeds from the auction benefit the Ashfall Memorial Hospital's pediatric floor."

"While the cause sounds like a worthy one, Mr. Smith does not give away his work, nor does he have any to spare."

"Please. If I could just speak with him for, like, a quick minute, I'd really appreciate it. I understand the value of his work, I really do, and I'm not asking for anything huge. Even a small sculpture would be a great addition to our charity fundraiser. All the local businesses get involved."

"I am sorry, Miss Caro, he does not take callers."

"Please, I—"

"Good day, Miss Caro."

Click. The line went dead.

Esme frowned at her cell phone and set it aside. "Dude, I think he has a butler. I mean, the guy sounded like I imagine a butler would."

"Like Tim Curry in *Clue*?"

"Yeah, pretty much like that. Very Alfred Pennyworth. I'm sure he calls him Master Alexander while delivering the morning paper and his coffee."

"Sorry you didn't get anything from him."

Esme shrugged. "Like I said, at least I asked. It was worth trying." Still, it stung a little. She'd long admired Smith's work, and meeting him would have been a thrill.

"Well, why don't you say we split up this list and tackle the soft hearts we know will donate?"

"Sounds like a plan."

A HEALTHY DOSE OF SKEPTICISM AND TOO MANY PRIOR disappointments led Esme to expect Luke would be a no-show. Then she stepped into the cafe and found him waiting at a table with another pair of hot peppermint cocoas and a big smile before sweeping her away from the building for a real date.

Esme warmed her hands on the cup as they embarked on their journey into the student lot. His arm fit around her waist like it belonged there, introducing her to the heat of his body and an expensive cologne she recognized from cruising the mall counters and staring at designer items she couldn't afford with her part-time wages.

Marie always teased her about having a nose like a bloodhound, good at picking apart individual notes, like the cedar, bergamot, and hints of vetiver clinging to his red hoodie. He wore his varsity jacket, white sleeves against a blue and silver body, too thin to provide real protection in the frigid mountain weather. But he didn't shiver.

Even his car was a real thing of beauty, an old classic restored to mint condition like he'd driven it off a showroom floor yesterday. She didn't know much about old cars except to appreciate how pretty they were. Luke's car had a metallic teal finish with silver racing stripes. She slid onto the glossy gray leather bench seat and buckled in. Then the seat warmers beneath her promptly chased away the remnants of the winter chill.

Esme sank down and sipped her hot drink. Heaven. "I don't know why bench seats like this went out of fashion. This is so comfortable. Especially the seat warmers."

Luke chuckled and pulled out onto the road. "Heh. Yeah. As soon as I was accepted here, I made sure to install those," he said. The streets appeared freshly plowed, but he cruised the car five miles below the speed limit, a prudent driver with vigilant eyes on the road.

When he paused at a stop sign, tourists rushed ahead of them down the pedestrian crossing.

"So, what made you come to Ashfall anyway?"

"Eh. A change in scenery I guess. It was something new."

"But didn't you have to sit out an entire track season just to change schools?"

He shrugged. "I didn't mind. Besides, a, uh... I guess you could call him a family friend, lives in the area. We hang out sometimes."

Esme twisted in the seat to study his expression as he maneuvered around a corner and pulled into the lot of the only theater in town. It was a small building, recently renovated with fresh carpets the previous year, and they never showed more than four movies at a time. "So, you moved here for a friend? That's really sweet of you."

He gave her a bashful grin, the kind of boyish smile that would have sent a pink flush across his face if he wasn't the golden shade of brown suede. "Since I'm so sweet, I'll let you pick the movie. We got four choices, superheroes, horror, comedy, or romance."

"Superheroes. I'm not in the mood for nightmares, and I won't make you sit through a romance. Um... speaking of romance. I have one tiny question."

"Shoot."

"Aren't you dating a supermodel?"

His brows shot up. Then he laughed so hard there were tears in the corners of his eyes. "Dito? No. Dito and I are like family. I haven't dated anyone in a long time. Feels like centuries."

"Oh."

Luke covered everything, including their overpriced popcorn, soda, and candies. He must have had a major sweet tooth, because he bought licorice, sour gummies, and chocolates for himself while she settled for a single king-sized Snickers.

They stepped into a semi-deserted theater room to watch their magical flick, the bulk of the evening movie-goers occupied by the recent new comedy release starring some popular Hollywood starlet and a sexy male antagonist. Luke guided her past a dozen scattered viewers to the middle of the back row.

At some point in the movie, he yawned and stretched out his arms, pulling off a classic move by lowering one around her shoulders. Since she couldn't decide if it was a legitimate attempt or her date's sense of humor, she let it slide and leaned against his shoulder, breathing in that scent of cologne and spice clinging to his jacket and neck.

They were among the last to leave the dimly lit room after waiting for the final after-credits scene.

Luke yawned after standing. "That was better than the reviews made it seem. So, wanna go grab a bite to eat?"

Esme shrugged into her coat again and fastened it. "After all that popcorn and candy? No thanks, I'm stuffed. Maybe next time we can just do dinner."

His eyes lit up, grin widening across a face made for magazines. "You asking me out on a date, or should I check for cameras?"

When she smacked his chest, his good-natured laugh wrapped around her like a warm hug inviting her into his embrace long before he pulled her close by one wrist. She melted into him, surrounded by strong arms and pressed against a hard, masculine chest chiseled by hours of training for his team.

Luke dipped his head for a kiss Esme had no hope of resisting. She'd never kissed anyone on the first date before. Some stubborn part of her psyche had always been resistant to the threat of being labeled easy. Loose.

But Luke's kiss sent sparks dancing along her spine and drove her pulse to a frenzied rhythm. Her skin was hot and electric, like a live wire sizzling each of her nerve endings and connecting in a tight ball between her thighs. Like she'd kissed this man a thousand times before and her body was amped up for more.

All of it came from one kiss. One moment. She dragged her mouth away and spent the next few seconds breathing against his cheek. "Wow."

"Yeah."

When Luke twisted to pick up where they left off, Esme lifted a hand to his lips. "Maybe we should head back. You know, keep things ending on a good note."

"Sure thing."

Luke held the doors for her on the way out and again at his car. It didn't take more than a few minutes to reach her driveway. The living room lights shone a golden glow beyond the drawn curtains, and the porch light was on.

"I had a nice time tonight, so thanks."

"Me too, Esme. I'm gonna hold you to that dinner."

She chuckled and ducked her head. Luke reached over and tucked her hair behind her ear. When the same spark zinged against her cheek, she leaned in and skimmed her lips over his, drawn in by the overwhelming compulsion to kiss him again—an urgent, overpowering need to have one more taste of his lips.

His kisses were like a drug, smothering her senses beneath a flourishing, heady desire to touch him and trace the lines defining his abs. When her palm slid over the hard layer of muscle beneath his shirt, Luke took it as encouragement. He tugged her sweater up and slipped a hand beneath the soft cashmere, caressing her with fingers like warm silk against her ribs. She shivered under the touch, on the brink of telling him to stop, but eager to experience one second more.

She slid closer across the bench seat and leaned into him. Luke stroked up and glided his fingers across her bra. Her nipples tightened.

Wanting to touch him in return, Esme ran her hands down his chest, delighting in the muscled contours. His slim frame and clothing style created a deceptive picture, because the body beneath his track jacket and shirt wasn't scrawny at all. She discovered only tight, lean muscle. He guided her hand from beneath his shirt to his lap.

Her hand closed around something hot and rigid, the throbbing length of bared skin beneath her fingertips. Startled, Esme jerked her head away and stared down at his lap, the open fly, and the hard cock wrapped in her hand. The same hand flew of its own volition, the sound of her palm clapping against Luke's cheek like a thunder strike in the car.

"The hell was that for!"

"You're a fucking dick. I knew it." She pushed away and slid back. "What the hell is wrong with you?"

"Was I not supposed to whip it out? I thought we were about to get busy."

"Um, at what point did I do anything to imply I was going to sleep with you tonight? Or do anything involving *that*?" she asked, waving her hand toward his crotch, and the hard length of him that was still proudly spearing up from his open fly.

To his credit, he did appear to be genuinely stunned, his perfect mouth forming a small circle of surprise. "You went out with me. I mean, hell, you kissed me."

"That doesn't mean I want your cock in my hand, asshole."

He fumbled his dick away as she threw open the car door and stepped out onto the gritty driveway. Before she could step away from the vehicle, he was at her side, reaching for her elbow, so damned fast she wondered how he didn't break his neck.

Esme jerked her arm away. "Don't touch me."

"I'm really sorry."

"I don't know what kind of girls you've been going out with, or how desperate you thought I was, but I'm not jumping on your dick in a car in my driveway on the first date."

"I know, I know, and I'm really, truly sorry about that. I misread you and where things were going. Like, baby, there are no words to express how sorry I am. I assumed. I'm an asshole—"

"Damned right you're an asshole."

She yanked her arm out from under his touch and

rushed onto the porch, nearly losing her balance in the process. Her heel slipped against the frost, but Luke—damn the man for being so fast and light on his feet even with patches of ice on the concrete—was somehow there to steady her.

Esme punched in the code on the doorknob and shoved her way inside while he babbled out another apology. She didn't even care that he'd probably seen the access code. She'd change it after he was gone.

"Shove off!" She banged the door shut in his face and stomped into the living room.

"Whoa! Why are we slamming doors?" Marie jumped up and ran over to peer out the peephole. "And why is Luke Tempest standing on our porch looking like he just got hit with a post-date final exam he didn't study for?"

"He's still there?"

"Um, yeah. Wait, nope, he's walking to his car, but he still looks like a little boy who just found out his puppy died. What happened?"

"He... he..."

"What, girl? Did he make you pay? I hate when guys do that."

"No, worse. He paid then expected payment back in the car. The sexual kind."

"What?"

"He whipped out his dick while we were kissing."

"He didn't."

"He did! And it was—"

"Gross? Malformed? Wait, no, let me guess. It was tiny, wasn't it? Tiny like Randy."

"Well, no, it was fine. I mean, it was, you know,

like big."

"Bigger than Daniel?"

"Well, yeah, but that's not the point! We were kissing in his car and, yeah, all of a sudden his dick was out."

"What a jerk."

"I know, right?"

Esme dropped down onto the couch and kicked off her boots. Marie grabbed beers and vanilla ice cream from the fridge before rejoining her friend.

"Seriously though, on a scale from one to ten, how was it?"

"He was a definite nine. I mean, if I'd wanted to jump his bones, I'm pretty sure it would have been amazing." Luke had been hard as marble in her hands, and long after he was gone, she couldn't clear the memory of him from her thoughts. She sighed, both irritated and melancholy.

Why couldn't he have pulled that move a few weeks down the road when she knew more about him aside from his name and how fast he ran a hundred-meter dash? After an afternoon cocoa and evening at the movies, what did she really know about Luke Tempest?

I know he's packing at least eight inches. She chastised herself mentally and focused on the horror movie Marie put on the television.

No one had worse luck than Esme when it came to dating, her ability to choose the wrong guys practically supernatural by design. With a wry smile, she stabbed her spoon into the pint of French vanilla ice cream and resigned herself to watching a creepy movie about clowns.

3

On Wednesdays, Esme had a single, three-hour-long evening class to attend, and when it released, it was always past dark and beyond frigid. It was also the one class she and Marie didn't share since her friend wasn't an overachiever with a minor in Architectural History requiring an additional eighteen credit hours. For the briefest of moments, she almost wished she would run into Luke, if only for the ride and warm seats.

God, for a ride home, she'd have volunteered the hand job.

In the week since their dating disaster, she'd managed to avoid him without even a brief sighting. She'd half expected to run into him Monday between classes or at lunch, but he hadn't popped up once to bother her, nor had he appeared the next day during her usual study session between classes.

Was it possible she'd overreacted, or had he lost interest because she didn't plan to bone him in his car?

Snow crunched behind her, and a familiar tingle raced up her spine, raising the hairs on her nape. Her pulse thundered behind her ribs at a staccato beat, ferocious as a galloping herd.

She glanced back over her shoulder but saw no one. Several shops remained open, but everyone was wisely inside where it was warm. Waving it off as snow falling from a roof, she continued on her way, until another crunch drew her attention. This time, she swore she caught sight of a shadow further back down the way. As the panic attack subsided, she looked back again after several more feet, and this time she made out a hulking figure in a dark coat.

Esme tugged her purse around to her front and slipped her cell phone out. She thumbed the recent call log and phoned her friend. "Marie," she hissed when the line picked up. "I think there's some strange dude following me."

"What? Why are you calling me? Call the police."

"But what if I'm wrong? I'll look like an idiot."

"Better to look like an idiot than end up in some bad man's sex dungeon."

"What the fuck? Sex dungeon? How does your mind jump to—you know what? Nevermind."

"Where are you?"

"Edge of Spruce and Main by the university library."

"Come to the cafe. Do you want me to tell Frank some guy was hassling you and send him out?"

Esme sagged in relief. Officer Frank would do

anything for Marie, especially if it scored him a shot at getting into her panties. "Yes, please."

"All right, I'll—*shit*. He's already in his cruiser and driving away."

At this hour, few tourists wandered the streets and most of the souvenir shops had long ago closed for the day. Nothing stirred on her corner of the street save a stray cat merrily prancing across a dirty mountain of snow created by the plows. The shadowed figure was gone.

"I am losing my damned mind. I'm freaking out over nothing. It's well lit, and if I can't bumble my way a couple blocks to the cafe in the safest, most open part of town, maybe I deserve to be snatched."

"You sure?"

"Positive."

"Okay. Love you, girl. I'll have a bowl of chili waiting when you get here."

"Make it a bread bowl. With extra cheese. I want more than a damn pinch this time."

"Extra cheese," Marie agreed.

Esme ended the call and continued down the road, shivering inside her coat. The wind cut through her gloves and numbed her fingers to the bone.

The growl of a rumbling engine echoed up the street. Esme peered over her shoulder and caught sight of a motorcycle coming around the corner a few blocks down. In this weather, she couldn't imagine how anyone could enjoy driving without a heater or walls to block out the wind.

Speaking of which, she was ready to be out of the

cold herself. With hands tucked in her pockets, she continued up the sidewalk at a quick pace.

"Hey there," a deep, husky voice called out.

She darted her gaze to the left. The biker coasted at her speed, a big man in a leather jacket and black-visored headgear designed to resemble an old Grecian helmet, complete with a scarlet brush comb on top. Despite the temptation to ask him about it, she picked up the pace and pushed on through the bitter cold.

"Oh, come on, can't you at least say hello?"

"Hello."

"Great, so she does speak. Pretty girl like you shouldn't be walking alone at this hour."

She grunted. He sounded like her dad, his tone oddly paternal... No, not paternal, warm and protective but not paternal. Marie was always telling her about street harassment and creepy old guys hitting on her when she visited her family in Sacramento, but Esme had never experienced it herself.

He paused the bike at the street corner while she waited for a long car to pass through the intersection. "I hear the recent influx of tourists have brought all kinds of shit to town. There's perverts out," he persisted.

"Are you one of them?" The words flew from her lips before she could reel them in.

The stranger chuckled and pulled off his helmet. Dark hair tumbled out around his shoulders, framing a face equal parts rugged and handsome, not as pretty and flawless as Luke, but breathtaking in its own kind of way, his bright blue eyes above a crooked nose that looked like it had once been broken and hadn't set right.

Esme stared, as petrified by his resemblance to the warrior of her dream as she was aroused by it. It had to be coincidence.

Despite his warm smile, he exuded a strong aura of don't-fuck-with-me that dissuaded Esme from approaching. Guys like him started bar brawls *and* finished them, the last man standing while all other bodies lay strewn among puddles of spilled liquor and shattered furniture.

"Nah. Not tonight, I'm not. You have a name to go with that pretty voice?"

Instead of telling him how much she wanted to sit on his face, she tersely said, "It isn't nice to follow someone alongside the road. Haven't you seen all those anti-catcalling videos on Facebook?"

He blinked at her, and a moment of awkward silence passed before he let loose a long laugh, the warm and comforting kind that didn't feel like he was laughing at her specifically. "You got me there, but technically, I haven't catcalled you. I don't do that kind of shit. Honest, I'm just offering you a ride home. You're carrying a backpack that looks like it weighs fifty pounds, and it's frosty as hell out here."

Esme hung back for a second. Her thumb was still hovering over the button to call 911.

"Isn't it dangerous to ride a bike in the winter?"

"No more than a car when you're with the right rider, and I don't crash. Ever."

"I don't know..."

"Look, ride or no ride, I'm gonna escort you along. So you can tolerate my company walking or have a break and let me drive you."

What would Marie do when faced with the impossible choice of potentially being swept away by a hot man on a motorcycle versus walking alone in the cold for ten minutes?

Her good and dependable, boring friend would take the long route, citing possible abduction and sex dungeons. "Fine." She wiggled her other arm into the second strap of her backpack then crossed the sidewalk to join him.

While balancing the powerful machine between his strong legs, he placed the helmet over her head and slid it neatly into place before coaxing her behind him on the enormous bike. She immediately felt like a bad ass. "Just put your arms around me, baby, and hold on tight."

It had to be one of her more foolish decisions ever, but she did as he said and gripped his coat. The body beneath it was rock-hard and warm as a furnace, heating through her clothes and jacket. She laced her fingers over his abdomen and let her overactive imagination carry her away.

When she relaxed and sank in against him, he throttled the engine and took off, the bike rocketing forward with more speed than she'd anticipated. Her mysterious—what did she call him when "stalker" had a negative connotation, conflicting with the reassuring comfort the stranger emitted—helper lowered his hand from the bar to her thigh, effectively steadying her.

The bike didn't wobble, didn't veer even an inch off course, but Esme freaked and buried her fingers into the leather. "Put your damn hand back where it belongs!"

"Damn. Sorry. You seemed tense."

"You not having both hands on the bars is making me more tense."

He laughed again and removed his hand. "Where to?"

"Ridgewood Lane. You can drop me at the cafe on the corner."

"You got it."

"So, what's your name, then?"

"Beau."

Esme laughed against the back of his shoulder. He looked like a Beau, the name a perfect match to those chiseled angles, tempting lips, and the scruffy shadow covering his jaw and chin.

"What's so funny?"

"It... fits. You look like a Beau."

"I hoped you'd say that."

"Huh?"

"Nothing."

The walk that would have taken her ten minutes took a couple on his bike, and despite the wind cutting through her clothes, Beau put off heat like a furnace. She almost resented arriving so soon, content to remain pressed against his back and soaking up the warmth.

Esme made herself release the absurdly hot stranger, climb off his bike, and step onto the curb. "Look, um, thanks for the ride."

"Anytime." He helped pull off the helmet. "Maybe I can catch you around some other day...?"

"Esme," she said in a rush.

"See? That wasn't so hard." He grinned and gunned

the engine, then pulled away before she could say anything else.

———

BEAU SET THE BAG OF CHINESE TAKEOUT ON THE COFFEE table and dropped onto the couch next to Luke, a widening grin on his face. Being the god of war didn't mean he couldn't celebrate and revel in every minor achievement too. And getting Esme on the back of his ride had definitely been a victory over the smarmy little asshole beside him.

"What were you saying before I left? That our Esme would never get on the back of a motorcycle with a man she doesn't know?"

Luke scowled. "She probably sensed something about you. Some part of her has to remember us after all of this time."

"Maybe. Or maybe you just struck out so bad she's eager to get to know a real man who won't pop his cock in her hand on the first date."

"Dude, are you ever going to let me live that down?"

"Nope," Beau replied.

"I think you deserved more than the slap she gave you," Alexander said. He sat opposite them, a huge man who barely fit in the seat even though Luke had personally bought the oversized recliner just for him. No amount of magic would shrink him or make him any smaller, his size part of his divine gift, so to speak.

"I'm sorry, okay? Look, I thought... I just figured she'd

be like the old Aphrodite, and once we started, she wouldn't be able to get enough of me."

Alexander leaned forward, a warm orange glow lit behind his amber eyes, turning them molten like flame. "You figured wrong, kid."

"As if you're doing any better. You stalk her in the shadows because you're too afraid of letting her see your face. You've been in this town with her for years, man. Watched her. There's a word for guys like you."

Alex was out of the chair in a flash, seven feet of man with fists as large as hams. Luke met the challenge and jumped off the couch.

And if those two clashed in this little apartment building, there'd be nothing left of it but rubble and cinders.

Beau groaned and stepped between his brother and friend.

"Guys, seriously? This is the shit that chased her away before. You wanna take this opportunity and fuck it up, be my guest, because maybe if you kill each other this time, she'll give me a shot and I can have her all to myself. All this sharing is caring bullshit we came up with won't even be necessary because she'll be all *mine*."

Alex grunted. "If it wasn't for my observations over the years, none of us would be getting this chance to win her back. Remember that." The giant stepped back first and returned to his chair. "I lived here before she was even born this time around. You wanna take it up with someone, go harass the Fates."

"Pus—"

Beau shot Luke a hard look, cutting him off before he

could finish the insult. "Drop it, Hermes," he warned in a low voice. "It's not worth a fight."

"Whatever. You want some rangoons?" Luke went back to the table to divide their takeout.

Beau snorted. No one else had wanted to go out into the cold and messy night again, so he'd been saddled with picking up the order for their shared dinner. They met at least once a month to play cards over beers and discuss their shared subject of interest, but lately they had gathered more often than that. "I was gonna take some whether you offered or not."

"Anyway, what's the plan now?"

"It's probably been long enough for Esme to cool off. You can probably try to apologize again," Beau said. At least, he hoped it had been long enough. For this to work, they all needed to be in her good graces.

Luke forked a huge shrimp and a tangle of lo mein into his mouth. "She's assisting the art director with an important fundraiser thing. I know you donated some money anonymously last year, Heph, but maybe you need to like... give them a piece of work this time around. It'd really brighten her up."

Alex grunted. "That was my plan. I decided to attend the fundraiser in person this year."

Beau fumbled his chopsticks. "Say again?"

"You two had your chance. This is mine. I have a piece to donate, and I'll be attending."

"But... but... that's unfair!"

Beau studied his brother. "Getting a bit of an advantage, aren't you? Posh event, artwork, tuxedos.

Ladies love men in tuxes the way they used to love seeing us in armor."

"It's not my fault you cling to your bad boy persona, or that Luke here is as dimwitted as ever."

"Hey!"

"You want me to do more than watch her from the shadows, so I am," Alex continued. "And as I've already said, my decision to live in the middle of nowhere is responsible for finding her in the first place. You struck out, Hermes. Be pissed at yourself if you want to be mad at anyone."

"She used to like it when I did that," he grumbled.

"Yeah, well, she used to like a lot of things, but she's the one who gave up her divinity to become mortal." Beau sighed. "She's had two dozen lifetimes to develop entirely different preferences."

"You afraid of a little hard work?" Alex asked.

"Me, afraid? Nah." Beau slouched back in his seat again and grinned at the other two gods—his former rivals, two men he'd once hated more than anything. "This only means it's up to us to figure out this new Aphrodite and win her back. All of us."

4

$\mathcal{A}$n uneventful week followed her meeting with the mystery biker. Since Esme and Marie alternated between their families during the holidays, they made the three-hour drive to San Jose the day before Thanksgiving to hang with the Caro family.

"We're home!" Esme called.

Her mother swept into the room from the kitchen, wearing her favorite holiday apron decorated with snowflakes and yule-themed designs. "Oh, you girls are so early. How was the traffic?"

"Surprisingly nonexistent. Where's Daddy?"

"Watching sports and leaving me be in the kitchen."

Her mother took their coats and gloves, tucking them and the scarves into the sleeves and hanging them on the rack as she always had since they were children. Then she ushered them both into the kitchen to taste the banana pudding she'd prepared for dessert.

"Hey, Daddy."

"Hi, Mr. Caro."

"Hello, girls. I hope you're prepared to gain a few pounds. There's about a thousand treats in there, and I imagine the pile is only going to continue growing by tomorrow."

Her mother frowned. "Don't exaggerate. I haven't made that much."

A pot of the prettiest roses Esme had ever seen sat on the counter. The attached card featured cherubs and hearts—apparently, an out of season Valentine's Day card.

"Daddy buying you late flowers?"

Her mother grinned. "Oh no. Those are for *you*. They arrived yesterday. You could have told us you have a new boyfriend."

Esme raised the card and opened it. "I don't have a boyfriend."

I'M SORRY. I KNOW I MESSED UP. PLEASE GIVE ME A CHANCE TO APOLOGIZE.

L

Marie stepped up to peer over her shoulder. "What's that. Oh, whoa. He sent flowers?"

"Yeah, maybe..." But how had he discovered her address? Esme was torn between being creeped out and touched by the sweet gesture. She glanced at Marie. "He didn't mention it to you?"

"Me? No, it's a surprise to me too."

"Seems like a nice young man if he understands he made a mistake," Daddy said, revealing he'd snooped and read the card, making her all the more grateful Luke's discreet message didn't mention his crime. That was a conversation she didn't want to have with her folks.

"I think you'd like him. He's a track star probably bound for the Olympics. Transferred here to help out a family friend last year."

Her father rubbed his chin. He loved college sports. "Sounds familiar. Wouldn't be Luke—"

"Tempest."

His eyes lit up behind his glasses. "Well, what are you waiting for? Give the boy a call."

"Daddy," she gritted out.

"What?" He looked innocent. "Rich, isn't he? I believe he's majority stockholder in an athletic shoe company."

"I didn't know that."

"It's a good sign when a man has enough humility to refrain from singing his own praises," her father said.

Luke had been exceptionally quiet about his personal life, mentioning little beyond his friends, hobbies, and present activities around the school. His money, his inheritance and supposed trust fund, and all those things had never come up.

"Anyway, you girls go ahead and make yourselves at home. It's always nice to have you over, Marie. The house is too quiet without you two running around."

Esme rolled her eyes and pulled Marie away by the arm. They retreated to her bedroom upstairs, which hadn't changed much over the years. The same rainbow polka-dot comforter from her high school days covered the bed, and a few peeling posters of old bands and actors covered the walls. Memories of Daniel occupied every corner of the room, from the sable football jersey-wearing teddy bear he'd gifted her last year, to a team sweatshirt tossed over the back of the desk chair. She'd even kept her prom corsage.

As soon as they were inside, Esme shut the door and pulled out her phone.

"Are you texting Luke?"

"No, e-mailing Dots and Burkes about their donation. They're catering the desserts."

Marie rolled her eyes. "Are you really going to work on that fundraiser here? Now? Girl, it's called a Thanksgiving break for a reason. It means you put down the work and enjoy some time off relaxing."

Her mother peeked into the room without knocking and entered to set a plate of gooey brownies in front of them. "Esmeralda Valentina Caro, put that phone away and at least *attempt* to relax. You always take your work so seriously."

"It's for a good cause."

"A cause that can allow you a few responsibility-free days. I mean it now, or I'll take the phone away."

Esme set her phone aside on the nightstand. She sulked at her mother and best friend but surrendered the fight. "Fine. Gang up and bully me."

Her mother departed again, leaving them alone in a room tainted by Daniel's old gifts. Esme frowned and sprawled across the bed.

"Ooookay. One second," Marie said. She vanished and returned moments later with a trash bag. "Fresh goodies for charity." After bagging the sweatshirt, she traveled around the room, trashing remnants of Esme's failed relationship. She even plucked a rectangle of photobooth pictures down from the dresser mirror and tossed them into the trash bin.

"Thanks. I guess I forgot how much of him was in this room."

"Ever notice how every gift he's ever given you is football or video game related? You know, when I think back, he wasn't even the best player on the team. Just the cutest," Marie said.

"Yeah, I guess. I actually liked playing games with him, though."

"Still, it's not like he was interested in your, well, interests."

Esme swung her legs off the bed and started with the closet, saying goodbye to a *Call of Duty* T-shirt she'd also stolen from Daniel. "True." A moment passed before she reclaimed it.

Fuck him. She loved *Call of Duty*.

"Well, here's to better luck with guys. Like Luke. Give him a chance, Esme."

"I'll consider it, but only if you promise no more boy talk this weekend. No work, no boys."

"Deal."

SNOW DRIFTED OUTSIDE OF THE STUDENT RECREATION center in waves of condensed fluff, almost hypnotic when

Esme stared outside the window too long. She had claimed her usual recliner in the student lounge to study for final exams, craving a peppermint cocoa but too stubborn to add even more calories to her waistline.

Screw it. I can go to the gym with Marie and hit the weights.

The moment she set her book aside to rise, Luke Tempest stepped around the front of the chair, bearing two extra-large hot chocolates and already fixing her with pleading, puppy-dog eyes, the kind of eyes only a heartless shrew could ignore if she had a shriveled little piece of coal where her heart should reside.

Damn.

"Thirsty?"

Esme lingered in the seat. "Maybe."

He held out a cup. "I wanted to apologize for that shit on our date. Really."

She crossed her arms against her chest. "Uh-huh."

"I misread you. I thought things were going somewhere they weren't, and I shouldn't have assumed."

"And?"

His dark brows squished together, clearly perplexed. "I'm sorry? I mean, I really don't know what else to say aside from promising to keep it in my pants next time."

"You're saying that next time bit like you're positive there's going to be one."

His face fell with genuine disappointment. "I really don't know how else to apologize," he said in a quiet voice. "But I can promise I won't do it again."

Esme sighed. She had the hottest, most sought-after

guy in school practically begging her for another chance, and nothing about it seemed real. "I believe you."

"And if you give me another chance, I swear my dick won't come out again unless you ask for it." He gave her a hopeful look, offering the cup again. "Beg for it maybe?"

After rolling her eyes, she accepted the cocoa. "All right. All right. Forgiven. We can put it behind us."

"Thanks, Esme. Really."

She let the warm and creamy chocolate heat her tongue. Liquid bliss. "Don't get too comfy. You're going to make it up to me."

"Anything."

"Well, I need a date for the Winter Fundraiser. It's formal, gonna be full of stuffy rich folk, and no good music, but the food is great and the drinks are free."

"That's the day after finals, right?"

Esme nodded. "Starts at five."

"Shit. Sorry, baby, but I already got plans made with the guys that night. The whole team is going out of town to Vegas for the weekend."

"Oh." She disguised the disappointment beneath a forced smile. Daniel had accompanied her last year to the fundraiser.

"I'm seriously sorry. I'd go if there was any way of getting out of it."

"No, it's okay. I mean, I totally hit you with this last minute."

"Tell you what. I can't go with you to your shindig, but at least let me help you prep for it."

"Oh, you don't need to do that. The resort hosts the gala, so they do all the setup."

"No, I mean, let me take you shopping for a dress and all the other overpriced things you need."

"You want to take me shopping?" Didn't guys loathe that sort of thing?

He nodded. "I'm best friends with a fashion model, remember?"

"Oh yeah." The best model to hit the scene in years too. Esme loved Dito's flair and sense of style, especially how they—the genderbending runway star insisted on "they" as a pronoun—had shaken up the modeling world. "Let me make sure I have this right. Are you offering to buy everything?"

"Yeah. Dress, hair, makeup—all that shit. I'll pay for it. I mean, it's the least I can do, especially since I can't come with you."

"Seriously?"

"Soon as you're ready to go, we can hit up the shops. I just need pictures. Like. Lots of selfies, girl."

"Excuse me?"

His big grin never faded. "You heard me. Since I can't be there, take enough photos to show me the good time you're having."

Outside, the flurries eased until the snowfall became nothing more than the occasional ivory fleck tumbling toward the pristine ground. Luke glanced outside and rubbed his chin. "I put snow chains on my truck today. If you don't have any plans, I'm down for heading to the shopping center now."

"Truck?"

"Yeah. This weather isn't so great for the Chevelle. The snow is dropping faster than the plows can keep it off the road."

As he had before, he snagged her bag before she had a chance to sling it over her shoulder. They made their way to the university garage and wove their way down the aisles to a parked Chevy the same metallic teal shade as his car. It must have been his favorite color.

"The roses were really pretty, by the way. Thank you," she said once they were on the road.

"I'm glad you got them."

"How'd you get my address anyway?"

"Oh, you know, Google is great for cyberstalking." He glanced over and grinned. "I may have looked you up on Facebook and got enough clues to figure out where you live. Sorry for creeping."

"Well, my parents thought it was a sweet gesture, so you can thank them for my change of heart. Marie and I were set to loathe you for eternity."

He stiffened, eyes widening in fleeting alarm that melted into uncomfortable silence. His fingers gripped the wheel, knuckles white and jaw clenched like she'd said he was a monster she never wanted to see again.

Esme touched his thigh. "Hey? Relax. You're forgiven, remember?"

"Yeah." His shoulders untensed. "Yeah, you're right. Sorry, it's just... I've made my share of fuckups in the past, this one the least of them. I really thought that was going to be the end this time."

He spoke little along the remaining half of the drive. Something about his silence troubled her. She hadn't just made him nervous—that was fear, true and visible fear.

Esme tended to hit up the bargain shops on the

edge of town out on the highway, but Luke drove them out of Old Ashfall and into the city proper, parking at an upscale shopping center closer to the hospital. There wasn't a mainstream department store in sight there.

Awnings stretched across the walkways to shelter passing shoppers and protect the walkways from the snowfall, and decorative heaters set at concise intervals provided a comfortable aura of heat.

Luke offered his arm once they were out of the truck and led the way into the maze of shops. Eventually they came across a window displaying party dresses and suits. He opened the door and gestured her to go ahead. "After you."

An attendant met them inside and offered to help in the search. It wasn't the sort of shopping Esme was used to, but she enjoyed the help. The woman pulled a few dresses from the racks she might not have grabbed on her own and led the way to the changing rooms.

"You gonna be okay out here?" Esme asked. "I hate clothes shopping and always take forever. Sorry."

Luke took a seat on the chair opposite the dressing rooms and unlocked his phone with a thumb press. "I'm cool. I can wait all evening."

"Are you sure?"

"Positive. Try on whatever you like for as long as you want." He pressed his lips together thoughtfully, and those honey-gold eyes twinkled with mischief. "Especially if you let me see some of the winners. Cool?"

"Fine."

The first dress clung to her like a second skin. She

tugged and pulled at it, hating the short hemline and the itchy sleeves. Luke whistled when she came out.

"You look hot in green."

"It itches."

"Oh. Well, try something else, then."

With help from the attendant, she had no shortage of dresses. Long ones, short ones, tight, loose, and all variety of styles. Nothing really made her feel comfortable, though, or won her over. She always managed to find some flaw, whether it was the way the dress emphasized her hips or flattened her modest bosom.

Fifteen more minutes passed before she emerged barefoot from the dressing room to show Luke the latest pick, a knee-length dress in taupe silk with a bloused waist. "What do you think?"

His gaze flicked up from the phone. He didn't disguise his wince. "Eh, it's okay. But kinda looks like something a grandma would wear."

"Try this one, dear." The attendant brought over another dress, as well as a shoebox. "I think you'll enjoy this one."

"I don't know. Maybe we should just call it quits, Luke."

He glanced at his watch. "It's only five. Rome wasn't built in a day, and you can't expect to find a 'knock 'em dead' dress in thirty minutes. C'mon, give it one last try, at least since Betsy went and found that for you."

"Fine."

One more dress, she could do that. She stripped off the unsuitable dress and situated it on the hanger.

Looking at it now on the wall, she agreed with his assessment.

Her grandmother would have worn that dress proudly to church services on Sunday morning.

Esme wrinkled her nose and examined the final offering. Hanging up, it didn't look like much, so she didn't harbor much hope for it being any better than the rest.

Then she wiggled into it, and the reflection in the mirror changed her entire perception of their evening shopping experience.

Esme smoothed her fingers over the soft curve-hugging cashmere, the perfect shade of wine red against her golden olive complexion. It flattered her shape and revealed a teasing hint of cleavage, enough to lure the eye without becoming tawdry and inappropriate. A flirty hem danced around her thighs in front and was longer in back.

"Winner."

Then she twisted and plucked at the dangling tag to reveal an outrageous $1,019 price. She gasped, dropping it. "Figures." The other dresses had been another label, nothing more than three or four hundred dollars.

"You doing okay in there?" Luke called out.

"Yeah, just taking this one off."

"But I haven't seen it. Come on out."

"But—"

"Please? You promised. Every dress I get to look at."

"Fine." She slipped into the shoes brought to match the dress. Velvet the same color as the dress covered the three-inch platform heels.

After a final glance in the mirror, she parted the curtain and stepped outside the dressing room. Luke rose from his seat and gave her a standing ovation like she'd performed in front of an audience.

"I think that's the one. Go on. Do a little twirl."

"I will break my neck if I twirl in these heels."

"You won't."

She didn't, but a man passing by rubbernecked long enough to stumble into a store display advertising a 10 percent off sale on lingerie. His wife scowled and slapped his arm.

"I don't know how models like Dito strut down a catwalk in heels like this."

"Nah, those are usually taller. I watched Dito try on a pair of six-inch stilettos that looked like a nine-hundred-dollar manslaughter attempt in the making."

"Nine hundred dollars."

He nodded. "Oh yeah. One basic pair of Louboutins will run that. Anyway, you look amazing, Esme. This is definitely the one you should wear."

"Luke, I can't take this dress. It costs a grand."

"So?"

"A grand," she repeated.

He nodded slowly. "Right. I caught that bit. Now why can't you take it?"

Heat rushed over her neck and flooded her face. Had the dress not been pulled off the rack, she would have assumed it had been designed with her in mind.

"Do you want it?"

"Yes."

"Then it's yours. Please. I think the cost is a pittance compared to what I did. Nothing can make up for that."

"Sweetheart, let him buy the dress." Another attendant stood stocking a display of five-hundred-dollar sweaters. Her makeup settled into the lines of her face, blue eyeshadow and hot pink lips clashing. "An apology doesn't get more heartfelt than that."

Mimi—as Esme dubbed the older woman in her thoughts, reminded of a character from a popular television sitcom—led Esme deeper into the women's department and helped her pick out a new strapless bra.

Luke glanced over when she passed by on her way to the dressing room to try it on. "So—"

"You do *not* get to see me model this one."

"Damn. Didn't hurt to try."

By the time they left the store, his arms were loaded down with shopping bags, because he wouldn't stop foisting expensive gifts on her. If she glanced at an object for longer than a few seconds, Luke wanted her to have it.

"Luke, you don't have to buy my affection. I like you. I really like you, and I forgive you."

"I know. I guess... it means more to me that I don't have to do it, if that makes sense. When I dated other girls, they expected that kind of shit. Wanted to be showered in presents, but you're not like that. Being around you makes me want to give you the world if I could."

"That's... it's sweet."

"C'mon. You said you were out of foundation, right? I think there's a Sephora about two miles away. You can make Marie jealous with all your new palettes and stuff."

"Are you sure you don't bat for the other team?"

He drew up short and blinked at her. "Huh? Why?"

"Because you know what a palette is and you actually enjoy shopping."

"Nah, girl, you don't have to worry about being some sorta smoke screen. I'm into you, believe me. Now let's get you everything you need for a night of rubbing elbows with affluent folk eager to burn up their disposable cash."

"You're still going to donate, right?"

Luke grinned. "Fill out a check in my book and I'll sign it."

LUKE RETURNED TO ESME'S PLACE ON FOOT. A FEW TREES littered the backyard and shrouded the area in shadows, though the dim yellow light from the back porch wouldn't have reached him anyway. He waited with his hands in his pockets, feeling out and listening with his divine senses.

Nothing. Whatever he'd felt fifteen minutes ago was gone, possibly even a figment of his imagination.

Something flickered at the edge of his perception, a ripple in the veil between worlds. Then there was a subtle pressure to accommodate the prolonged presence. It didn't move. Like him, it waited.

"I know you're there," he said, speaking to the empty night.

A few seconds of silence lapsed before Beau stepped into sight. "You felt it too?"

"Yeah. Something was here earlier when I dropped her off. It left, but I wanted to make sure it didn't return."

Beau grunted. "What do you think it was?"

"No idea, but something's been following her for a while. Heph's walked home behind her from the school a few times and said he felt something too. Something stalking her but too far for him to perceive what or who it is."

"Whatever. It won't appear with us standing guard."

"Fine. Tone down your aura though."

Beau nodded. Moments later, he was so dim, Luke couldn't tell the god of war was there if he closed his eyes.

They both faded across the veil and retreated to the In-Between. It was a nebulous sort of space, like the insulated zone between two walls of a house filled with support beams and studs, but little else, existing only as a pathway for supernatural beings and creatures of the other worlds. He'd heard some gods refer to it as reality's glue, or the bond that kept all the realms together.

Waiting there, some time passed, and it was all the more dull since his cell phone didn't operate in the nowhere space and he couldn't even text Esme to ask if she was awake.

Luke grunted. "I think we're worried for noth—"

It shot out of the sky, all feathers and foulness, and crashed through the living room window and into the house.

Beau moved first. "Shit!"

But Luke was faster. He emerged from the In-Between inside the living room and caught the filthy bird in the chest with his arm. After clotheslining it, he flung it with all his might into the In-Between, crashing through the barrier with it and losing track of Beau.

In the real world, lights popped on, and both women rushed out of their rooms. Esme had a baseball bat, and Marie was clutching a shotgun.

"What the hell was that?" Marie asked, cradling the weapon to her chest rather than pointing it at any possible danger.

"Maybe the wind knocked that branch into the window? I told you we should have trimmed it back. And why did you even let your dad give you that thing if you're just going to hold it like a teddy bear? *God*. Give it here."

Another harpy rocketed toward the barrier, only to encounter Beau's sword. The god of war sliced it into two distinct pieces with the flaming blade and dove toward another member of the flock descending with her outstretched talons aimed toward his face. Now the air of the neutral plane smelled like sizzled bird droppings.

The screeching harpy tore at Luke with its claws and screamed in his face, her offensive odor bringing tears to his eyes. He slammed her into the ground and summoned his caduceus. Once the rod appeared in his hand, he drove the sharp tip downward into the flopping bird-woman, effectively spearing it through her naked breast.

More were coming.

Two. Then three. There were five suddenly, their dark bodies rushing the curtain, savagely scratching and fighting to get to the woman Luke and Beau loved. Luke fought alongside the man who had once been his rival—one of his *greatest* rivals when it came to Aphrodite—

though his chest heaved, and he couldn't recall the last time he'd cared to fight anyone for any reason at all.

One of the harpies ripped the staff from his hands, grasping it in her dirt-encrusted talons. He caught it around the shaft, but it became a tug of war battle to retain possession of it. A second bird landed on Luke's back and knocked him to the ground, smearing her foulness on his clothes, making him reek just like her.

Throwing his jacket off dislodged her. He spun up from his prone position, off the ground with a move worthy of a Capoeira championship and snapped his foot into her human face. She screeched then lunged at him again, but he caught her beneath the wings, which flapped and buffeted his cheeks. All of her flockmates were dead now.

Beau yanked his sword from the gut of the one who had taken Luke's caduceus, which only threw the creature into a desperate frenzy.

"Kill it already!"

"Then stay still, otherwise you'll end up missing a hand."

Still? Luke grunted and turned his face into his shoulder. He closed his eyes, felt the wind from the swing, and the sporadic jerks of the body still struggling even after the head tumbled to the ground. Grimacing, he dropped the creature. Its blood was on his hands and had splattered his body.

Through the hazy black curtain of the veil, he watched Esme retrieve the vacuum from the closet while Marie picked up larger pieces of glass from the floor around the couch.

VIVIENNE SAVAGE

"Ugh. This sucks. What the hell do we do for the window?"

Esme plugged in the vacuum. "Saran wrap and a blanket for now, I guess. I'll call someone first thing in the morning."

"Something smells like shit," Marie muttered.

Esme tensed and glanced around the room, a deep wrinkle in her brow until she locked her gaze in Luke's direction. He stilled, even held his breath, positive she could see him.

"We better go," Beau murmured.

"What if something else comes back?"

Beau dragged the harpy's corpse away into the yard and impaled it on a spectral sword, the glowing length of spirit matter glaring red against the dark tones of the neutral ground. "I don't think anything will tonight. That should last a couple days until it disperses." Corpses in the In-Between didn't last for long, usually dissolving into energy and matter that fed the different realms, seeping into them by a kind of magical osmosis.

Luke blew out a breath and nodded. "Yeah, okay. We should let Alex know too."

"I suppose you're right. We have some work to do and some asses to kick, because someone sent that bird to do more than trash her living room. Who knows that we found her?"

"I didn't mention it to anyone. Why would I? Did you?"

Beau shook his head. "I mentioned it to Dad, and he isn't telling anyone. I guess we just have to figure out who

64

hated Aphrodite enough to hold this kind of a grudge. Heph should remember most of her rivals."

"Who *wasn't* her rival back then?"

"Everyone dicking her."

Luke hit Beau in the shoulder before he thought it through. "We fought plenty."

"With each other. Not with her. Now, you gonna hit me again, kid, or we gonna go see Alex and figure this the fuck out?"

"Fine, let's go."

5

*A*lex wiped the blood from his hammer and glowered at the smashed remnants of the snakes he'd fought while Esme enjoyed a book behind the store counter at Memory Lane.

She hadn't so much as looked up, completely oblivious to the battle happening beside her. Humans never noticed anything that wasn't right in front of them. While there were a few rare souls who seemed to sense the In-Between, they only caught the haziest glimpses through the Fog.

He grunted and grabbed one of the serpentine carcasses from the floor. Esme's head jerked up abruptly, and she stared through him, eyes wide with alarm. She blinked a few times and shifted in the chair with tension in her shoulders. Eventually, she relaxed and returned to her book.

Luke was right. She did have a hint of her senses. Like

the last drop of soda left in a can, a breath of divine spirit remained in her mortal body. Just enough to perceive something had happened nearby.

While he watched, she plucked a truffle from the box on the counter and nibbled it. The differences and similarities to the Aphrodite he had known fascinated Alex, though he was satisfied to discover her sweet tooth had survived the passing of several dozen reincarnations into the human world.

He left the shop and took his kills with him, already aching and stiff from fending off her would-be assassins. Their bites covered his brawny forearms and blood glistened on his chest and thighs. It might have been a problem for another god, but Alex was immune to the effects of their venom. It stung, a mild irritant and nothing more, though it was capable of putting someone like Ares or Luke down for a few days.

It would have killed Esme in one bite.

Alex emerged from the In-Between when he reached Luke's apartment. Most gods surrounded their domains with spells and different protective hexes in the In-Between to prevent trespassing, but Luke had designed his to allow both Beau and Alex free reign.

Both were on the couch embroiled in a video game battle, aware of him but distracted until the moment he stepped into the real world and dropped both bloody corpses beside the coffee table.

Luke spared a brief glance away from the television. "What the hell happened to you? You okay, dude? And what are those? What *were* those, I should ask."

"Stygian serpents I intercepted at Memory Lane. They were on their way to a rip in the veil."

Beau jumped up from his seat. "And you handled them *alone*? Fuck, that impresses even me."

"I don't need a sword."

"No, I suppose you don't. I forget sometimes what you are." Beau frowned. "That's one of Mom's tricks."

Alex nodded. "Yes. It is."

"You gonna go ask her about it?" Luke asked.

"No." Alex wanted to punch Luke for even asking such a stupid question.

Beau sighed. "Hey, man, I know she did you wrong and all, but it's been a couple thousand years. Are you still not ready to just bury the hatchet and move on?"

"She tossed me out like trash. I'm not going back."

"But—"

"You do it. She always preferred you to the rest of us, right? Find out if she's up to her old tricks and meddling in mortal affairs again. In the meantime, I'm going to create something to protect Esme at home and at the job."

Alex faded into the In-Between and returned to his estate. Contrary to the taunting he received from Beau and Luke, he'd lived in Ashfall Springs for years before he'd even realized Aphrodite was alive again. Stalking her had never been part of his plan, though he had been her silent protector for the last few years of her life.

And as much as he loved Esme, as much as he wanted to protect her, facing down the mother who had hurled him from a mountaintop was the last thing Alex could do.

BEAU HATED CROSSING INTO OLYMPUS. HE DIDN'T VISIT often, preferring the liveliness of the mortal realm with all of its imperfections and flaws.

Like the world they pretended to lord over, Olympus evolved with the times, although some hints of the olden days remained. Alabaster statues and marble pillars decorated the manicured fields designed to resemble the hanging gardens. He spotted Apollo and Artemis playing golf together. The sport had become the new archery. The twins waved at him, so Beau forced a smile, waved back, and kept on walking.

His mother lived in a lavish home on a cul-de-sac between the goddess of youth and goddess of childbirth, both her children with Zeus. Peacocks roamed her yard and foraged through the lush plant life.

Beau frowned at the birds when one ventured close and pecked at his feet. The jewel-toned creature followed him to the door, tempting him to kick it, but no one— even her preferred children—messed with Hera's favorite animal. He ignored his feathered harasser instead and knocked on the door.

"It's open!" she called from inside.

He took in a deep breath to steel his nerves and opened the door.

The house smelled like cookies and wine. He wandered down the hall into the living room where Hera sat on the couch. Instead of a television, she watched something in a shimmering pool set on the coffee table.

"Morning, Mom."

A warm smile spread across her face. "Ares, dear, how nice to have you over for a visit. Let me make you something to eat."

"You don't have to do that."

"Nonsense. I'm your mother, and I know you've been hanging out in the mortal plane. You must be starved for something that's actually fulfilling."

"You never cooked when I was young, so don't bother doing it now. I didn't come to hang out."

"Oh." Hera's face fell, and if he didn't know her so well, if he hadn't watched her devote every waking moment to stalking her adulterous husband instead of spending time with her numerous children, he would have thought he hurt her feelings. "I take it this isn't a social visit, then."

"Nope. What do you know about a recent attack on Aphrodite?"

"Aphrodite?" She scoffed. "That girl ran off centuries ago."

"Well, she's been reborn, and we know where she is. All *three* of us. We're going to bring her back."

"And you think I care? No, I didn't send anything to kill the little bitch, though if I'd known she was around again, it might have occurred to me. Why? What happened?"

"Hephaestus intercepted a pair of Stygian serpents on their way to her from the In-Between, and a few nights ago, Hermes and I slew a harpy that burst through her window. Barely got it out in time before she realized what was happening. Then a whole fucking flock descended and we had to take care of it. We've been taking turns keeping an eye on her ever since while trying to figure out who sent them."

"Oh." Hera pressed her lips together, and then she chuckled. "While I can't claim to feel any pity or concern, I can say it wasn't me. I haven't tamed a serpent in some time."

"I bet you know who has. You're a product of the times, as nosy and gossipy as every other woman down there in the world."

Her scowl furrowed her brow and darkened her eyes. "Why should I bother helping when you won't even let me cook for you?"

"Because deep down I know you wanna make up for what you did to Hephaestus, and he'll be crushed if she's hurt. You want him back, help me out here."

Hera uncrossed her legs and rose. "I'll talk, but while I'm cooking."

Given no choice, he followed her into the kitchen.

"Stygian serpents come from only one place, you know that. None of them can leave or be taken without special dispensation."

"Hades."

"Or his wife." She sliced a golden apple and smiled at him. "And you know how our lovely Persephone feels about your lover."

"But why should she give a damn about Aphrodite now? She left our divine realm and became a human. She doesn't even know any of this shit exists right now."

"Exactly. But if you three convince her to return to our

VIVIENNE SAVAGE

realm, she'll recall all past squabbles and victories." Hera smiled slyly. "She'll remember Adonis, whom Persephone has kept all to herself these past centuries thanks to you sending him to the Underworld. She may even want Adonis back again since my dear ex-husband forced them to share."

Ares scowled.

"Murdering him certainly wasn't one of your best moments."

"I shouldn't have let Persephone manipulate me into that," he agreed, "but I guess my lack of impulse control comes from you and Dad. How's the old man doing anyway?"

Hera shrugged and moved to the cold box to remove a decanter of wine. "How should I know?"

"I still can't believe you left him. You're the goddess of marriage and family."

"Why should I stay? Times have changed." She paused, and after a moment she said, "Still, you should go see your father. Be a good son and visit your parents sometimes."

"I don't have much to say to the old man. He exiled me over Hephaestus crying foul."

"And I convinced him to allow you to return. Now go sit down and let me finish this apple pie. You can take it back with you." Her expression turned wistful. "Take half to Hephaestus, but don't tell him it was from me. He'd never take it."

"Regular apples? No ambrosia?"

"Sorry, love. There's a shortage. Haven't found a crumb in all of Olympus recently. The doves who once brought it have all vanished, and there are no signs of more coming soon."

With nothing left to do but wait, he dropped down on the sofa, kicked his feet up, and closed his eyes. At least if he napped he wouldn't have to talk.

6

*E*sme fastened her winter coat over her sweater dress and leggings before hurrying outside into the frigid afternoon. The skies were a uniform gray over Ashfall, but the day was somehow bright, making the pristine snow appear more ivory than ever.

Given a choice between popping into the resort to oversee placement of last-minute donations and spending time with her friends, she'd decided to decompress with the gang at the rink.

It had been touch and go during the middle of the semester, her entire college career circling the drain as she struggled through her architectural graphics class, but it was all done save for one art project requiring its finishing touches, and she could deliver that in the morning. She wanted to add a pair of dwarf pomegranate bushes like the ones she'd seen in an editorial spread about Dito's Manhattan penthouse a couple years back. For a clothes model, she had excellent taste in décor.

Esme had painted the design in watercolors, creating a cozy conservatory with enormous windows spanning its walls to shed light over the plant life within. She'd added numerous wooden chairs and benches with cushioned seats for relaxing alongside the circular, in-ground hot tub.

The hot tub had been one of her favorite parts to sketch out and bring to life in color. She'd given the room high, vaulted ceilings with spacious skylights and an iron hearth surrounded by stone. Windows made from many glass panes added a touch of warmth with several potted palms and ferns.

Last night, right before bed, inspiration had struck and she'd painted in a glass table for two in the corner by the brightest window, adding two teacups on the bamboo placemats.

Esme slogged through a mile of snow to meet up with her friends at the rink on the borders of Old Ashfall and the city. After showing her annual pass at the fence separating the skaters from the spectators and meandering pedestrians, she took a seat.

"About time you got here," Jordan grumbled, folding his arms against his chest and pouting. "We've been waiting for like thirty minutes. All that time, and you don't even show up with a full face of makeup? Girl, bye."

"Dude, it's too cold for all that. The moment I blow my nose, half my foundation will be on the Kleenex. No thanks. Besides, you two could have totally skated without me for a while."

"We're waiting on Ashley too—oh, there she is!"

After Ashley laced up her skates, they moved onto the

ice as a group. Conversation drifted between grade predictions, boys, and winter plans interspersed between moments of Jordan and Esme showing off on the ice.

"So, you going home for the break or nah?" Ashley asked.

Esme shook her head and twisted to skate backward in front of the other two, gliding effortlessly into the reversal. Marie scowled at her. "I'll stay here. I went home for Christmas last year."

Jordan mimicked her while adding in fancy step work. He'd been a junior figure skater before quitting during his teens. "My parents want me to come home but, ugh, nobody wants to sit around the table and listen to my drunk uncle discuss politics."

"Same," Marie said. "Minus the drunk uncle. My personal Christmas hell would be listening to Dad bitch and moan about my major because he wants to know how I'll get a *real* job."

Esme wrinkled her nose. "Eww. Dad fail. I'm not worried about anyone hassling me. I just figured I'd stay here for once, maybe spend some time with Luke."

Jordan perked up and skimmed near them again. "Oh yeah? How's that going anyway? He still making it up to you for his spontaneous game of hide the sausage with your hand?"

The girls all giggled at the imagery, but heat spread over Esme's face. Thinking back to that night stirred up more than embarrassment—part of her, deep down, wished she'd dared to give in to his expectations. "Good. He helped us both study this weekend, and I gave him a *hand* with his programming stuff."

Jordan and Marie cackled again.

Ashley broke off from the group. "I am freezing. Y'all, I seriously need a hot cocoa break. Anyone coming with?"

"That's because you weigh ten pounds. Anyway, yeah. I'll take one," Marie said.

Jordan skated off to join them. "Me too."

"I'll stay here."

While they were gone, Esme practiced her sit spin, wishing for a quieter rink where she could do more. Sometimes, when the ice wasn't busy, Jordan gave pointers and taught the simpler moves. She'd learned to go from a single to a double salchow since meeting him sophomore year.

"Looking good there," the deeply masculine voice rumbled when she came out of a twirl.

Esme jerked to her right and narrowly avoided colliding into a passing skater. "Beau?"

Her motorcycle-riding savior flashed a big grin. He steadied Esme with a polite hand to her upper arm, and he released her the moment she regained her balance. "Sorry. Didn't mean to scare you, sweetheart. Just happened to see you across the rink and figured I'd come by to say hello."

"Oh. Well, hi."

A guy of his size should have been awkward on the ice, muscled and tall as he was, a direct contrast to Jordan's lithe frame. He wore the same jacket and black gloves but no other winter protection, the most underdressed man on the ice compared to the others in scarves and muffs. He wore his jeans fitted, hugging a flawless ass.

Esme jerked her gaze away. "Aren't you cold?"

"No. Why? You offering to warm me up if I am?"

Her body flushed with heat. A vivid image played in her mind of Beau shrugging out of his leather jacket and peeling away his shirt to reveal a chiseled, hard chest and defined abdomen. The guy had to be ripped.

Angered at her own imagination, she glided away until there was a comfortable distance between them. "*No.* Sorry, I have, um, I have a boyfriend. Kinda."

"Damn. Okay if I hang out then?"

She bit her lower lip. Her attention drifted to the concession stand a few yards from the rink where elephant ears, hot cocoa, and other hot snacks awaited skaters and spectators. Jordan and Marie stood at the end of the line while Ashley sat on a nearby bench beside a portable heater. "I should probably go to catch up with my friends."

Undeterred, Beau circled around her, spinning a 360-degree turn. "Your 'kinda' boyfriend that jealous or is it just me?"

"No. I don't think he's the jealous type."

"What's the harm then?"

The harm was that she wanted to bone him, and he was definitely *not* her boyfriend. One look at Beau's face made her imagine the things she wanted to do with it. Like ride it. He was the guy mothers warned their daughters about, the bad boy who deflowered virgins in the back seat of the car. He was sin in a black leather jacket and a handsome devil bent on torturing her.

"Afraid?"

He pushed the right button. Esme scowled and moved back to his side. Beau grinned.

"So, do you live around here or are you up for the slopes?" Esme asked.

"I'm in town visiting my brother and monitoring a mutual interest. He's a bit of a loner, so I gotta come and keep him company every once in a while." His tone gentled, and a hint of unexpected pity warmed his voice. When he spoke of his brother, his eyes went sad.

The unexpected answer made her look at him with new understanding. She studied his jawline and admired his full, firm lips. Lips she really shouldn't be thinking about. She tore her gaze away, ducked her head, and swept her hair back behind her ears. "That's nice of you. Anyone I'd know?"

"Nah, probably not. He doesn't get into town much, the old hermit."

"Talking about Alex?" a husky, feminine voice spoke up from behind Esme. She turned and came face-to-face with a tall, lean young woman with dark hair styled into a faux hawk, the sides braided toward the top of her head. She looked like an extra for a movie about Vikings or the lead guitarist in a punk rock band.

Beau's jaw tightened, but then he smiled, making Esme wonder if she'd imagined his irritation. "Yeah," he replied.

"I'm Eris. Beau's sister." She snickered.

"Oh, hey, nice to meet you. I'm Esme."

"So I've heard," Eris replied.

"I didn't know you were in town," Beau said.

"Well, what kind of sister would I be if I didn't pop in to check on my brothers? Alex told me where to find you."

"I'm sure Alex could use the company more."

Eris frowned. "Well, I'll leave you two lovebirds to skate alone. See ya after the date." She glided ahead, punctuating her departure with a flawless quadruple Lutz jump.

"Lovebirds?" Esme slanted a glance up at Beau. "*Date?*"

"She's a pest, what can I say?"

"You talked about me to your sister?"

"I mentioned you, that's all."

"Uh-huh." She smiled, amused by his discomfort.

"Anyway, back to our conversation."

She raised her brows at him. "We were having a conversation?"

He scowled and bumped his hip into hers. "We were. I was gonna ask about you. You only up here for college?"

"My grandmother lived in town. She was an art history professor over at the college, and I guess there wasn't any doubt about where I wanted to enroll." She brightened as she thought of her grandmother, visiting the museums and traveling abroad with her. They'd traveled to Paris together one summer, and from there backpacked their way to Italy. Every beautiful moment had been seared into her mind, memories of a fond time with a wonderful woman.

"So that means you're probably the artsy type, huh?"

"Something wrong with that?"

"Nope, it just means you can probably do more than draw a stick figure like me."

Skating backward, Beau weaved in and out of the crowd without ever seeming in danger of crashing into anyone. She envied his perception of his surroundings, or his luck, whichever one was great enough for a guy of his size to maintain extraordinary grace.

Five years of figure skating lessons, and she'd never felt as confident as he appeared.

She could have let him go and continued her own leisurely skate, but instead she pushed herself forward and caught up to him.

"You can't draw that bad."

Beau smirked. "Trust me, princess, there's not an artistic bone in my body, but you're more than welcome to find that out for yourself if you'd like. I think my younger brother stole all the creative genes."

"Younger brother? Sorry, from what you said, I assumed he was the older one. Or do you have more than one?"

"Nah, I got several, but I was referring to Alex. I just call him an old man because he acts like one. He's boring. Doesn't go out in public, doesn't have any friends." He edged in closer and slipped an arm around her waist, and then he twisted them both into a controlled spin. Esme grabbed at his sweater to keep her balance, which only brought her in closer.

"What are you doing?"

"I don't bite. Come join me at the Hot Spot."

"I don't know..."

"Seriously. All that skating has me ready for a pizza, and I'm down for sharing. It's not a date."

Pizza. He said the magic word, an ideal way to celebrate the end of another semester, with gooey and hot, delicious cheesy pizza. Then she glanced across the skating rink to where Marie sipped cocoa while resting her feet on a bench outside of the rink, distracted with a hot tourist and oblivious to Beau's presence.

"Only if my friends can come."

"Deal." He leaned down. "I promise I won't take offense at you wanting a chaperone."

She smacked his chest, which only made him laugh, but he released her waist and took her hand instead. They made one more circle around the rink before skating to the exit.

Ashley and Jordan had disappeared—likely visiting the restroom, but Marie was stuffing her face with a sack of hot candied pecans. The moment Esme stepped off the ice, her friend stared at their linked hands.

Esme tugged free from Beau's grip.

"Who's this?" Marie asked.

"Marie, this is Beau. Beau, meet my bestie, Marie."

Marie's mouth fell open. For a moment, she appeared to be incapable of operating her vocal cords, an awkward three seconds passing before she squeaked out, "*You're* motorcycle hottie?"

Beau chuckled and offered her a leather-gloved hand. "That would be me. I hadn't realized Esme talked about me."

"Oh, well, you know how it is. She thought you were a serial killer who was gonna toss her in a sex dungeon."

"Marie, I did not!" Esme hissed.

Beau laughed, a rich, deep sound that made Esme's insides turn to liquid mush. Judging by Marie's glazed look, she experienced the same.

"Sorry, ladies, no sex dungeons. I was thinking pizza and a pitcher of beer or something. You wanna join us?"

"Did someone say pizza?" Jordan reappeared from around the bleachers. He looked Beau over from head to toe and back again. "Who's your friend, Essie?"

"Jordan, this is Beau. Beau, meet Jordan. The cute redhead behind him is Ashley. Don't let her size fool you, she can put away an entire pizza on her own."

"Hey," Ashley said.

"Nice to meet you all." Beau smiled. "So... pizza?"

"Yeah, that sounds great," Jordan said. "Thanks, man."

"No problem. I'll meet you all there. Unless Esme wants a ride on my bike?"

"Oh, um, I'll pass this time. Won't your sister need the ride?"

"Nope. She'll be fine. So, you game or not?"

Esme shook her head.

"Suit yourself. I'll see you all there."

The group all watched him go. The moment he was out of earshot, Marie turned on Esme and pinched her.

"Ow!"

Ashley placed the back of her hand to her brow and feigned swooning. "Oh my God, he's gorgeous."

"Totally drool worthy," Jordan agreed. "Definite A plus on the 'Would Wreck Him' scale."

"Pretty sure I told you both that already."

"I know, but I mean..." Marie sighed dreamily. "He

really is. He's hotter than Luke, which is saying something, 'cause you know I like me a chocolate man."

Esme rolled her eyes. "Sure, I guess, if you like the bad boy look. And can we please not refer to people with brown skin as food items?"

Marie fixed her with an unimpressed stare. "Uh-huh. Whatever, chocolate is delicious. C'mon, we better get moving before he thinks we ditched."

They hurried through the process of changing out their shoes and tossing their skates in the car trunk. Marie drove, which meant Esme clutched the armrests and Ashley asked at least five times for her to slow down. Jordan zoned out while texting on his phone, unaffected by Marie's NASCAR impression.

Beau already had a table, pitcher of beer, and a two-liter of soda. Marie claimed the spot beside him in the booth, but Esme took the seat across from him with Ashley and Jordan. Their feet bumped together.

"So, Beau," Jordan began, setting aside his phone. "What do you do? 'Cause I know for a fact you aren't a student. I've never seen you on campus, and I know *everyone.*"

"Guilty as charged. I, uh, work out of the country a lot. This is a bit of a long-overdue vacation. In fact, I've just returned from Afghanistan after wrapping up some shit in Iraq."

"Army? Marines?" Ashley asked.

"You could call me a contracted agent."

Marie's eyes lit up with interest. "Ooh, does that mean you can't talk about what you do?"

Beau nodded, but the warm grin never faded from his

face. "Pretty much. One of those, 'if I told you, I'd have to kill you' things. Besides, you'd never believe me even if I did say."

"Wow, I've never met a mercenary before. That's so cool."

"I've also been a stunt advisor for a few Hollywood hits. I'll be filming in New Zealand this summer."

Their evening progressed into friendly banter over four shared pizzas. Beau charmed them all, funny and charismatic enough to win over even Ashley, the shyest of them all. The time flew by, and soon enough they were chased off by the staff so they could close up.

"Hope we see you again sometime, Beau," Jordan said.

"Yeah. I'd love to learn more about those self-defense classes," Ashley added.

"Anytime. Drop by the gym and I'll set you up. I'm there every weekend, Tuesday, and Thursday."

Beau walked them to the car parked in the lot. His motorcycle occupied a spot out front on the curb. And like a gentleman, he held the door open for Marie as she slid into the driver's seat.

"Hey, Esme. Got a sec?"

"Sure. What's up?"

Beau stepped away from the car and gestured her over. Jordan flashed her a thumbs-up before he got in the back seat. Esme rolled her eyes, but inside she had butterflies flapping around in her stomach. She followed Beau away a few steps and smiled up at him.

"I had fun tonight. You've got some good stories."

"Told ya." He smiled and reached over, adjusting the

scarf around her neck. "Listen, I just figured I'd toss my hat into the ring in case this boyfriend of yours fucks up. And even if he doesn't, I wouldn't mind doing this again. I can keep my hands to myself. Completely platonic."

"Uh-huh."

"Men and woman have had friendships and nonsexual relationships for centuries, sweetheart."

"You make a convincing argument."

"Good. Then I'll see you again soon. Oh, and Esme?"

"Yeah?"

"Were you really worried about being followed and thrown into a sex dungeon?"

"That last bit was all Marie, but yeah, I guess. Walking home alone at night can be scary. It's been a long time since I took a self-defense class."

"Come by the gym and I'll teach you a few things to refresh your memory. I mean it. Here's my number." He passed her a card.

"We'll see. Night, Beau."

She hurried back to the car and scooted inside.

"Damn, girl, not even a goodnight kiss?" Jordan asked.

"We're just friends. That is only my second time meeting him."

"Didn't you kiss Luke on the first date and second time you met him?" Ashley asked.

"Shut up."

Marie dropped Ashley and Jordan off at the school dorms. He smooched Marie noisily on the cheek before hopping out and promising to give them a call later. Ashley slid out behind him with a quiet goodbye.

Marie waved out the window then backed out of the

lot. She glanced over at Esme and smiled. "That was fun, right?"

"Yeah. Beau wasn't half bad company."

"Esme, he's incredibly hot. Like panty-melting, makes you want to shove him into a closet and go down on him right the fuck now kinda hot. Like get boned in a dingy restroom in the club hot because you've had too many drinks and don't think you'll encounter that kind of hot again. Like sexier than Henry Cavill hot, and you know how I feel about that man in spandex. He's a stunt coordinator. I bet he knows all those big actors."

"Yeah, he is. And he seems like a nice guy. He said he came here to look after his little brother."

"I wonder if the little bro is as sexy as him. Think it runs in the family?"

"Probably."

"Since you have Luke, um, you wouldn't mind if... maybe I took this one?"

A lie hung in Esme's throat, heavy as an iron weight, displeasure gluing her tongue to the roof of her mouth. She tried to speak, but she couldn't, couldn't make herself utter a blessing. Finally, the tension eased, and a suitable response followed. "He doesn't belong to me."

"That's not the same as it being okay with you. I mean... you've never had two guys actively into you before like this."

"No, I haven't."

"And I totally get it if you don't want to let it go. I mean, maybe you're waiting to see if Luke lasts and you wanna hold this guy on the shelf like a benched player waiting for his chance to bat at the plate."

Esme sighed in relief, reminded not for the first time what an awesome best friend she had. "Do you mind holding off a lil? I mean, if he shifts his interest to you, that's, you know, fine, but for now...?"

"I got you, girl. Besides, there's always the younger brother, right?"

7

*M*arie applied Esme's makeup in the resort restroom, her steady hand preferred when it came to drawing flawless cat eyeliner.

"I feel ridiculous."

"Well, you look hot," Marie said. "Luke may be a presumptuous douchebag, but the man knows how to shop."

"He's not that bad."

"Uh-huh, says the girl who ended up with a meat sandwich she didn't want. I know we forgave him for that, but I still... No wonder you want to hold on to Beau for a while."

Esme rolled her eyes and changed the subject. "Did you see it yet?"

"See what?"

"The Alexander Smith piece." The last minute donation had arrived while Esme was helping with the final preparations that morning. She'd practically fainted when she saw the name on the crate and rushed to rearrange the entire exhibit area to place it front and center as the star of the auction.

And then a second donation had arrived from Mr. Smith that shook her so deeply, affected her profoundly, she didn't understand why. She'd stood for nearly a half hour inspecting what had become her favorite piece of work from him to date.

Esme wished more than anything that she had the money to purchase it.

"Ready to go mingle and convince people to spend money?"

"Let's do it."

Each item up for auction had a clipboard beside it for people to write down their bids. To maintain anonymity, participants received a number when they checked in for the event.

Esme, Marie, and five other students had the challenging task of encouraging guests to raise their bids throughout the evening. She made her first round of the room, pausing to speak with people she knew from town or the campus. Several of her professors were in attendance, as well as the elite of Ashfall. She recognized the mayor, several business owners, and the woman who owned the resort.

She wound her way back through the room to her favorite area—the sculptures. She had tried her hand at it once, but never managed to make anything that resembled the idea in her mind.

A shadow fell over Esme and blocked out the light to her left. She glanced up to see a large man wearing a tuxedo that must have been tailor made to fit the enormous breadth of his shoulders. He had the height of a professional basketball player and the build of a football pro, the rugged features of a war veteran, and the sad eyes of a lost puppy. A thick, pink scar emerged from his crisp white collar and twisted over his neck. Had someone once tried to cut his throat?

His brows were thick and heavy above eyes the golden brown of topaz chips, though for a moment, she thought they were red. Another scar slashed his right brow and crept into his hairline where the rest was concealed by a full, thick mane of blond hair.

Was he a war veteran? As it would be rude to stare, she stole glances at him out of the corner of her eye instead. He was missing a piece of his ear, and all his features appeared exaggerated—from his prominent brow to his strong jawline. The lantern jaw of a comic book hero matched his barrel chest. Despite those physical flaws, there was something more attractive about him than all the models, movie actors, and boy band artists she'd ever admired.

Although he wasn't standing at his full height and gripped a cane in his right hand, he towered above her. "What do you think of the sculptures?" the man asked.

She startled. One heel skidded and turned, threatening to drop her to the floor, but a strong hand beneath her elbow steadied her. His grip was iron hard, his fingers scorching against her bare skin, calloused and rough as sandpaper.

But one touch lit a spark through her and raised the fine hairs on her arms. Her nipples tightened beneath the strapless bra, and she thanked any god who was listening that the consultant at the shop had insisted on a padded style to accentuate the girls.

"Sorry. I didn't mean to scare you."

"No, no, no, it's not that. It's these stupid new shoes," she said. "I never wear heels this tall." But she'd felt empowered and confident the moment she emerged from the dressing room in them.

"Well, you look lovely in them."

"Oh, well, um, thank you."

The stranger withdrew his hand and fell silent. His gaze lingered on her face without unsettling her, and each time he opened his mouth to speak, he only shut it again until he finally looked away.

"You asked me something about the sculptures?" she prompted.

"I wanted to know what you think of them."

"Other than the fact we have more to auction off this year?"

A small smile upturned the corner of his mouth and softened his harsh features. "Yes. Do you have a favorite? A least favorite? I'm debating what to bid on."

"Oh, well, in that case..." Esme took a small sip from her champagne flute and looked out over the gallery. "I wouldn't say I dislike anything, but if I had to pick the one I like the least I'd have to say this one over here."

She led the way over to a pedestal displaying a three-foot-high figurine carved from pink marble. A card placed before it named the piece *Love Divine*. The feminine construct had been donated by Alexander

Smith, but it hadn't wowed her in person like the other works of his featured in magazines or the dragon.

What did wow her about *Love Divine* was the resemblance between herself and the figure—the upturned, almond-shaped eyes, high cheek bones, and full lips—but it couldn't be Esme because she'd never met Alexander Smith before.

It had to be a coincidence.

"Why this one?"

"I don't know. It's beautiful, I mean, an absolutely beautiful and stunning work of art from Mr. Smith, but I don't look at this statue and feel warmth and love. More like... arrogance. As if the she knows she's better than everybody else. That's not love to me."

He studied her with a quiet intensity. Reminded of a disapproving professor, Esme resisted the urge to squirm under his scrutiny. She must have sounded like a romantic idiot.

"That is a unique perspective. Insightful," he finally said. "But I suppose you're right. You seem to like Alexander Smith's work."

"I love it. I've followed his career for years, ever since I was a child I wished I could sculpt like him, but sculpture and metalwork isn't my artistic talent."

"What medium do you prefer."

"Water colors and charcoal."

"I see. Both are respectable and beautiful forms of art. So which of these do you like best?"

"Oh, that's easy. My favorite is this one."

She bypassed several other donations and moved to the back wall where the largest piece in the auction occupied a space beneath two spotlights. Copper, bronze, and black steel made up the sculpture that had been fashioned in the likeness of a dragon. The entire piece stood seven feet tall, and it had taken a guy with a forklift and several men to bring it in and get it into place once they'd opened the crate. The title card identified it as *The Fire God*.

"You like dragons?" he asked.

"I've never really cared for them much, to be honest. I wasn't into that sort of stuff as a kid."

"So why choose this piece?"

"I can't really explain it, but this one calls to me. Even though it's crafted from metal, there's a life to it. Even though it's a dragon, the artist was able to depict an expression on its face. While the other statue appeared arrogant, this one is... majestic," she finally murmured after a pause to collect her thoughts. "And the wings are unfurled just ever so slightly, indicating the dragon is poised to take off or pounce. See the amount of detail in the individual scales?"

"I see what you mean." He turned to her and smiled again. "And if you could purchase this piece, would you?"

"If I could afford it, yes."

He nodded. "Thank you for your time, and your assistance Miss..."

"Esme. Esmeralda, really, but all of my friends and family call me Esme."

He took her hand and bowed over it, brushing a soft kiss across her knuckles. The old-fashioned gesture made her stomach flutter.

"A pleasure, Esme. Thank you again."

"You're welcome."

Her mystery man stepped away and moved into the crowd. As tall as he was, she was able to follow his progress for a moment until he disappeared around a corner. She hadn't even asked his name.

"Oh my god, Esme, you lucky heifer."

"Huh?" She blinked and turned toward Marie's voice. Her friend hurried over, eyes wide. "Why am I lucky?"

"Girl, that was the big-time artist. The guy you couldn't get ahold of on the phone, remember?"

"Alexander Smith?"

"Yes. I only know what he looks like because—okay, so you know Jasmine is a nurse at Lakeside General Hospital, and last year she was stuck pulling a twelve-hour shift on Christmas Day. She says this guy—this really scarred guy with a cane—showed up with an assload of toys and gifts for everyone, introduced himself, and said he'd received permission from the director. Then he spent hours reading and gaming with all the kids who didn't have visitors. He let her take his photo with a few of them. Like, he specifically asked to meet the kids with parents who never visited them."

"Oh no." The blood drained from her face and a sense of vertigo overcame her. "Oh my God, Marie. I was gushing over his work like a clueless idiot while he just nodded along and humored me."

"At least you didn't say anything bad, right?"

"No. I didn't trash any of his work, thank goodness." She didn't particularly like the piece of work that she suspected was the goddess Aphrodite, but she did see the skill involved in its craftsmanship. The flawless lines and polished curves made the statue hyper realistic, bringing to mind myths about gorgons capable of turning humans to stone with a stare. He'd chiseled and shaped every wrinkle of her gown, added the illusion of silk draped over nipples hardened into tiny pebbled points.

At any moment, she expected the statue to walk down from the pedestal.

"—know if it's that crazy new cocoa diet you're on or those perfumes you bought online, but if it is, I need to buy some."

Esme realized Marie had been talking the whole while and turned a sheepish look on her friend. "Sorry. I was thinking about where I could dig a deep enough hole to hide in."

"Well, buckle up, girl. We still have a dinner to get through. If you're lucky, you won't have to see him again tonight."

ALEXANDER HAD PAID A MEMBER OF THE STAFF FIFTY dollars to change his assigned seat to Esme's table in the banquet hall. Then he'd paid the guy another two hundred to pretend they'd never met.

Sometimes a god had to make his own miracles happen, and he definitely needed every helping hand he could get.

When he reached the round dining table, Esme had just arrived before him. She stood behind her chair, eyeballing the small white card displaying his name on the setting to her left. Her friend stared directly at Alex then leaned in close to whisper.

Esme stiffened, jerked around to look at him too with widening, horrified eyes.

Shit. Alexander didn't know much about socializing with women, but tense shoulders and a straight spine seemed like a bad way to start the dinner.

He took the risk and closed in on the table until he stood behind his chair. The other diners hadn't found their table assignment yet, which gave him a moment to break the ice on his own. "Good evening, ladies. What a pleasure to discover such fine dining company," Alex said amicably, although he towered over both of them and Marie craned her neck in the close distance to look up at him.

"Hello, Mr. Smith," Marie said, taking her seat on the other side of Esme.

Esme turned to smile up at him. The tension vanished, her smile radiant, and he wondered if he'd imagined her discomfort, perceiving something that wasn't there. "Hi again."

Beau or Luke would have said something charming, and as he stood there fumbling for something remarkable to say about meeting her again, he floundered and realized he was never going to be like them.

He drew her chair out instead. "After you."

Once Esme settled, he took the seat on her left. His knees touched the bottom of the table. When he glanced up, both girls were staring, and he wondered how much he looked like a gorilla in a suit.

A waiter brought fresh water and lingered long enough to take requests for tea or coffee.

Alex asked for tea. The ladies requested coffee.

Servers moved into action and swept over the room with carts loaded with salads. Alex didn't care for salad, but eating it passed time.

"I am so sorry for what I said about your sculpture," Esme blurted out.

"Why? You told me your thoughts on it. That's all any artist can ask for."

Esme picked at her salad, pushing spinach and orange segments around. "Why didn't you say who you were?"

"Forgive me for the deception. I'm not used to..." He gestured with a hand, feeling helpless. Aphrodite was —*Esme* was in her element, at ease and comfortable with the crowd of diners. The room felt too small to Alex, tiny. Cramped. It hurt to remain in the uncomfortable suit for so long, and he realized quite sadly that he could never be the posh gentleman she wanted. Couldn't be Luke in a nice suit or Beau in his leathers and jacket on a motorcycle. His back had ached from the moment he left the estate, but he wanted to do this for her and was no quitter to skulk back home in failure over mild discomfort.

"It's okay, Mr. Smith."

"Please call me Alex."

"Alex." She tasted the word on her mouth, repeating it with a smile on her gorgeous face that cleaved through his pain like a sharpened ax. "All right. If you don't mind my asking, what changed your mind about attending our fundraiser."

"The children."

"You like children?"

"Sometimes. I, ah, did donate last year. Anonymously."

An arched brow raised. "Really?"

"I didn't offer anything for the auction, but I gave a monetary contribution."

"And this year you donated two."

"I did." He wasn't even sure himself why he'd added the sculpture of Esme at the last minute. "I'm told you called me."

Esme blinked and set down her fork, turning her full attention upon him. "I did, and I'm sorry if I crossed a line there."

"No, it's fine. Augustus passed on your message, and I decided it was time to step out of my comfort zone, as it were."

"Which part is out of your comfort zone?" Marie cut in. "Fancy banquets or socializing with other people." Esme shot her a hard, impossible to miss glower, but her friend ignored it. "Your face is such a mystery, Esme didn't recognize you earlier."

"I value my privacy," Alex said, avoiding eye contact with Esme's pushy friend. "So both are, I suppose."

Two more diners arrived, one of them a woman in a plain black dress contrasted by her jewelry. Diamonds sparkled around her neck and at her ears, rubies flashed from her fingers, and emeralds gleamed against her wrists. She had on enough bling to stock a jewelry store.

Esme smiled across the table at the two, but it didn't reach her eyes. The warmth had dimmed, leading Alex to suspect the two diners wouldn't be the best company. "Good evening again, Mr. and Mrs. Griswald. I'm glad you were able to attend again this year."

"Yes. As are we, honey. Once again, you and Director Coolidge have put together a magnificent event for the children." Mrs. Griswald looked down her nose at Alex, as much as one could when standing but still eye level with the man placed beside your chair. Then her eyes darted to the folded card identifying him. Her expression changed from appearing as if she'd smelled curdled milk to false geniality, her smile a thin veneer over her initial reaction.

"Alexander Smith? *The* Alexander Smith?"

"Yes."

"What a pleasure to be seated beside the man who has decorated so much of our estate."

The man accompanying her chuckled. "My wife has bought several of your pieces."

"Yes, including your *Love Divine*. As soon as I saw it, I wrote my number on the buy-out line. I would have been devastated if someone else took her home."

"Congratulations." Alex glanced sidelong at Esme. "You were right."

She blinked at him a few times, and then she laughed, her amusement as musical as chiming bells.

He'd always loved her laugh the most, and it pleased him to discover it hadn't changed over the centuries.

Servers came around and swapped out their salads for dinner. Alex examined the miniscule filet mignon on his plate and held back a sigh. Four bites of meat and a flimsy bacon strip? That was it? These modern humans had a strange way of providing a banquet. He remembered the days when the tables would be overflowing with food and drink, more than enough for everyone to eat. He often missed those times.

Of course, he also missed the days when artisans would build temples in his honor and throw festivals celebrating the god of fire and crafts.

When Marie engaged the rich couple in conversation, he turned to Esme. "If you are truly fond of the dragon, there are many more in that particular style in my home. You're welcome to visit and view them at any time."

Esme's fork clattered to the plate. She fumbled for it, reclaiming it before it tipped off onto her lap. "I—really?"

"Of course." He paused, considering the nature of the invitation, and cleared his throat. "No pressure of course, I completely understand if you—"

"I would *love* to come look at your work, Mr. Smith."

"Fantastic. And please, call me Alex. Perhaps you might join me for dinner tomorrow as well, so we might discuss another donation for the hospital."

Mrs. Griswald's eyes grew larger than the small saucer holding the dessert.

"I would love to," Esme said, looking starstruck.

He passed her a card with his personal number, different from the landline manned by Augustus. "Text me at your convenience tomorrow."

Coming out had been worth it, if only to hear her laughter and see her smile.

pproaching winter had dumped another two feet of snow on Ashfall Springs and the surrounding area, so there was no finer day for a double feature at the theater. Luke had returned from Vegas and picked her up sometime after noon that Sunday, and they'd driven to a popular dine-in, only to discover most customers had stayed home to avoid the snow and poor weather.

They'd watched an epic fantasy movie, a thing of beauty with elves, dwarves, and magicians, while gorging themselves on pizza, concession candy, and alcoholic beverages. Afterward, Luke convinced her to stay for a second film.

He bought another pair of tickets and led the way. Esme followed him to the rear of the theater to his preferred seat, farthest row in the back, middle chairs. "Kinda empty."

"That's fine. Less people cackling during the movie.

Less people standing up and blocking your view with their big heads." He chuckled, and memories of their last outing came to mind when the enormous man in front of her had stood up during the movie and searched for his misplaced phone for almost five minutes.

The screen was still blank, the lights dimmed but not darkened for full theater ambience. No one else had arrived yet for the six-thirty showing of the current brain and guts comedy slasher starring sentient zombies.

They sat in silence, perusing the drink menu and writing down dessert treats on small order forms, but she felt the weight of his attention occasionally settling over her, a palpable thing, like a gentle caress on her nape.

"What?" she finally asked.

"Nothing."

"You keep looking at me."

He grunted, gaze darting away. He twirled the pencil between his fingers and didn't look at her again. "I was not."

"You were."

"Okay, so maybe I was. Can't a guy appreciate his beautiful girlfriend?"

It touched her heart, because from Luke, it didn't feel like a load of bullshit to get into her panties. "So, girlfriend?" she said in a gentler voice, lowering to a whisper because people were entering again. "What's happening here? With us, I mean."

A crease formed between Luke's brows. "I'm not sure I'm following."

"Are we an item now? Is this just a few dates for fun? We've never really spoken of it and..."

"And what?"

"I've sorta been asked out by someone else. I had coffee with him yesterday, but it wasn't a date," Esme said in a rush. Technically, she'd been sitting at the cafe with a novel when Beau helped himself to the other chair at her table.

If he'd been anyone else, she would have left. But his company had been... oddly satisfying, and she'd set the book aside to talk about Old Ashfall's Norwegian style architecture with him. Before leaving, he'd convinced her to meet him at the gym next Sunday for boxing lessons.

She didn't bother to mention the dinner with Alex. That had been business, though there were so many moments of fleeting sexual chemistry between them she'd had to excuse herself to the bathroom twice to pace in a panic.

Whenever Alex looked at her, she felt bare and exposed.

Those were the wrong feelings to have about a stranger, even if she did stalk his online art gallery.

"Oh... okay. That's cool."

"That's it? It's just cool?"

"Well, what did you expect me to do? Rampage and ask who the fuck it is so I can go choke him out? I mean, you're hot. If someone else didn't want you, I'd be concerned you were hanging around blind dudes."

"I'm not hot."

"I beg to differ. Anyway, like I said, go for it."

"Just like that?"

Luke shrugged.

Esme nibbled her lower lip and shooed the tiny,

niggling feeling of self-doubt chiseling her confidence. "Are you only saying this because you want to stay open too?"

Now Luke looked offended, unconcealed irritation flickering in his golden eyes, like she'd dealt him a serious insult or blow to his masculinity. "*What?* No. As far as exclusivity goes, I don't plan to date anyone but you, but I'm not going to lose my shit and lurk outside your window at night if you go out with another dude."

"Uh-huh."

"Seriously. Call the guy up and accept the date if I'm what is holding you back. All I care about is that you're happy."

She pursed her lips, studying him. She'd developed a good method of determining if Luke was fibbing with her, because his fidgeting intensified and he had a difficult time leaving his sleeves alone. Or his buttons, messing with his jacket zipper or anything else attached to his clothes.

His hazel gaze didn't flinch from eye contact, his serene expression still and serious.

"That's... a little unusual."

"Let's just say I've learned my lesson when it comes to smothering chicks and wanting too much too fast. I don't have anything to fear, and well, if you do date some other guy and like him more..." He shrugged. "Anyway, you do you."

"All right. Maybe I will." She leaned across the armrest between them and slanted her mouth over his lips. He tasted like gummies and sour sugar again, sweet lime flavoring his tongue along with a hint of the tropical mixed drinks they'd sipped during the previous movie.

Once she started kissing him, she couldn't stop. Something small, like a kernel of confidence she hadn't known could blossom inside her, took over completely and guided her hands. Guided her mouth and her tongue until she was delivering kisses over his jaw, his throat, nibbling his earlobe and taking her sweet time with exploring the way his pulse beat beneath her lips when she returned to his neck. Her fingers slid over his thigh until she found the prominent, impossible to hide bulge beneath his fly.

A month seemed like years ago.

Esme unzipped his jeans, ignoring the empty rows ahead of them, the faded rectangle of light that shone directly above their heads at the screen, and the fact that someone could walk up on them at any moment.

"What are you—?"

"Shhh," she whispered against his lips. She eased his cock out into the open air. "No one's here to see us."

Esme discovered something oddly empowering about having her hand around Luke on her own terms, her fingers wrapped around the silken and smooth heat of him. She explored at first, her grasp loose, fingers wandering and trailing up and down, tracing the vein that pulsed his need. He arose so hard so fast in her hand, it seemed almost magical.

"Esme, you're killing me, girl."

"Should I stop?"

"No!" He jerked beneath her touch and clutched the armrests.

"Then shut up and enjoy before we're caught."

A glistening droplet beaded against the slit in his smooth cockhead. She smeared it with her thumb and smoothed it over his soft skin. Luke groaned softly and tipped his head back against the seat. His hips shifted, lifting slightly so he pumped into her hand. Esme firmed up her grip and stroked his full length down then up again.

His breath quickened, and then the rhythm of his hips became frenetic. Desperate. He groaned her name again, prompting her to lean forward and smother his pleasure with another kiss, muffling him.

"You're going to get us in trouble," he mumbled.

She chuckled and nipped his lower lip.

Her pumps quickened, skin sliding against skin. Luke trembled beneath her, every muscle in his body taut. When he came—and it was going to be soon—it would be all over his jeans or the back of the seat in front of them. She didn't want that, which left only one option. One daring, ballsy option. Esme tucked her hair behind her ear and ducked down, capturing him between her lips.

Luke practically came undone, one of his hands white-knuckled over the seats, the other tangled in her hair. He pumped twice, lasting mere seconds after she put her mouth on him.

It wasn't as bad as she expected, the salty sweet taste of him forced down in a swallow. Then she leaned back and tenderly tucked his cock inside his jeans then zipped him. He was spent in every definition of the word, slumped in the seat with his head back, looking like he'd been hit with a dose of a strong narcotic instead of fellated in a movie theater.

"Whoa." It came from him about five minutes later. She wished she'd timed it.

"You okay?"

"Yeah... I'm good. Just wanted to lay here and savor it for a few."

"You're not gonna sleep through the movie, are you?" The lights had dimmed, and the first trailer was up on the screen. The theater doors opened and light from the corridor cast the shadows of three people before they came into view and took their seats in the middle.

"Nah. Trust me. I'm wide awake."

"Good." She snuggled into his side when he didn't shy away from kissing her afterward and felt even happier when his arm slid around her waist.

Luke held her throughout the movie, occasionally turning his head to kiss her brow, skimming his fingers beneath the edge of her sweater. She'd never seen him so relaxed. So still.

One date with Beau wouldn't hurt. Once she had the rugged biker out of her system, Luke would receive the attention he deserved.

MORE FLOWERS ARRIVED FROM LUKE MONDAY MORNING. Daffodils this time, with a few red rosebuds included.

Marie squinted at it. "Is this seriously a blow job bouquet? I have *never* gotten flowers after giving head."

DIVINE AMBROSIA

"It wasn't a full blow job," Esme muttered, shrugging into her coat. She had a morning and afternoon shift at Memory Lane before plans to meet Beau at the Krumkake, a Norwegian-inspired restaurant popular among the tourists.

"He must really wanna make sure you come back to him after your date with Beau. Or is it Alexander you're having dinner with later? I can't keep up with your multiple admirers anymore."

"Alex isn't an admirer. I had dinner with him Saturday to discuss an additional monetary donation, remember? Then he invited me over to see his work Friday afternoon. That's all."

"Uh-huh. The rich recluse who doesn't see anybody invited you to his private house no one else has ever seen. If he's not aiming to get you in bed, then I'll eat my shirt."

"Hope you're hungry."

"Whatever. How do you even keep track?"

Esme winked. "The Amazon Echo did a great job of reminding me this morning with my alarm." She wound a scarf around her neck then stepped into her fur-lined snow boots. "I'll see you later."

"Bring leftovers."

"If there are any."

The last thing she heard as she stepped outside was Marie muttering about what a lucky heifer she was. Not that Esme could disagree. Her private and professional lives had finally flourished, with two men pursuing her on a personal level, and a wealthy billionaire intrigued by her artistic eye.

Eight hours of relative peace gave her a chance to

catch up on a book behind the store counter. She humored the occasional tourist and showed a few regulars around but ultimately spent most of her time devouring a romance novel.

By the time Esme locked up, darkness had fallen, the moon a pale silver crescent in the sky. The street lamps were all aglow, and Christmas-themed ornaments glittered from every corner and every intersection. Light strands shone from building storefronts, wound around light poles, and decorated trees. There were ribbons and tinsel dangling from signs, and festive snowmen with carrot noses.

A few Christmas ornaments to the left flickered. One by one, the pieces of the Nativity to her right-hand side, lovingly situated on the front lawn of an apartment, dimmed and went dark.

Esme tested the soles of her new snow boots, confident enough with the traction to pick up her speed and dash down the next corner. The restaurant wasn't far, only another two blocks.

A strand of twinkling lights in green and red went out, as did the lights inside the souvenir storefront that always kept its Christmas decor lit throughout the night. The lights all popped and sizzled, crackling until a wave of darkness swallowed the area and only the faint hint of white moon above her remained.

She wondered if it was a citywide blackout until she realized, in the great distance, she saw there were lights at the school over a mile away. She veered off her path and cut across the road, only for the darkness, the persistent and stubborn darkness, to overtake her and dim the entire block.

Her heart lurched, and that terrifying sense of doom returned—the dismay of seeing a cop in the rearview mirror with his sirens screaming, the terror of seeing your beloved dog charging toward a busy intersection, and the absolute pants-shitting terror she imagined her parents must have felt when she climbed onto the bathroom sink as a child, fell, and cracked her head on the toilet.

Pins and needles spread through her fingertips. Somehow, she fumbled her phone from her purse, only to encounter no service.

Breath quickening, she shoved her hand back into the pocket and palmed the stun gun her anxious father had given her the day she moved to Ashfall on her own. While he was a peaceful man, he was willing to set aside that nature when it came to her.

An impossible thing emerged from the shadows, barely visible against the gray slush and trampled snow. It was all mottled black and brown with disfiguring scars twisting against its furry hide, as large as a Great Dane, but... there were two snarling mouths dripping thick saliva. It smelled like sulfur and smoke—living nightmare fuel.

Not real. It's not real. This isn't real.

It padded closer, a low and menacing growl rumbling from its barrel chest, hot spittle dripping to the snow and sending up curls of steam. At this distance, she saw its tail looked more like a snake than anything else, thick and scaled.

Not real. It can't be real. This isn't real.

Esme stood her ground and decided to wait for the nightmare to end. In a moment, it would collide with her. Then she'd awaken at the shop counter, or perhaps at home in her bed, heart pounding but otherwise prepared to embrace a day at work and delicious dinner with Beau.

It lunged and snarled, washing hot, fetid breath over her before she spun on her heel and dashed toward the street because she lacked the willpower to put her theory to the test.

A blur shot by her peripheral vision. A split second later, the dog yelped and trash cans toppled over behind her. Esme continued running and darted to the right through the empty, rear parking lot of a charcuterie known for its smoked meats and exotic cheeses. The employees were gone. They closed early on weekends.

Shit. Although she didn't hear the sound of the mutant dog pursuing her, she lunged toward the opening of the narrow alley.

Hard, rough fingers closed around her right wrist, restraining her.

"Esme."

Despite years of laughing and doubting it would ever be used, let alone recalled, everything she'd ever learned during a few self-defense classes with her mother boiled to the surface. Panic and intuition thrust the stun gun forward, striking somewhere in her attacker's thigh. She hit him again with it, the crackling noise startling her as much as his cry. He staggered and wobbled on one leg. That split second was enough time for her to lead in with her knee to his groin.

When it connected, the large man dropped to his knees, although he was so tall, so enormous, he was still almost eye level with her, down on the dirty snow with both hands cupping his balls and bellowing in pain.

She leaned to dash past him when his hood slid back, tumbling away from a familiar scarred face.

"Alex?" she cried. No wonder her attacker hadn't lifted a finger to stop her.

He grunted. "That hurt more than it should have."

"What the hell are you doing here?" Her gaze darted toward the mouth of the alley where she'd last seen the *thing*. It had run on four legs but hadn't resembled any dog she ever saw.

"Protecting you. Or trying to."

Beau skidded into the alley, gripping a short sword in his hand with a bright tongue of flame blazing over the edge. Esme jerked back and slammed against the brick wall of the building behind her.

"Is she hurt?" Luke demanded, suddenly present to her left, placing a hand on her shoulder. "Are you okay, Esme? Did that thing hurt you?" He guided her toward the corner where two buildings connected. Three short stairs led up to an alcove and the back door of another closed tourist attraction.

"Breathe, baby," he coaxed as he helped her sit down on the step. "How's it coming over there?"

"Shut up and keep her safe," Beau snapped.

A snarl preceded the creature's return. A dark shape blurred through the alley and pounced on Alex. Growls and snapping teeth echoed against the alley walls, and strange, terrifying shadows crossed Esme's vision. Golden red light shifted and flickered, and it took a moment for Esme's mind to connect it to the sword—the impossible flaming sword.

"Just keep looking at me, baby," Luke said. By crouching in front of her, he blocked her view of what was happening. Maybe that was for the best.

A sharp crack accompanied by a pained whimper filled the air, followed by silence. The burned stench reached Esme's nose, like blackened meat, and nausea shredded her stomach. One by one, the lights came on again.

Beau stepped into view without his sword. "All right. It's done. How is she?"

"In shock I think. Where's Heph?"

"He felt someone disturb the veil and went to check it out."

"We need to get Esme home. Persephone's hounds tend to hunt in pairs, if not packs."

No one provided answers. Only discussed her. A visceral blend of terror and fury welled inside her and burst out at once. "Someone tell me what the hell is happening."

Luke sighed. "All right, but I'm gonna get you inside first. You're freezing, and I only live around the block from here."

"I—"

"No. No arguing this." He scooped her up into his arms and then... then it was as if she were in a windstorm. Her hair whipped around her face, and suddenly she was out of the cold and inside a warm room. Luke set her down on his couch and drew a blanket down around her.

"What? How?"

"I'm fast. It wasn't just a brag."

"But we were... we were blocks away."

"It's hard to explain, and we should wait for the others. Lemme get you a drink or something to warm you up."

"I don't want a stupid drink. I want answers."

"They're coming, I swear." He pushed a glass into her hand and stepped out of her sight again. Esme dropped her gaze to the golden liquid inside and then tossed back the drink in one gulp. The whiskey burned down her throat and warmed her all the way to her toes.

Luke returned to drape another fleece blanket over her lap. Then he ducked down beside the couch and plugged in the cord.

Esme stared at it. "This is just like the one in my room at home." The similarity wouldn't have bothered her if not for the hint of dried red nail polish on the edge. She'd spilled some on her own electric blanket three nights ago. "It *is* the one from my room at home."

"Yeah..."

"All right, I don't give a damn if the others are here or not, I want to know what's happening, and I want it—"

The door opened. Beau and Alex stepped through, though the latter had to duck to fit. All three of the men in her life, all in one place.

Life had to be pulling one cosmic joke over on her.

Beau spoke up first. "I know how this must look."

"Really? How does it look, because right now it looks

like I'm going fucking crazy because a weird creature chased me down the streets and now the two guys I'm dating are here with... with..." She gestured toward Alex, unable to put a title to what he was to her, though something in stomach did an anxious flip whenever the scarred man came into view. "Am I going insane? What's going on here? Why are you three together? What was that *thing* in the alley?"

Beau rubbed his face with one hand. "I didn't lie about being here to see my brother. Alex is my younger half-brother. And the thing in the alley—"

"It was a hellhound," Luke said. When the other two stared at him, he threw up his hands. "What? Better to rip it off like a Band-Aid at this point, man."

She was trapped in an apartment with three crazy men. Three absolutely crazy men who would probably throw her into a car trunk and drive away with her, if they didn't dice her to pieces right now.

His sword couldn't have really been on fire. It had been a trick of the light, or maybe a child's battery-operated toy with clever LEDs. Her brain rushed to explain what she had seen. Her attacker could have been a rabid dog or even a black bear with a skin disease.

Esme forced a few even breaths through her lungs. "Why are you three here? If you two are brothers, why is *he* here?"

"Hermes is a friend," Alex said in his deep, rumbling voice.

"His name is Luke."

"Actually, my name *is* Hermes. Luke is just the name on my legal stuff this time around..."

"Like the god?"

"Yeah. Just like the god. And his name is Ares."

Alexander nodded, concern setting deep creases across his rugged face. "And my name is Hephaestus. We are gods, as are you."

Cold swept over her. Her eyes searched their faces. In the time since they had started dating, she'd noticed Luke was the playful one. A jokester who was always up for making her laugh. She'd seen him maintain a straight face before when making mischief.

Then why was her heart still slamming in her chest, pounding against her ribs with the ferocity of a bass drum?

IF ALEX HAD HIS CHOICE, THEY WOULD HAVE BROKEN THE news to her in a gentler way. The plan had been to take it slow or get her to remember on her own.

Finding her had been the easy part. Breaking the news of what she was and convincing her they weren't three lunatics was where the plan fell apart and became a complicated mess.

Beau sighed. "Do we have any damned reason to lie to you? You've known us for how long? Wait, don't answer that."

"A month. Barely that. For all I know, you weirdos are on some kind of drug. Maybe I've been drugged and that's why I saw things."

Luke snorted. "I mean, if you need visual proof, that'll

work too. We can let this play out like one of those superhero movies instead and each demonstrate our gifts until you believe us."

"Demonstrate them then. Prove it," she challenged.

He shrugged. "You want some coffee, babe?"

"Coffee? What the hell kind of random question is that?"

"Just humor me." Luke's grin widened. "You still like those caramel ones, right?"

Alex shifted his weight from foot to foot and watched the way Esme stared at Luke. Everything hinged on this moment, and as much as he hated to admit it, Luke's powers were the least likely to send her running in terror. She finally nodded and then Luke was gone, moving so swift even Alex had a hard time tracking his movements.

"Where did he...? He... he just vanished."

"He does that sometimes," Beau said, amused.

When Hermes reappeared, he had a frothy caramel-laced coffee, the name Annette scribbled across the cup in black marker. He must have taken it right out of the barista's hand.

"Here you go. Just the way you like it."

Esme stumbled back, right into Alex's arms. She didn't jerk away. "How did you do that?"

"I told you, we're gods and you're a goddess. Our Aphrodite."

"*Our?*"

"Ours," Luke confirmed. "When I said I didn't mind sharing, I was speaking for these guys too."

Beau stepped forward, morphing his clothes into armor. It ended the moment of peace and sent Esme into a full panic, a fighting, spitting, and clawing kind of panic instead of the petrified silence and terror they were accustomed to with normal humans. That was more like the Aphrodite they knew. She may have lacked the skill and the knowledge of how to fight, but she still had her fire and spirit.

"Stay back!" Her knee struck Beau in the groin. She started past him for the door, but Luke caught her in his arms. In the split second between her darting away and him moving to intercept her, he'd donned his divine raiment in all its white and gold glory, down to the winged helmet on his head and sandals on his feet.

"Hey, we're not going to hurt you."

"Let me go! You're crazy, all of you! I'm not some fucking goddess, so you can stop with this sick, perverted trick and leave me the hell alone!" She threw a punch, busting Luke in his perfect nose, and darted past. The door slammed shut behind her.

None of them followed.

Beau groaned from the floor, still cupping his balls until Alex helped him up. "Fuck, that hurt."

"Yeah. That seems to be the new trick in her repertoire." It would have amused him if he hadn't been on the receiving end only minutes ago in the alley.

"Should we—"

Alex shook his head. "No, let her cool off some. If we push her too hard, she'll shut us out forever."

Beau shot him a dirty look. "She did that once before, and it ended with her saying she never wanted to see any of us again. Because of you. Because you had to humiliate her for loving me."

Alex crossed his arms over his brawny chest. "Don't you blame this on me. Who killed Adonis? Was it me? No. You ruined that."

The moment Beau stepped into Alex's face, Luke slid between them. "Stop it. We were all dickheads to her," he said, nose honking until he pinched the bridge of it and squeezed. The injury began to heal at once, but he still had blood all down the front of his tunic. "And we agreed if we could get her to come back, there'd be no more fighting. Fighting is what drove her away."

"Fine," Beau grumbled.

Alex sighed. "You'll have better luck than me. She fears me, and why shouldn't she when I have a face no amount of magic can repair."

Luke shot him a glance and raised both brows. "Nah. If you ask me, you have the better chance of getting her to come around. Besides, you were her husband. I'll put money on it that when she's ready to come around, you're the one she seeks first."

Alex snorted and glanced away. "She hated me. Hated me from the beginning."

Beau shook his head. "No, twinkle-toes is right. She calmed down some when you touched her. I... she also didn't hate you as much as she let on, man."

"Perhaps. I suppose we have no choice but to wait and see." And they would wait. Because if they could wait centuries to see her again, what harm was there in sitting by a few more days.

But first, one of them had to shadow her home, because they had come too far to let anything hurt her now.

9

*W*henever humans talked about the afterlife, they seemed to have the same two places in mind—cloud filled heaven and fiery hell. Luke always found that amusing, because nothing could be duller than the Underworld.

Luke skipped the scenic route into the Underworld intended for mortals on quests. As the messenger of the gods and the guide of the dead, it was as easy as dragging Beau across the thin boundary and into the heart of Persephone's realm.

"Damn. Last time I came down here, I wandered lost for days," Beau murmured. They were already at the gates.

"Yeah, well, your uncle is serious about his privacy. He's probably going to lose his shit over me bringing you along, but Persephone owes you one."

"Heh. It seemed like a good idea at the time. I should have told her to kiss my ass."

They walked past the Fields of Asphodel, which looked more or less like an average suburban neighborhood filled with identical houses in recent years. Plain. Dull. Repetitious. A Homeowner Association Board's wet dream. Mediocre people who weren't worthy of a heroic afterlife or endless torture went there.

Hades's palace remained unchanged since his last visit. The structure, carved from marble and gemstones, never failed to impress and awe. The pale golden stone gleamed amidst the subterranean darkness.

Luke led the way up the winding path through Persephone's garden, where pomegranate trees grew in abundance. They reached the enormous front door only to find it open and the lady of the realm herself waiting for them.

"Persephone, you're looking lovely as ever," Luke began. "Right, Ares? Isn't she pretty?"

"Well, that was record breaking. I've never seen you start a visit off with kissing my ass."

Beau snickered. "Hello, Persephone."

"What can I do for the two of you? It's not every day I see you playing nice with one another."

"Can we come inside?" Luke asked.

The goddess pursed her lips. "I suppose." She gestured for them to follow her and led them into a small sitting parlor lit by the warmth of a golden hearth. A skeletal servant appeared with a tray bearing a tea service for three.

"Um, no thanks," Luke said. He made it a rule to never consume anything she or Hades served.

Beau shook his head too.

Persephone sulked and waved the skeleton away. "As lovely as it is to have visitors, I sense this isn't a social gathering."

"We want to know if you're behind the two attacks on Aphrodite."

Persephone blinked at them. "I don't know what you're talking about."

"Oh, don't play coy," Luke said. "One of your hellhounds attacked her in the mortal realm, Seph. Come on. If you did it, you did it, be an adult and at least admit it. I thought we were friends."

"We *are* friends. I'm not going to confess to something if I didn't do it. I didn't even realize Aphrodite was alive again. Look, unlike the three of you obsessed psychos, I don't keep tabs on her soul or where it goes. She comes here, she passes onto the tapestry of life again, and she's born into another world. Do I look like I have time to torment her?"

"Well, I thought—"

Persephone interrupted Beau. "You thought wrong. Your former lover hasn't been a blip on my radar since you killed Adonis. When she left her divine life, she did me a favor. I've had him all to myself."

"And maybe you don't want to share if she returns," Luke said. "Look, we didn't come down here to accuse you of trying to kill her, but two creatures of this realm have tried, and nothing leaves without your say so."

"I haven't taken anything to the mortal realm or allowed anything to escape. It's winter. I *can't* leave, and if you don't believe me, you can take it up with Hades."

Luke sighed. "No, that won't be necessary. I'm sorry,

sweetheart, really. It just looked really damning from our point of view, okay? Hellhound in the mortal plane causing trouble? Creatures from the Stygian Marsh stalking her?"

Persephone's lips pressed together. "I'm not angry. Just hurt that you think so poorly of me. For the love of Olympus, I'm not Hera. I don't have to go around orchestrating the deaths of people who piss me off, and I certainly don't murder them in cold blood while hiding in the guise of other creatures."

"No, you just turn them into plant life," Beau growled. "Isn't that what you did to the river nymph who flirted with Hades?"

When she stiffened, Luke groaned into his hand. "Guys, please."

"You can both see yourselves out of the palace."

Luke jumped out of his seat and followed her to the door. "Seph, come on."

"You've come into my home and insulted me. I'd like you to leave, and I won't ask nicely again."

He could wring Beau's neck. Luke drew in a deep breath and forced a smile while racking his brain. "My apologies. Really. We'll go, but do you think you could at least help us figure out who snuck a hellhound out? I mean, it's gonna look pretty bad for you when the big man finds out."

Persephone arched one perfect brow. "It wouldn't. Many of the other gods have received hellhounds from us over the years, and Father *knows* how selective I am about my babies and where they go. But fine. Try Hekate. She's good at this divining thing, maybe she can find some answers for you. If I hear anything, I'll pass it along, but... what happened to the hellhound?"

Luke sighed. "We killed it. The damned thing was rabid. Like, it tried to take a piece out of *me*. I've been petting your beasties for centuries. Why would one try to attack me?"

Frowning, she gestured for them to follow her. They traveled outside of the palace to the kennel hugging the exterior, a building devoted to Persephone's hellhound breeding program. The moment she passed through the gate, two calf-sized pups scrambled over and danced around her legs.

"Hello, sweetlings," she crooned to the drooling monsters. She crouched and let them lick her face. "Agape! Xenos!" Two more bounded to meet her. "Xale! Philos!" A third dashed over to join its littermates. "Philos!" she called again.

Luke and Beau exchanged glances.

"We *are* missing one. A pup."

"The one we killed had been beaten badly. There were whip marks all over it, like it had been driven mad by pain."

When Persephone straightened, tears glittered in the corners of her eyes. She blinked a few times. "One of my pups was beaten?"

Beau nodded. "I'm sorry, sis. I know I was an ass, and I know how you feel about your pets, but someone mauled it and set it on our woman. We *had* to put it down."

Her features darkened, lips pressed into a terse line. "Whoever is responsible will pay dearly. You go see

Hekate if you like. I'll question everyone who has access to the hounds and let you know what I find."

"Thanks, Persephone, that's all we ask," Beau said, seeming to find his tact again. "If there's anything we can do to help, don't be afraid to reach out and let us know."

BEAU DIDN'T EXPECT TO FIND HEKATE ENTERTAINING HIS sister in the fragment of the underworld realm dedicated to her control. The goddess of magic and witchcraft kept a humble home that reminded him of a *Lord of the Rings* hobbit hole built into the dark earth. A campfire burned out front, crackling blue and purple flames, where both women sat on a thick carpet of grass while sipping wine out of enormous jugs and nibbling treats from a meat and cheese plate.

"Good evening, ladies," Luke said as they approached.

"Told you," Hekate said. "Pay up."

Eris groaned and passed her several golden drachmas. "You have an unfair advantage."

Both men exchanged glances, and Beau cleared his throat. "Betting on us? Really?"

"When we saw you come down, we decided on a little wager to see if you'd make your way over here," Eris explained, grinning. "You know, since you two have a history. I didn't think he'd have the guts to come over, but looks like I was wrong. Playing the role of the wingman tonight, Ares?"

Luke shuffled his feet and glanced aside, avoiding eye contact with Hekate. "It's not that kind of visit."

Too bad Luke had left his longtime lover and set his sights on Aphrodite instead, further complicating an already challenging relationship. The goddess of magic wasn't a bad looking woman, but Beau had to wonder sometimes what happened to split them up.

"Good to see you up to your old tricks, Eris."

"Long time no see, brother."

Beau snorted. "You visited me almost two weeks ago."

"Then you ditched me for the princess. When are you coming back to help me out? It's no fun in Afghanistan without you stirring up trouble."

"You're doing a badass job on your own. You don't need me there."

She frowned. "I can't believe you aren't bored with that snowy little town yet."

"Between the snakes and the hounds, it's been rather exciting, actually. Look, I'm sorry for burning off on you, okay? You picked a shitty time to visit, sis. Come back whenever you want, and we can bat around a harpy together if more return."

A big grin spread over her face. "I'm kind of seeing someone now too, but maybe I will come and liven up the place a bit."

"Enough you two," Hekate said. "Hermes, Ares, please join us."

"Thanks," Luke mumbled. He took a seat across from his ex-lover and folded his hands in his lap. Beau dropped down beside him.

"Wine?" Hekate offered.

"Thanks, but no, we only have a few questions if you don't mind," Beau said.

"You want to know if I can help you with your Aphrodite problem."

Eris perked up. "What problem?"

"Someone stole one of Persephone's hounds and sent it after her," Luke said.

His sister leaned forward and studied them over the fire, blue eyes twinkling with interest. "That's a serious accusation. Tell me more."

Beau rolled his eyes. "We're not here for your amusement."

"Yeah, we were hoping you could help, Hekate," Luke said. "Please."

"It could be any number of gods. Aphrodite has certainly made enough enemies over the years. But I wouldn't give anyone but Athena or Artemis enough credit to have the wit to sneak into the Underworld and make off with one of Persephone's prize pups."

Eris cackled and clapped her hands. "I'd put my money on Artemis. She's never forgiven Aphrodite for casting that love spell on Hephaestus to punish him for getting you kicked out of Olympus, brother." She lowered her voice and leaned closer. "I heard he pulled it out after dinner and humped her thigh like a little poodle. Can you believe it? What kind of man does that?"

"Yeah, what kind of man does that?" Beau asked.

Luke flushed. "*Anyway*. Do you think you could use your magic to help us track the assassin?"

Hekate tossed something into the fire. The flames roared upward and deepened into an indigo hue. Beau waited, unable to see anything in the flames, but Hekate's mismatched eyes reflected the firelight and he knew enough not to interrupt her when she was focused. Eventually the goddess blinked and shook her head.

"Something shrouds the person you seek. I cannot see them."

"Well, fuck," Beau muttered. "Then, can you at least tell us if she can regain her immortality?"

"She could if there wasn't a shortage of Ambrosia in Olympus—in all of the worlds for that matter." Hekate gazed into the distance and pursed her lips. "The doves are all gone. One hasn't flown to deliver any Ambrosia in a while. It's driven up the price."

"Damn. Do you have any?"

"None I'm willing to part with, even for you boys."

"What about you, Eris?" Luke asked.

"I don't keep that stuff on hand. Too busy."

"Well, damn." They were back to square one with nothing much to show for their efforts, and Beau hated the time wasted. Time he should have been using to check on Esme.

10

*E*sme huddled on the couch beneath a blanket and watched another Hallmark Christmas movie. In the days since the attack in the alley, her mind had tried everything to discredit Luke, Alex, and Beau's claims. Nothing made sense, and none of the three contacted her. A sort of silence fell over the trio until Saturday afternoon when Luke sent her a single text.

Just checking in. Don't gotta talk to me, just let me know you're okay.

She glanced at the message, then tossed the phone back onto the empty cushion beside her. A few moments passed before she plucked it up again and returned his message with a curt, *I'm okay.*

What if they were right? What if she was a former divine creature trapped in a fragile human body? Not any goddess, but the goddess of *love* who never kept her legs shut. Every story she'd ever read about the mythological

Aphrodite described an adulterous jerk who picked on mortals and started wars.

That wasn't her. That kind of person wasn't anyone she could ever be.

"Hey, Esme?" Marie asked gently from the doorway. "What happened on your date with Beau? You've been... really different."

"Hmm?"

"Are you all right? Did he like...?" Her friend took in a deep breath then joined her on the sofa. "Did he do something to you? Do you need someone to talk to?"

"What? No! It wasn't—he didn't *do* anything to me."

Marie practically melted against the couch. "Oh, thank fuck. Watching you around here, after how you came back, I just thought... I was so scared and ready to ask if I needed to whoop ass or call the cops."

"I never got to even go on our date. Something happened and... I don't want to talk about it, really, but I swear, he didn't touch me."

"Okay. Well, if a time comes when you do want to talk about it, I'm here for you, okay? Jordan is on his way to Las Verdes, and I'm going with him. Wanna tag along?"

"Nah. I'll just... actually, can you both drop me off somewhere?"

"Sure. Where you going?"

"To see Alex."

Marie's brows disappeared beneath her bangs. "Really now. I wondered if you were still going to catch up with Mr. Moneybags."

"I *did* make plans with him to meet last night for a viewing in his personal residence."

"But that was before whatever happened with Beau on Monday night."

Esme twirled a lock of hair around her finger and gazed at the television screen. The flick had reached its predictable conclusion, a happily ever after around the Christmas tree with carols and eggnog. How much could she share with Marie? In all their years of friendship, she'd never held anything back from her. "I found out Beau is Alex's older brother."

"*What?*"

"Yeah. My feeling exactly. And you know how Luke told me he transferred to help out a family friend who lives all alone?"

"They all know each other? No way! With those kind of odds, you should either stop dating or go play the lotto. Nobody has that kind of luck."

"I do." Esme sighed. Though it had nothing to do with luck if they could be believed about her being a goddess in a mortal body. "Anyway, long story short, they're all trying to be really nice about it and no one is angry. Nobody demanded for me to pick one of them. Luke kind of implied I could be with all of them, and it creeped me out."

"Seriously? Ew. Or... I dunno, kinda hot. But ew. Brothers?"

"Yeah, I can hardly believe it myself."

"So, wait, Alex is the *younger* brother? Damn." Marie whistled. "Life has not been kind to him. Or does Beau just look really good for his age?"

Yeah, I guess that happens when your mother throws you

off a mountain. "Beau looks really good for his age. A mix of both I guess."

She made herself get up and into the shower. After she finished dressing and putting on her makeup, Marie rushed her outside to Jordan's car.

"Hey, girl, looking good today." Jordan smiled at her through the rearview mirror. "You got your eyeliner on nice. So where am I taking you?"

Esme entered their destination into Jordan's GPS, and their adventure to the outskirts of town began. Ten minutes into the ride, Marie shot her a sly look from the front seat.

"Hey, Jordan, guess what?"

"Marie, no—"

"Those three guys into Esme? They all know each other and two of them are brothers."

"Lucky bitch."

Esme groaned and kicked the back of Marie's seat. "Look, it doesn't matter. It's all just too weird."

"What's weird?" Jordan asked.

"No one is jealous."

"So?"

"It was hard enough dating two guys, and I really wanna do more than date. Any time Luke or Beau are around, it's hard not to rip off their clothes."

"And Alex?" Marie asked.

"He's... like a big teddy bear. I don't know. I've only met him twice. He was sweet at the charity event, and... dinner alone with him was nice, but that was to discuss another donation for the hospital."

"Yet you spent Sunday morning texting him until your date with Luke, and you're going over to his house."

Esme scowled. "To see art."

"Uh-huh." Marie snickered and smiled over her shoulder.

"Um, are we going to ignore that two of them aren't related?" Jordan asked, turning onto the road that led to Alex's billionaire mountainside retreat. "If you don't end up in some kind of sexy man sandwich, I will never forgive you for leaving that opportunity at the door. I will etch that shit on your gravestone. 'Could have had two hot friends DP her but was a prude.'"

Marie stared at him, mouth open. "*Jordan.*"

"What? It's true. Luke and sexy-ass Beau look like the type who won't care if their balls touch."

Plows had recently blown through the area, piling fresh snow along the sides of the road. When they reached the gates—both of which were wrought iron sculpted into two big dragons—Jordan lowered his window and pressed the intercom button.

"May I help you?" the fancy British butler asked.

"Esme Caro is here to see Mr. Smith."

"Please bring her to the end of the driveway." The gates opened.

Jordan drove her down a quarter mile of smooth, dry concrete. There hadn't been any snow on the gate either. He parked at the end and peered out at the house. "Have fun."

"It's not that kind of meeting."

He winked at her. "Make it one."

Marie and Jordan waved goodbye before embarking

on their journey to the road again, leaving her at the foot of a dozen stairs leading up to a literal mansion carved into a mountain.

"Now or never."

Her discussion with Luke flooded back, because Alex's place *was* something out of a *Cribs* episode, all glass and metal, and secluded several miles out of town without another road in sight. If he turned out to be a psycho after all, she was fucked.

AFTER THE CATASTROPHIC MEETING IN LUKE'S APARTMENT, Alex had returned to his home and work, taking comfort in forging metal into beautiful shapes.

He had a few pieces ready to drop off in town at various shops and was contemplating sending Augustus to deliver them when the truck showed up at the gates. He eyed it and its occupants through the security camera poised above the console.

Augustus's voice cut through the intercom. "Master Hephaestus, a visitor—"

"I saw through the security cam," he said. "Send them through. I'll greet her myself."

"As you wish."

He stopped his work and met Esme at the door, pulling it open a split second before her finger pressed the buzzer. "Good afternoon, Esme."

"Hey, I, uh, hope you don't mind me stopping by. I'm sorry for standing you up last night."

"I understand. You don't have to apologize." He moved aside when he realized he was staring at her. He cleared his throat. "Please come in."

The others had been right after all. He'd expected her to choose one of the handsome two. Luke would have been his bet, since she seemed to prefer his attention the most.

He took her coat then led the way to the living room, aware of Esme's curious gaze touching everything they passed. He'd never given much thought to his home beyond its security and his personal comfort. Now he found himself wondering if she liked it, yearning for her approval.

"Have a seat anywhere you like. Can I get you something? Tea or coffee?"

"No thank you." She settled on the end of the sectional and brushed her hand over the leather armrest. How did she see her surroundings through her mortal eyes when his home was a dull museum occupied by a single man?

Alexander cleared his throat. He didn't know how to entertain a guest, unaccustomed to receiving any visitors who weren't there for business matters. A few awkward seconds passed before he settled opposite her and laced both hands together between his knees. "I didn't expect to see you again."

"Yeah, well, I wasn't sure if I'd want to see any of you again, but..." She took in a deep breath and let it out in a rush, words tumbling from her too fast. "I've been having weird dreams, okay? And they started before I met you, so now everything in my head is a mess, and I just want answers."

He listened with his head cocked. "Dreams about what?"

"I dunno. Things. It's stupid," she mumbled.

"If they bother you, they aren't stupid," he said, calm as ever.

"Aphrodite was a horrible goddess," she blurted out instead. "She cheated and she slept with, like, everyone, and she was childish sometimes. Cruel even. I mean, she played around with people's hearts for fun. That's not who I am."

He startled, flinching as if she'd struck him instead. "What? No. Never. She was—you were never an awful goddess." It spilled out of him in a fierce rush. "You were always a good woman, kind to your followers and all who loved you. And there were many who were jealous of that love, and they told lies once you were gone."

"That's a lot of lies to have lasted this many centuries, don't you think? Didn't she start that whole Trojan war thing by helping Paris seduce another man's wife? That doesn't sound very nice at all."

"Ah." He chuckled. "If the wife truly didn't want to leave her husband, she would have remained. Aphrodite could influence our hearts and show us our innermost desires, sometimes forcing us to act upon them. The stories say nothing of Helen's unhappiness with King Menelaus." He spread both of his hands, and then he sighed before dropping them down to his lap.

"Her meddling caused a war."

"It was a simple mistake any god could have made.

Unfortunately, when we err, hundreds, if not thousands, of mortals are injured in the process. And therein lies the reason we have withdrawn from the world. We grant a desire and there are ripples, a thousand ripples few of us can foresee the inevitable outcome of."

"Let's say I believe you about you three being gods, at least. Why? How could anyone give up that much power? I mean... I'd think Beau would be out there in the Middle East, North Africa, or Korea, or even somewhere down in South America reveling in the bloodshed."

When he looked at Esme, he could see hints of the goddess she'd once been, mostly in the fullness of her lips and the curve of her high cheekbones. Some of those features had survived the centuries of her life as a human, reborn again and again no matter where reincarnation took her.

"Yeah. About that. It goes back to what I said about making things worse. You see, as much as he revels in war, he doesn't enjoy endless war. There needs to be a time of peace. Imagine you had a chocolate cheesecake, and I told you to eat it right now. Then I set another in front of you, and every time you ate that cake, I produced another. No break in between to savor and enjoy what you've been given."

"Okay, that bit makes sense I suppose. Still, it seems hard to believe you'd give up people worshipping you and tending to your every need. And what about the others? Is Zeus out there? Athena?" She paused a moment, then added in a softer voice, leaning forward with wide eyes. "Hades?"

"You gave up more." His shoulders dropped a little

further, and the natural curve returned to his spine. It ached after a while of attempting to appear normal. "Most of us merely discovered there's more to life than living for the worship of the humans. We also realized they're good at screwing up their own lives without our help. Why complicate things more? Athena owns a well-known publishing company in New York. Zeus founded an airline. We each found things we love more than meddling in human affairs. Even Hades."

"Wait, hold up a sec. You're saying Zeus, god of lightning and all-powerful ruler of the gods, is just some suit in charge of an airline? And to think I've been stuck flying coach all these years. Damn."

Hephaestus chuckled. "You always preferred catching a ride with Helios in his chariot, but yes, you've missed out on a fair bit."

"You were the god of blacksmiths, right? And, um, volcanoes. So when Mount St. Helens blew, was that you? I mean, did you actively decide one day to set it off or did Ares piss you off and you lost your temper. 'Cause he does that a lot in the old stories."

"We're not to blame for every disturbance, Esme. Though I'm sure some of us would like to take credit for every disaster, I'm not responsible for that one. I could, if I wanted, but I prefer to prevent them from blowing these days. Yellowstone requires a lot of my attention." Then he rubbed his nape and looked away. "And yeah, he does. Claims it's brotherly love."

"And you were Aphrodite's husband, right? She was sort of given to you. So, if I'm Aphrodite—and I'm not saying I believe it yet—where does that put us?"

"Yes. Once, you were mine." Hephaestus glanced away, avoiding her eye contact for that moment. "You were wronged, and we failed to make it right then. So now I put the ball in your court, as the humans put it."

"What happened? You guys may be incognito, but you have your powers. What would make a goddess give hers up to become *me*? I'm nothing special. I'm plain and I'm dull. I'm not rich."

"We were fools and fought over you as we always have," he answered in a quiet, rough voice, dipping his head down. After a moment, he exhaled the deep, pent-up breath. "I believed I knew what was best for you. The more we tried to control you, the harder you fought, until finally, you broke away and did what no other god has ever done, renouncing your gift."

"Aphrodite was a cheater. If she was married to you, she shouldn't have needed other men, right? There should have been no fighting over her." She sighed and leaned back on the sofa, frowning. "Why do you even want me back?"

ALEX LEANED FORWARD AND REACHED ACROSS THE distance between them to place his hand over her knee. It sent warmth coursing through her and a strange, familiar sense of comfort, like sitting with an old friend.

"I don't blame you. It never would have happened if Zeus didn't offer you as a bargaining chip to whoever could convince me to free Hera from the trap I laid for her. But once we were wed, Aphrodite made the best she could of an awful situation. Each time I drove her away to Ares, I didn't want to admit I was to blame." His frown deepened, and his brown eyes grew sadder by the moment.

"Where does Hermes come into this?"

"You and he were lovers before you fell for Ares. When the war god stole you away with promises of battle and excitement, sonnets and poetry were no longer enough for you, and you wanted much more."

Esme dragged in a deep breath. "I still think you're all nuts," she muttered, but with less heat and conviction than before. She laid her hand over his much larger one and squeezed. "Tell me more about you. I don't want to hear about Aphrodite anymore. Not yet. Why do you stay up here in this huge house all by yourself?"

"Where else am I to go? It's private, and I have the space I need to work. It seemed like the ideal place to live."

Alex never seemed to meet her gaze, and when he did, it didn't hold for long. It seemed more than shyness. Had she done that to him or was it something else?

"You still do artwork in metal. Guess old habits die hard, huh?" She'd seen his work in shops all over town. Beautiful precision stopwatches, iron sculptures, one of a kind fire pits with fascinating designs. The resort had a large one in their courtyard that looked like a burning sun.

"Smithing and artwork are what I do best, my only true talents, and I suppose... my only other love. What else could I do?" He glanced over one shoulder toward the rear of the room at a pair of double doors. "Would you like to see my forge?" he asked suddenly.

"I'd love to. I wasn't lying to get your donation when I said I admired your work."

He offered her an arm and escorted her through the doors and into a wide corridor decorated with lavish art from around the world. Soon, they were outside on a snowless veranda. In the distance, there was another building, revealing his estate was more of a mountainside compound than anything else.

"Do you have any of my pieces?"

"Me? Oh, no. We don't have anything fancy like that in our place."

His face fell, and he glanced at her sidelong from beneath his heavy brows. He had one of those faces that looked stern even when she thought he wanted to appear happy.

"How big is this place? I had no idea it extended so far back. From the road, this all looks like forest and rock."

"A bit of magic blends the rest of the grounds into the forest. You can't have airplanes and busybodies noticing anything is amiss. I don't like the snow, so Augustus casts spells to keep it cleared from the paths."

"Spells."

"Yes. Magic."

As they reached the end of the stepping stone path, he moved toward the outbuilding and pressed his palm against the door. When it slid open, she saw it was an enormous stone slab. If it was solid stone, it should have taken at least six men, maybe even eight or ten to budge it.

A great wave of heat rolled over her from the huge glowing fire inside. From outside, the building couldn't be much taller than him, but inside, it was easily twenty feet high and three times as long, a circular chamber with rows of tools in a variety of sizes, some that seemed to belong in a giant's hands. The anvil stood taller than her.

"Holy crap," she whispered in awe. Once she realized she wouldn't burn to a crisp, and that it was nice and toasty compared to the frigid air outside, she followed him inside and gazed around in wonder. "How do you even lift some of these things? They're huge!"

"With my hands. This is much like the forge I once worked in Olympus. A little cramped at times, but good enough."

"Cramped. Right." Within a matter of seconds, her hair clung to her cheeks. She didn't see a single welding tool or blowtorch in sight. "So how do you weld things together? And please don't tell me your pinky is a flamethrower or something. Then again, that might be sort of cool. Scary, but cool."

He stared at her initially before glancing down at his hands. He snorted. "No. The blowtorch is a modern convenience. I use a stone from the sun, gifted to me by Helios."

"Yeah. Okay. A sun stone. Sure, nothing at all crazy weird about that."

"He and I are good friends, and he's always had a great appreciation for my work. I created his chariot, after all. Prior to that, he flew across the skies by pegasus."

"By pegasus," Esme repeated, staring at him.

"They are winged—"

"Winged horses. Yes, I know. Sorry. I'm just a little overwhelmed here. Helios is the one who told you Aphrodite was sleeping with Ares, right?"

"Correct. As god of the sun, he sees all and is privy to many things."

"There must be a lot of blackmailing going on in Olympus."

Alex shook his head. "Ah, to the contrary, he is a good man of great honor. What needs to be kept in secrecy is kept close to his heart. The same cannot be said for Luke, as he told you right away Helios was behind the discovery, and it led to a great rift between many of us." He paused with a grimace on his face. "Forgive me, that was worded poorly. Hermes is also a good man, though he stumbles from time to time, as do I."

Esme pulled her sweater off and tossed it onto an empty bench, leaving her camisole on. He had a bench lined with some of his smaller pieces—beautiful sculptures made from brass, iron, copper, and metals she couldn't identify. When she touched sundial and traced her finger along the polished surface, rainbow patterns shimmered beneath the surface of the white metal.

"Should I call you Alexander or Hephaestus?"

Alex kneaded his neck with one big hand. He was slouching now, and she noticed he wasn't using his cane. "Whichever name you prefer."

Which name *did* she prefer? One was the god, but the other name was the man. The man she'd become enchanted with at the dinner, touched by Marie's story of him visiting sick children. Now she knew why.

Esme decided she wasn't yet ready to acknowledge

the god just yet. "Tell me why you want me around, Alex."

"I missed you. You may not remember your past life, but I do, and I know the same traits I valued in Aphrodite exist in you. You have her compassion, her desire to help others, and the depth of her love for mortals and mankind. More love than any other god."

"But you miss her. Why do you want *me* around? If I wasn't the incarnation of Aphrodite, you wouldn't pay me any mind, would you? I've grown up as a human. I have my own interests and dreams, but all you three seem to want is Aphrodite back. None of you have asked what I want. Do I, Esme, interest you at all? Or is it just Aphrodite?"

Alexander quieted. His shoulders had dropped another two inches, uneven, and he was grimacing. "I can't explain it, and I don't know what else to do to make you happy."

She watched the way he rolled his shoulders, then tugged his hand. "Take a seat, I'll rub your neck."

He grew quiet and settled on the bench in silence, leaning forward with his arms resting against his thighs. Esme moved around behind him and kneaded his shoulders. She started at his neck, trying to press away tension that felt like rock-hard boulders sculpted into a vaguely masculine shape.

Alex sighed in relief and closed his eyes, practically reduced to pliable putty beneath her hands. "I'm not handsome, not like Luke or Beau. So I stay here and tend to my art as I did in the old days, as it is better than overhearing speculation from mortals that I am an ogre."

"You're not an ogre. To be honest, first time I saw you, I thought maybe you were a veteran who'd been wounded in a war or something. But I'd never call you an ogre."

A moment of silence passed before Alex spoke again. "Why did you come to me, Esme? We would have honored your words and let you be."

"I don't know. I guess because I thought you'd be the more understanding. Besides, I like discussing art with you, I enjoyed dinner at the banquet, and I just... Let's say I believe this crazy thing about being Aphrodite. What then? Are you three going to start fighting over me again? Do I have to pick one of you over the others?"

He shook his head. "No. When you walked away, we swore if we crossed paths with you again, we would be better men. *I* swore I would be better. Hermes always made you laugh, and Ares, he gave you the passion you needed, but I stole you away and behaved like a child when you didn't bend to my will." He relaxed beneath her hands again. "Would you want to be a goddess again? If it were at all possible," he added after a very telling pause.

"I don't know. I need time to figure out my life and where I fit in. Being a goddess sounds complicated. So... a question for another day, yeah?"

"Time? Is that all you wanted?" Alex chuckled at her this time with genuine humor and warmth. "We have nothing but time. We waited centuries for you, Esme. Trust me when I say a few weeks longer won't hurt. The love is gone from this world, and though it needs you, each of us would gladly wait even longer if it means you'll happily return."

She moved her hands a touch lower, working the next knotted section. After a moment, she grunted and plucked his sleeve. "Off with it. It's hard to work properly with this in the way. Did you know I took a massage class with one of my friends for fun?"

He glanced over his shoulder at her, eyes lit up with interest. "No, I didn't, but I would be pleased to hear more."

He unzipped the sweatshirt first and shrugged out of it, left in just a T-shirt that was almost a size too small for the sheer bulk of him. All muscle and bronzed skin, though he wasn't flawless.

She wiped her brow against her shoulder. How he managed to sit in this sweltering sauna in a sweatshirt was beyond her. God magic, she guessed. "Ashley is learning to become a physical therapist, and she suggested a beginner's massage class. We went together a few times for fun, but she still takes classes. Best part is, I let her use me for practice. In return, she let me decorate her place for a class project I had."

"What inspires you when you decorate a room?"

"I don't know. Sometimes it's the person who lives there, or the way the lighting plays against the walls. Sometimes it's the season. I just sorta go with my gut and things tend to work out. At least my professor thinks so. What inspires your sculptures?"

"Memories," he replied. "And sometimes my dreams."

"That must be sort of sad then, to sell them away to

people who have no idea what they mean." It made her wonder.

"Sometimes. I always hope they'll be loved no matter where fate takes them. I give them shape and form, it's up to someone else to appreciate the beauty, isn't it?"

"I suppose so."

She worked her way down to his shoulder blades, starting with the left. He always seemed to favor that side more. While Ares had the sculpted body of a model, and Hermes could have been a male dancer, Hephaestus had the thick, solid build of a laborer, a man who was muscled for function not form, strong for a purpose, not aesthetics. She continued working out the knots in his back until her belly made an unladylike grumble.

"I take it that's my cue to feed you," Alex said. He twisted around and smiled. The expression brightened his eyes and lessened the prominence of his scars. "Augustus is an excellent cook. Will you stay?"

"I'd like that."

11

*E*sme ate like a pig. At the conclusion of a four-course meal served in Alex's expansive dining room, she leaned back in the high-backed chair and tried not to die. She hadn't known roast beef could be so tender, potatoes so succulent and savory, or that a chocolate mousse so perfect could exist.

"More mousse?" Alex asked, seeming to read her mind.

"No. I seriously cannot stuff another bite into my stomach."

He chuckled. "You have made Augustus a happy man today. The opportunities to flex his culinary talents are rare indeed, and I am easy to please."

"I'd be happy to let him cook for me all the time. I mean, I'm not half bad in the kitchen, but this is amazing. Also, thanks for letting me come and talk. I feel... a little better, I guess."

"I'm glad." When Alex smiled, his eyes lit with

pleasure and he became truly attractive, as if happiness and warmth smoothed away the rough edges and let him shine brighter than a polished ruby. She gazed at him across the table for a moment, searching his face and hoping for even a fragment of a memory from her past life.

Nothing came.

"Esme?"

"Yeah?"

"I've lived here a long while now, but this place doesn't feel like a home. Would you help me?"

"Really?"

"Why not? You're a decorator and I have a home in sore need of your talents."

"Sure, I'd love to. I can take a look around and get some ideas then sketch out a plan for you. Why don't you tell me a little about what you'd like for your house. Do you like warmer colors or cooler ones? I mean, what color is your favorite?"

"Cool colors. I'm surrounded by fire and heat all day. It's nice to be around something different."

"Okay, I can work with that. You don't want to have things remind you of the forge when you're away from it. Do you mind if I walk around and take some pictures with my phone before I leave?"

"Leave?" He blinked and twisted to look at the time on an old grandfather clock. "Forgive me, I hadn't realized the late hour."

"Waiting for the food was worth it."

Alex remained quiet. He sipped his tea, still watching

the clock, before finally turning back to her. "How will you get home?"

"I can call Marie and see if she's back in town yet. Unless you plan on going into town? I don't want to put you out or anything."

When she stood, Alex rose from his seat to join her. "You're welcome to stay overnight, or even the weekend, unless you have somewhere to be in the morning. There's plenty of room, and I'll grant you full access to the house."

Esme nibbled her lower lip. "I have a self-defense lesson tomorrow with Beau. We made plans, but I dunno if those are still on."

"Augustus will drive you, and Beau will meet you as planned, I promise."

"I don't have any clothes or anything with me."

"It will be taken care of."

Before she could protest, before she could even question his promise, Alex placed both hands on her hips. His thumbs slid beneath her thin camisole and glided over the bare skin beneath. Her pulse leapt, like a spark zinged up her spine then back down, straight to the junction between her legs with an urgent need to be filled, reminding her of the months-long dry spell she'd endured since dumping Daniel.

Daniel who?

Esme swallowed, mouth dry despite the half bottle of fancy red Augustus had served. Her entire body flushed warm and hot.

"Then I'll... I'll just let Marie know I won't be home. I

can get a chance to look around, and you can tell me what you'd like."

"Yes. Yes, of course. Tell your friend whatever you must."

God, he was still stroking her, petting her ribs and caressing her like he'd done it a thousand times before, growing increasingly confident with each passing second, until he abruptly stepped away. "I will be in my forge."

"Great. I'll go call her then and wander around some."

It took a moment to gather her senses after Alex left. She called her friends, and, once she assured Jordan and Marie she was safe, she hung up and started her self-guided tour around the house. Everything was aesthetically pleasing, full of hard, masculine lines but still light and spacious. But it was empty—a big blank canvas waiting for her touch.

After peeking into the upstairs bedrooms, she wandered into a solarium filled with tropical plant life.

It was the conservatory from her dreams, the one she'd sketched with painstaking attention to detail for her final project, though there were some fixtures and furnishings missing from her design.

How was it even possible? Had she remembered this room from her other life? Had Alex read her mind and hastily thrown it all together? No, it was too well-lived in, contrasting the other rooms she'd explored so far. Of all the rooms, it had the most personality. She lingered for a few minutes to admire the various orchids, miniature fig trees, dwarf pomegranate bushes, and hibiscus, then passed back into the house, though it was difficult to leave, and she could have lounged within its warm atmosphere for hours.

Eventually, Augustus showed her to a guest bedroom with every comfort she needed, down to the soap and shampoo she preferred. The same brand of toothbrush and toothpaste awaited her in the bathroom on the marble counter.

"Creepy."

But convenient. Maybe Augustus was a fairy or a genie, or some other implausible magical creature.

"Augustus, before you go, where's Alex?"

"The forge, madam. Shall I send for him?"

"No, I'll go out myself. Thank you."

The moment she stepped outside, she regretted leaving her sweater. The cold night air whipped against her bare skin and tightened her nipples. As if that weren't enough, a heavy snow fell from the sky. She hurried down the path and rushed inside the forge.

"Damn, it feels nice in here. Sorry to barge in, I—" Words failed her. Alex stood at the foundry, shirtless, sweat gleaming against his golden skin. He poured red-hot liquid metal into a mold, his focus and gaze never wavering from his work.

"It's fine," he grunted.

"What are you making?"

"Seraphs for Eros. He likes to leave them at the nursing homes around the holidays. Then I need to get on forging a new sword for Beau." He wiped the sweat from his brow with the back of his hand and guided her to an unoccupied area of the adjacent workbench. An enormous pitcher of iced tea awaited him there with its cubes still tinkling together.

"Isn't Eros...?"

Alex nodded and took a long drink. "Aphrodite's son, yes. By Ares."

He may as well have told her the world really was flat. Despite the days she'd spent researching Greek mythology and reading old stories about the gods, she'd never considered that part was true.

"I'm a mom?"

Alex nodded again. He set her on the edge of the bench—either tiring of looking down at her or sensing her knees had gone weak. "A good mother. You bore Hermaphroditus by Hermes, then Harmonia, Eros, Anteros, Adrestia, Phobos, and Deimos by Ares. They miss you, but they understand it may take time before you are ready to meet them."

The number of children overwhelmed her. "Yeah... yeah, that's gonna take some—so why are you making Beau a new sword?"

"He shattered the last one during a spar with Athena yesterday."

The tight feeling in her chest eased when Alex didn't push the subject. "Beau got beat by a girl?" The idea of ultra-masculine, testosterone-fueled Beau losing a fight to anyone, even a goddess made her giggle. The more she thought about it, the funnier it became, until she leaned back against his workbench and held her stomach.

Alexander's bewildered look pronounced the creases in his face and deepened his crow's feet. "Why is that so surprising? You've beaten him before." He quieted, and a chastened look came over his face before he offered an apologetic smile. "Aphrodite has bested him before. Anyway, I didn't say Athena beat him this time, I said he shattered his sword."

Esme chuckled again, wishing she had seen the fight. Her thoughts ran wild with vivid imagery inspired by her favorite Grecian historical flicks, and she pictured the god and goddess battling across Olympus.

The idea of being Aphrodite—*their* Aphrodite, became less scary by the moment, and perhaps that alone should have been enough to frighten her out of Alex's forge and out of their lives.

Alex's sigh dragged Esme out of her reverie. "You're right," he said. "I thought your laughter was the same as hers, but it isn't. It's different. Better. Warm and inviting. Like a hug given sound."

"That's the sweetest thing anyone has ever said to me."

Alex snorted. "I find that hard to believe. Do men no longer speak sweet words to their women?" He caught himself at the end, and the same boyish smile resurfaced. "To women they appreciate, rather?"

"Pretty sure romance like that is dead in this modern age. My last boyfriend, he tended to compliment me on things like my ass or my tits, when he cared to offer a compliment at all."

"Ah..." Heavy lines furrowed his brow as he frowned. His gaze dropped, but he didn't step away. "So, have you decided where to start your decorating? Is my bank account in danger?"

"Don't worry, I'm not planning to make you a beggar."

She studied him a moment. Of the three men—gods—Alex was the quietest. She laid her hand over his on the table and stroked her fingers back and forth across his warm skin. "I thought I'd start with your bedroom."

"What's wrong with my bedroom?"

"It's so dark. Everything is in shades of gray, and since your first name isn't Christian, we need to fix that. Besides, when I look at you, I don't see dark and dismal. A dark person wouldn't make such beautiful things."

ESME'S TOUCH, AS INNOCENT AS IT WAS, SENT SPARKS shooting through Alex's body. "You can have whatever you need for your work. What will you change?" he asked after he found his voice.

"Well, I'd pick a different color for your walls to start. Change out your drapes too. Your bed frame is nice." She swept her thumb across his fingers. "Strong, sturdy, and masculine. I'd leave that alone. And the comforter, even though it's gray, is an attractive slate shade that I actually like. But the charcoal sheets should go."

"Masculine and sturdy? Thank you, I suppose." At least she appreciated the one item he'd made there, on a whim more than anything else.

Following an impulse, he turned his hand over and curled his fingers loosely around hers. Her hand was so much smaller, he expected it to disappear within his bearlike grip, or for her to withdraw altogether. She didn't. One success encouraged him to aim for another, so he brushed his thumb over her knuckles and stepped in closer, until he was between her legs. Esme's breath caught in her throat.

"I, um... hope you don't mind that I helped myself to your room. It seems like the best place to start. A place for you to relax in after a long day. Unwind."

His pulse sped, beating with enough intensity he was positive she could hear the powerful thumps inside his chest. "I did tell you to make yourself at home and to explore to your heart's content," he reminded her. "That included my bedroom." The bedroom he didn't do much unwinding in because he often slept in the forge.

He dipped his head down and breathed her in, nose skimming over her throat. She smelled like sin personified, rich chocolate and warm vanilla against her skin, daring him to have a taste. She exhaled a soft, quiet breath and closed her eyes, tilting her head to the side, freeing him to explore her throat. His whiskered jaw scraped against her skin, and she sighed again, this time with his name on her lips.

The sound, and the longing behind it, startled him. Before he could pull away, she lifted her hands to his shoulders, sliding them to his nape, and pulled him back in. She leaned in and slanted her mouth over his.

Her kiss startled him as much as the raw surge of lust it provoked. He stepped forward into her, thrusting his hips between the soft junction of her thighs. Dragging her against him by the waist of her leggings, practically shredded them in the process.

For a moment, his mouth was demanding and rough

against her lips until he gathered control of himself again, gentling. She dropped one arm from his shoulders, wriggled her hand between their bodies, and stroked him through his pants. His stiffening cock jerked up so hard it took him by surprise, though it was trapped painfully beneath denim. With a groan, Alex turned his lips from hers but continued his kisses down her throat.

And still he couldn't stop. Esme's pebbled nipples stood out against her thin top, her breasts bare beneath her camisole. He took the first into his mouth, suckling it through the thin cotton while he palmed the other. It wasn't enough. He ached for her, driven to hear his name on her lips again and again.

"Lay back for me, beautiful," he whispered when he released her breast.

"But then I can't touch you," she said, breathless.

"But I can touch you."

He yanked off the remnants of her leggings, then removed her panties before they became another casualty. They were skimpy, black lace, and he wanted to see them on her again.

Esme's thighs trembled beneath his touch, and her left leg jerked as he skimmed his palms over a ticklish spot near her knee. The discovery delighted him, like finding a secret treasure. Careful to keep his touch light, he traced his fingers upward again and sought out the warm junction between her thighs. He teased his thumb over the neatly trimmed dark curls, then dropped a kiss below her navel.

"Alex, please."

"Tell me what *you* want, Esme."

"I want... I want you to touch me. Taste me. I want your mouth on me."

Having Esme stretched before him was a gift he couldn't take for granted. He watched her face while he stroked her. Her silken heat tempted him as nothing had before, and his cock strained against his jeans, but he resisted the urge to claim her in favor of granting her the bliss he denied himself.

Did she want to be filled with him as much as he needed to be inside her?

His fingers thrust to the rhythm of her hips, curving inside her to find the tender spot that drove her wild. Her breath came in pants, hitched when he found what he wanted and delivered what she needed.

At the last possible second, as Esme's body tightened around his fingers, he knelt and answered her plea, putting his mouth to her sweet folds. He flicked his tongue against the sensitive pearl and growled his mutual pleasure when both of her hands tightened in his hair. Then he captured the tender bundle between his lips and sucked.

Esme cried out. She called his name, and the sound of it swept through him, burning soul deep with hope and love. Sweeter than any ambrosia, he lapped every drop her body offered, until her limbs went lax and she lay breathless on the table.

Had he ever experienced anything so beautiful?

With infinite care and tenderness, he kissed his way up her sprawled body. He stroked her hair and watched with bated breath as she came down from her euphoric high.

"Would you like to come to my bleak and boring bedroom?" he teased, deciding she would be the shining rose against the dull gray tones.

Her mouth curved into a smile, though her eyes remained closed. "Alex, you can take me anywhere."

———

ALEX WRAPPED HER IN A SMITHING APRON AND MOVED HER from the forge to his bedroom. Esme's mind remained in a fog during the silent transition, and she didn't care that the gray sheets were so boring and inaccurate to his colorful personality.

She sighed toward the ceiling after he placed her beneath the covers. He'd even taken off her camisole, and she couldn't be bothered to care. He'd just had her in his mouth. Just fingered and licked and sucked her to climax. Baring her breasts seemed trivial.

"Your fingers are definitely godly. I think I am spoiled for the rest of the evening."

"I aim to please."

"I've never... I've never had an orgasm so good. Everything about this is like a dream."

Alex only chuckled and lowered to the bedside before kissing her sweat-dampened brow. "I'm glad."

"But what about you?"

"Pleasuring you was reward enough."

Pleasuring her was enough? What kind of selfless,

wonderful, beautiful lover had she found in Alex that going down on her was enough to satisfy him? Her mind drifted to the foggy memories of the past that sometimes seeped like vapor into her thoughts. "Have we ever... before?"

"No. Though I've waited centuries to have the honor of touching you like this."

She leaned up and feathered kisses against his neck. "I wonder if Aphrodite knew what she was passing up."

"I doubt it. Looking back, I can't blame her for refusing to lay with me, I suppose. She loved Ares, and I was the interloper who forced her into marriage."

"Still, she didn't have to agree to Zeus's deal."

"She didn't," he agreed. "She thought it would drive Ares to action and force his hand to seek her as his wife. Perhaps she erred, but we gods are not perfect. We are powerful, flawed beings. And for a little while, for a short time, I did feel loved and blessed to have her in my life."

A long silence passed between them before she spoke again. "Alex?"

"Yes, my sweet?"

"How could you feel loved if she wouldn't sleep with you?"

"I suppose that never mattered to me as much. There is more to intimacy than sex, Esme. I like to think that toward the end, before I discovered the affair, there was affection between us. Friendship. There were times when I would be working for days in the forge and she sought my company. She'd sit on that same workbench and watch."

"Still it seems unfair to both of you, a sexless marriage like that."

He shrugged. "Despite the circumstances, I saw to her needs and crafted her things to make up for where our marriage lacked."

"Wait, are you saying you made her dildos?"

"My creations may have inspired a certain... improvement."

"*You* created vibrators?"

He ducked his head and dropped a kiss on her shoulder. "Yes."

"Wow." A few quiet seconds passed before she murmured against his ear. "I kinda wore out the rechargeable battery in old faithful last semester. So is old Aphrodite's privilege mine too?"

He laughed. "I see you are as shameless as her. Yes, whatever you want will be yours. And perhaps one day, if you'd like, I'll take you to the palace I built for her in the heavens."

She stared. "A palace?"

"Yes, though... I understand if you would prefer a new home of your own built for you—"

"Alex, I would take anything you gave me happily."

He drew her down beside him beneath the covers and cradled her close against his chest. Esme snuggled in, twining her legs with his until the rough denim chafed her legs.

"Aren't you going to undress?"

"I didn't want to make you uncomfortable."

Esme lifted her head from his shoulder. "You don't."

"I'm sorry. Old habits die hard, I suppose."

"Then we'll make new ones, and I say, first good habit is no jeans in bed."

He chuckled but obliged her request. Esme knelt on the mattress—ever aware of how his gaze darted between her naked thighs—and helped him tug his pants off.

Alex wore nothing beneath them. She sucked in a sharp breath, caught by surprise, and awed by the absolute, masculine beauty of him. Even semi-flaccid, his dick hung at an impressive length against his thigh.

Stunned as she was, it took a moment to realize Alex had gone still. So still he seemed to not even be breathing.

As she saw it, she had two choices, and the wisest one was to lay back down and go to sleep as planned, cradled in his warmth. Except she didn't feel very wise.

Her poor impulse control won. Needing to touch him, she claimed him in a hand. He was huge in her fist. She couldn't help but trace its silken contours and explore the stiffening length.

He hissed in a breath and squeezed her thigh. "Esme," he murmured. "Do not start something we can't finish."

She met his gaze. His eyes were the loveliest shade of brown she had ever seen, closer to red sometimes when the light hit them just right. "Whoever said we wouldn't finish?"

Following impulse again, she straddled his hips and drew his hands up from her thighs to her waist. She held one there and guided the other to her breast.

"I want this, Alex. I want you." She leaned forward, trapping his hard length between their bodies, and kissed him. The hand on her waist tightened.

She tugged his shoulder, urging him to roll her

beneath him. Once their position shifted, Alex's careful restraint vanished, his touch firmed, and their kiss deepened.

Esme opened her mouth at his coaxing and lost herself to the sweet taste of him. Like fire, whiskey, and cinnamon, flavors she would always associate with Alex. He was smoky and exotic, warm against her tongue. He took control, and she gladly surrendered.

Alex drew her arms above her head and pinned them in one strong hand. One moment he was tenderly worshipping her breasts with his tongue, teasing the nipples and alternating between them—in the next, he nudged her thighs apart and plunged forward, taking her in one smooth stroke. She gasped out his name, his true name, and in response, he withdrew and drove forward again, edging her up in the bed. Her fingers brushed against the iron headboard, so she grabbed hold and held on tight.

"Don't stop."

"I won't. I dreamed of this moment, Esme," he murmured against her ear, breath a warm caress against her skin. "I dreamed of the day you would be mine in body the way I was yours in spirit."

He continued moving within her, treating her to every magnificent inch. It should have hurt. It should have been impossible to take him all, but she did. Releasing her wrists, he propped his weight above her on both forearms and glanced down to where they were joined.

"Look at how well we fit together, Esme."

For a moment, she watched, mesmerized by the smoothness of their rhythm. She caught his whiskered face between both palms and kissed him for every lost moment. Kissed him until she clenched up and his name became her mantra, her prayer, the only word she could utter in the throes of orgasm.

When it seemed it couldn't get any better, Alex proved her wrong. He never slowed, pushing through each clench of her body, revving her up again before she had a chance to recover from the first rippling waves. Then he teased her with those magic fingers and coaxed another climax from her, the second chasing the heels of the first.

Trapped in a cycle of pleasure beyond what seemed humanly possible, she grasped his muscled shoulders and her nails scored his skin.

On his next thrust, Alex spilled within her, calling her name—both of her names. "Esme. My Esme," he gasped. "My Aphrodite."

And at that moment, she would be anyone he wanted her to be.

*B*eau didn't need a legitimate human job, but if he was going to spend months away from the world's many battlefields, he needed something to occupy his time in little suburban Ashfall. He'd located the nearest gym with self-defense classes and physical trainers, offered his services, then proceeded to lay all three of their best instructors on the mat.

After he established he was top dawg in their little neighborhood, he made a name for himself, and decided he preferred his new life. In the two years since he'd abandoned the war in the Middle East, he'd taken on dozens of elite clientele, from pop princesses to famous stunt men. He'd even worked on and off at movie sets as an expert advisor, and it jacked his pride up a notch when he saw his name in the credits at the end. Even if it wasn't his *real* name. To fix that, he'd started asking them to credit him as Beau "Ares" Castle.

Back in Ashfall, he flew under the radar and spent too

many hours at the city's only gym whipping the excess fat off their clients and teaching women to make a man *hurt*.

Not that Esme didn't already know something about that. His balls still ached when he thought back on it. But her talent was raw and unrefined, and he thought with a little training she'd show promise.

He waited for her at the gym's front desk while tuning out a pretty blonde fitness trainer in tiny shorts to his right. She'd been chatting his ear off for ten minutes about... fuck if he knew what she was talking to him about.

"Beau?"

"Huh?" He blinked and glanced to his right.

"You live nearby, right? I was wondering if maybe you want to come over to my place sometimes. We can hang out. Watch Netflix."

He stared at her, judging her stupid waterproof, sweatproof makeup, her too perfect, surgically enhanced nose, and her perky boob job that made both tits sit up on her chest like two hard grapefruits had been stashed beneath the compression tank.

"Ah..." The gym doors opened, blowing in a gust of winter air. Esme stepped inside. "My client is here." Excusing himself from behind the counter, he crossed the room to her in a few long strides. "I didn't think you would come."

"I didn't either." She glanced past him briefly then looked back up at his face. "Are we still on for this?"

"Yeah. Scan in then follow me." After Esme scanned her gym tag at the desk, he guided her from the lobby and into the private training room devoted to personal physical training lessons. The last trainer hadn't picked the mats off the floor. When he shut the door behind them, he turned to face her. "What made you change your mind?"

"I... talked to Alex."

"And?"

Esme shrugged. "I've been presented with undeniable proof that gods are real, and I may be one of them. I don't have many choices. I can be rational and accept it, or freak out and waste more time hiding at home. I choose to face it."

"That's the goddess I know." He grinned, the sting of her going to Alex first soothed by her decision. "So, time for you to show me what you already know so I can see what I'm dealing with."

He led her through a few easy, basic scenarios, playing the role of assailant while she tried to defend and get away. Wherever she'd taken her initial lessons wasn't bad.

"Not awful. One word of advice though?"

"Sure. That's why I'm here, right?"

"Couldn't help but notice you seem to have a signature move you fall back on when you're threatened. It's a good move but..." Beau grimaced. "A kick to the balls won't take every man down."

"It took down two gods."

He resisted the urge to kiss her gloating face. "I wasn't prepared for it," he grumbled instead.

Esme smiled up at him. "For what it's worth, I'm kind of sorry, even if it is a feather in my hat I can never brag about. How many girls get the chance to say they kicked the god of war in the junk?"

He grunted. "You caught me when my guard was down, that's all."

"Mm-hmm."

"Anyway, as I was saying, the balls won't always work. Going for the groin is great, but the face is also a good weak spot in general. Put a guy's eyes out if you can, with whatever weapon you have on you or with your fingers."

When the lesson began, Beau didn't go easy on her. He demonstrated classic moves and dirty tricks, how to break out of a choke hold, and an effective eye gouge. He put her through punching drills on the heavy bag and admired her lithe limbs.

"You're a fast learner, but I guess I'm not surprised. You used to be great at those pressure points."

"Really?" She didn't bristle up, brows perking instead.

"Really. Aphrodite didn't like a fight to go on for a long time, especially if it was going to mess up her hair. She'd incapacitate an opponent as early as possible with as few moves as necessary."

Esme wiped one wrist against her perspiring brow. "Yeah, that's not going to be me today."

"Definitely not," he agreed.

She jabbed him in the stomach, but he danced back, laughing.

Afterward, they returned to punching drills on the focus mitts while Beau picked apart her fighting form, occasionally corrected her stance, and marveled at how fast she adapted, even as a human, to his lessons.

She remembered. Some part of her soul or her subconscious recalled their old spars. He was positive of that, certain the old Aphrodite was somewhere buried beneath the mortal flesh and dulled by centuries of human life. He just had to find her.

"All right, gloves off. I should be teaching you this with mitts, and the manager would definitely fuss if he saw I had you going bare hands, but if you're in a *real* fight, your opponent isn't going to wait until you're gloved up."

Esme unstrapped the training gloves and tossed them aside. "Right. That's why I'm here. I want to be ready for the real world and a real situation so you three stop following me down dark alleys at night."

He grinned. "Good. I actually have better things to do with my time than to be your benevolent stalker."

Once she raised her guard, he did the same and feinted toward her chest. She weaved to the side.

"Watch the footwork. That was clumsy."

"Why was it clumsy?"

Beau repeated the feint, and when she moved, he swept his foot against her ankles and took her off her feet. Esme tumbled to the mat, swearing the moment she landed.

After he helped her up, she eyed him. "Teach me how to avoid that."

"Sure."

He taught her two methods then made her take a water break. Afterward, the lesson carried on while he eyed the clock and wondered what else he could squeeze in during the remaining hour he'd scheduled into their session. Not much. He didn't want to overwhelm her.

Deciding to test her instead, he lunged forward for

her throat with both hands. She came up with her arms, drove his down with surprising strength, and stepped forward with a brutal knee for his groin. He twisted his hips to the side and struck with his leg again, taking her down to the mat.

Although Esme toppled over, she rolled away before he came down on her.

"Good. You can't always avoid someone taking you down, but what matters most is that you don't *stay* there. Maybe I'll teach you ground fighting next time once you get this move down."

Her chest heaved. "But I want to learn it now."

"You can't learn it all in one session, Esme. It takes practice."

"Fine."

Over and over, they repeated the same move, though she landed on the padded floor as often as she avoided him. And when she did avoid him, he snuck in with an open palm to her chest that thrust her off balance anyway.

"You're faster than this, Esme. I'm only moving at quarter speed."

Her jaw dropped. "*Quarter* speed? There's no way I can block everything you send at me."

When the corners of her mouth dropped into a frown, he touched her chin and raised her face to his again. "You can. I know you can do better. I know you're faster than this."

Her brown eyes remained on his face, lips an alluring temptation he ached to kiss.

Beau dropped his hand and stepped back again. "Ready?"

Esme raised both fists. He went after her again, practicing the same attack pattern, going for her throat, aiming a soft jab toward her face, a feint toward the stomach. She fended him off and traded hits in return he easily blocked and swept aside despite the sweat dripping into her eyes.

"You're tiring, babe. Let's call it a ni—"

Esme adjusted her stance, a fluid transition that brought her nondominant right to the forefront in a jab aimed for his throat, only for an unexpected left cross to break through his guard. The blow rocked his head back, and Beau stumbled a step.

Through the haze of sudden pain, he heard her cry, "I'm sorry!"

He held out a hand and shook his head, holding his nose with the other palm. "I'm good."

"But I—"

"Broke my nose again. Yeah. You seem to have a talent for that too."

"Again?"

"Long story." The bleeding had already stopped, but he excused himself to make sure she hadn't made a mess of his face.

When he returned, Esme bit her lower lip. "Are you okay?"

"I heal fast."

She raised a hand and tenderly touched the tip of his nose. The hint of bruising would be gone by the next day.

"Are you going to tell me the story of how it was broken before?"

Beau studied her. She'd rolled up her sleeves and tied her shirt up around her midriff. Loose strands of dark hair escaped her ponytail and clung to her perspiring face. Despite that, she'd never been sexier to him, never more attractive, not even when she'd been in her divine body.

"Well?" she persisted.

"I'll tell you for a kiss."

Esme quieted.

"Too high a price?"

"No." She sniffed as if he'd insulted her. "Maybe I was only waiting for you to tell me *where* you wanted my lips. Your face might be too tender from me beating on it."

His cock jumped up, her words shooting arousal right to his groin. He lurched toward her in a step and claimed her mouth, hungry for the first taste of lips he hadn't tasted in centuries. All his hunger, all his need conveyed in one unending kiss, eager for the tease of her tongue flitting between his lips, the soft curves of her body pressing close. She wiggled in, grinding against his erection.

Hot and wanton passion surged between them. Her palm slid between them over his cock, stroking him through his gym shorts and pressing against the unrelenting force. He groaned into her mouth.

"Touch me, babe."

She nibbled his lower lip. "I *am* touching you."

"Skin. I want to feel your skin. Your hands on me. Your body against mine. I need to be inside you." The breath rushed in and out of him, chest heaving with excitement.

He'd shared her long enough with the others, and in this moment, for these brief and precious seconds, he didn't have to share. Every fleeting brush of her fingertips took him down the road to ecstasy.

Her fingers slid between his skin and waistband, beneath his boxers, then stroked over the tip of his cock, sending a jolt of bliss trembling through his body.

A fist hammered against the door. "Hey, Beau, you almost done with this room or nah?"

Esme jerked away from him. He could have killed the trainer on the other side until he glanced again at the clock and saw they were five minutes over the block he'd scheduled.

"Shit."

Esme stepped away from him and dipped down to grab her bottle of water. She chugged it in the corner then fanned herself. He was arrogant enough to think she was cooling off from their make out as much as the training session.

Then Beau recalled the dozens of times his sex kitten love goddess had tackled him into bed, desperate for him, unable to go a second longer without him inside her. He smirked. She was definitely cooling off because of him, and soon, he'd give them both what they needed.

"Yeah, we're cleaning up. We'll clear out in a sec."

Beau sent her off to the showers while he finished tidying the room. Then he hit the locker room too.

Esme showered in the women's locker room after their lesson, wondering what would have happened if his coworker didn't interrupt.

Absolutely nothing, considering she'd spent the previous night with Alex and he'd wrecked her so completely she was fortunate to be at the gym at all.

Beau had been a delicious temptation to test the resilience of her body, however.

No wonder Aphrodite had continued her affair with Ares centuries ago. Who could give up kisses like that? Then she thought of sweet Alex's gentle kisses, the passion that surged between them while his skilled fingers coaxed her to orgasm and he asked nothing in return.

Even if she wanted to pick up wherever everything left off, that felt impossible now. Everything ached, from her shoulders to her hamstrings. Beau hadn't gone easy on her, and she'd appreciated that in a weird way. The few times she'd ever gone to the gym with Daniel, he'd always lowered the weights, steered her away from certain equipment, and generally treated her like she should be there to look good rather than actually work out.

Beau was different, treading some fine line between treating her like a woman but also holding her to higher expectations.

Although it was a lot to take in, she'd had lots of time to think things over since their revelation.

Beau waited for her outside at the juice bar where he'd already ordered and an enormous orange and purple layered smoothie. She eyed it.

"It's your favorite," he said.

"How do you know my favorite?"

He cocked one dark brow. "I know your favorite everything."

"Fine." She took an experimental pull through the straw from the rich fuchsia layer, filling her mouth with blended raspberry and pomegranate followed by a tangy and sweet peach mango bottom. She didn't stop until the inevitable brain freeze punished her greed.

He chuckled. "Like I said. I know your favorite everything."

Esme took her time with the rest of the drink. "I had a good time with you this evening. Thanks for the lesson."

"No need to thank me."

"So, I was wondering... could you call the others up and tell them I wanna talk tonight? They can meet us at Luke's place."

"I could, but how about I give you a lift to Alex's instead? Luke is already over there." When she raised a brow, he added, "It's game night."

"Are we going on your bike?"

The rakish grin she'd come to love made an appearance on his face. The girl behind the juice counter sighed. Esme couldn't blame her.

"The roads are clear. Why? Afraid?"

"No, I was actually hoping you'd say yes."

ALEX'S MANSERVANT MET ESME AND BEAU AT THE DOOR

and welcomed them into the estate. He took their coats then guided them into the living room where Alex and Luke were embroiled in a game of cards.

Did gods seriously spend their Sunday evenings playing gin rummy?

"Hello, Esme," Alex greeted her. A smile lit his entire face. She wasn't the only one to notice either. Luke looked between them with one raised brow.

"Oh, hey. How'd the brawling lesson go?" Luke asked.

"Pretty well. I managed to bust him once in his nose."

"Awesome. Just give us one second to finish this. I got Alex on the ropes."

Fifteen minutes later, after Alex had thoroughly trounced Luke, they moved to the couch where the guys had pizza and craft beer. From what she understood of Luke's awful taste in beer, she assumed the latter belonged to Alex.

"So, to what do we owe the pleasure of this meeting, Esme?" Alex asked.

"I made up my mind about our arrangement and wanted to offer the three of you a deal. Together. You three say you can share, that we can do this together without any fighting. As long as you can honor that, I'm in."

Luke's eyes brightened. "Really?"

"Yeah. I gave it a lot of thought after what happened Monday. The truth is that ever since I met you guys, I've come to care about you all for different reasons that have *nothing* to do with who I was." She glanced to Alex and smiled. "So as crazy as this is, I'm game to make it work. At *my* pace."

"Absolutely," Beau said first, while Luke and Alex echoed his agreement.

"We meant what we said. No more fighting," Luke said. "Just tell us what you want us to do."

"Well, for starters, if I'm going to get my powers back so I can keep up with you, I'm guessing it means I need to talk to the guy in charge."

Anticipation and fear created a frenzy of warring emotions. On one hand, she still expected to awaken alone in bed to discover the past few weeks had been a wicked fantasy, a product of her imagination after one too many drinks with Marie on the couch. On the other, she wasn't yet sure if she believed it was all real and the three weren't mistaken.

Powers. Godhood. It was too unreal. Too spectacular and unbelievable.

"Then you will need to go to Olympus," Alex said.

Beau groaned. "Luke, you up for taking her to see Zeus?"

Luke sighed. "You two are pussies. Yeah. I'll take her."

"Wait, why can't we all go?" she asked.

"Bad blood, so to speak," Beau replied. "I was kicked out. Mom and Alex convinced Zeus to lift my exile a couple decades ago, but still..."

Luke snorted. "And Alex—"

"I don't go there," Alex said for himself.

"Anyway, I'm Zeus's personal messenger, and I know all the shortcuts to Olympus and the other divine realms. It's better if I take you."

"Well then, what are we waiting for? Let's go see Zeus."

13

*E*sme's first time in the In-Between while aware was an eye opening and odd experience. When they finally stepped out into the real world again, she shook off the dizziness and looked around. They stood in an office lobby, a quiet room with aerial views hung on the walls in gilded frames.

At a nearby desk sat a pretty blonde woman in a navy blue uniform. She smiled at them and touched the wireless device curled around her left ear.

"Welcome to Elysian Airlines International. May I help you?"

"What's up, Iris? You're looking good. Is the big man in?"

The woman cut her eyes from Luke to Esme, a frown on her perfectly bowed lips. "Mister—"

"It's okay. You can relax. Esme's in the know. Don't you recognize her?"

"Um, Luke, she and I have never met," Esme whispered.

"Sure you have. Well, the old you knows her."

Iris's eyes lit up with interest, shifting from dull gray to vibrant green. Esme blinked, certain it had to be a trick of the light, but then the woman's eyes were an unmistakable shade of lilac.

"Wait, do you mean this is *her*?"

"In the flesh. So, is the boss here or not?"

"Go ahead. He's probably expecting you."

Iris passed Luke a golden key and waved them off. He led the way to a door across the office marked as a stairwell.

"What? No elevator or magic portal?" Esme asked.

"Nah, the old man likes the classics."

A normal stairwell was visible through the narrow window set in the door, gray walls and stainless steel railings, but when Luke pulled it open he revealed something else entirely.

The warmth of a balmy spring day greeted them, and sunlight shone from every direction. Instead of the standard staircase, wide steps spiraled upward without any railings, and vanished somewhere far above them.

"What the hell is this?"

"Stairway to heaven, baby. Come on." Luke offered out his hand and smiled.

As she stepped out onto the landing, Esme realized the steps weren't connected. To anything. Each one hung suspended in the air. Her fingers tightened around Luke's, but she didn't try to turn back. The marble didn't shift or move, and the air was still, a windless and ideal day. Once she overcame her fear of falling, she was able to appreciate the world below them in its dazzling array of unusual colors. The mountains were blue and purple, arising from plains and valleys of fertile green.

Miles and miles of unspoiled beauty stretched for as long as she could see, kissed by golden and pink skies as radiant as the dawn.

But it wasn't dawn. Or sunset. These were the colors all times of the day, and somehow despite never setting her mortal eyes on the view, she knew that.

"It's like we're walking in the sky."

"In a way, we are, only not in the sky as you know it. This is Olympus, realm of the gods. And here we are, the big man's office."

A door leading to seemingly nowhere hovered on the next landing. Luke unlocked it with the golden key and pulled it open. An office was on the other side. Esme marveled a moment. Through the door was a room worthy of any wealthy CEO, but when she looked around the frame, there was nothing but open air. Luke chuckled and stepped through first.

"Pretty neat, right?" he asked.

"It's amazing." She followed behind him and the door closed on its own.

A man stood with his back to them at the far end of the room. Floor-to-ceiling windows let in the diffused golden light, highlighting broad shoulders clad in a tailored suit.

"Why does everything look so normal?' she whispered to Luke. "I mean, I expected roman baths and gardens, not an executive office."

"Changing times, remember?"

"Is that him?" They hadn't moved from the door, and the man staring out the windows remained still as a statue.

"Yeah," Luke whispered back. "We've gotta wait for him to acknowledge us. He doesn't like when people just barge inside."

"He's... smaller than I envisioned. No white beard or robes either. Shouldn't there be lightning?"

"I can hear you, you know."

The deep voice came from directly beside her. Esme jumped, a scream caught in her throat. Zeus had crossed the room and appeared beside her. He towered over her, smaller than Alex in height though her perception made him seem larger than a mountain.

"Sorry," she squeaked.

"Hey, Uncle Z. How're things going?"

Zeus turned an unimpressed look on Luke, his lips turned down and his gaze hard. "A little respect, please. This isn't the mortal world."

Luke's easy grin faded, and he ducked his head, shifting his weight from one foot to the other. "Sorry, sir. May I introduce you to—"

"Esmeralda Caro. College student attending University of Ashfall. Human. I know who she is. And I know who she *was*." Zeus looked her up and down, from head to toe then back again. Steel-gray hair coursed over his shoulders and framed a stern, unforgiving face that might have once been handsome, could be handsome if he smiled. "What brings you here?"

"Oh, well, um..." She looked to Luke for help, but he

tucked his hands in his pockets and stayed quiet.

Zeus gestured for her to follow him to a cabinet where he poured two glasses, though Esme had no idea what it was. The liquid shimmered like a sparkling rainbow. Zeus pressed a glass into her hand and kept the other for himself while Luke remained by the door.

"Yeah, well, I was pretty surprised myself. I don't exactly remember anything about my former... life. Existence. Whatever you'd call it."

"An existence you threw away."

Esme sniffed her drink. At first it smelled like candy canes, but another whiff brought to mind chocolate covered cherries. A tentative first sip exploded like liquid sunshine against her tongue, bright and tart citrus that mellowed to a spiced sweetness. She'd never had anything so delicious in her life.

"I don't remember any of that, to be honest. I'd sorta hoped you'd help fill in some blanks. Or at least let me have the chance to come back and make things right."

"I hear what you're saying, Esme, but you haven't given me a reason. *Why* do you want to be a goddess again when you were so happy to toss it away?"

His stare worsened her anxiety, both palms so moist with sweat rubbing them against her jeans didn't help. She wiped them on her thighs again, flushed and hot. Vulnerable under his gaze. "I've learned things since then. Learned what it means to care about others. Learned how it feels to be human. I've read stories about the old Aphrodite I used to be, but I'm *not* her anymore."

"Why should I return your gift?"

"Because I can do better. Alex—Hephaestus believes

the love has gone from the world and has faded more and more since I left my powers behind. If that's true, give me this chance to put everything right."

Zeus snorted and knocked back the remainder of his drink. "The Aphrodite we all knew was a self-absorbed bitch. Why should I believe you're any different now?"

"Why wouldn't you?"

"There are three gods chasing you across a shit town in the middle of nowhere California, each of them with more mortal currency than you can spend in a lifetime. Convince me this is about the greater good and not wanting to prosper."

"That is part of it," she confessed.

Zeus raised a brow. "Well, now. You told the truth."

"A part of it, sir. I don't want power, but I *do* want to be their equal. I don't want their wealth and magic, or whatever you call it. I want... to be on equal terms with them, because they're three incredible men who I care about for different reasons. Because I feel something here," Esme said, placing a hand over her heart, "every time I look at any of them. And I... I don't..."

"Don't what?" he prodded. "Out with it, girl."

"I don't want to leave them again," she whispered. "I don't understand any of this or why I feel how I do. It's not something I can explain in words. Someone tried to harm me, possibly to stop me from coming back this way. Now the guys are petrified, and I can *sense* that somehow. They waited forever to find me. It wouldn't be fair to wait for the next lifetime to bring me around. Maybe the next me wouldn't forgive and forget."

Zeus's stony expression didn't change. He moved

around her again, eyes traveling down her body in an appraising manner that sent trickles of apprehension dancing over her spine. "Let's say that I believe you, that you care for them and genuinely love someone besides yourself. Nothing proves you can handle the divine gift again."

"I can learn."

"The responsibilities of a god are vast. Long over are the days of starting a war over trivial matters, of dooming families and lovers over jealousy."

"I understand. I wouldn't anyway."

"Good. If you want to reclaim your powers, you'll have to prove you can handle the gift of dominion over love, recognize true beauty, and because I'm a bastard, win a war."

"War?"

"You were once the goddess Astarte, or rather, the evolution of her. Didn't you ever wonder how Aphrodite started so many wars? It was in her blood, part of her, and what attracted Ares in the first place. Do these three tasks, and I'll consider restoring you to the goddess you once were."

"And how am I supposed to do that? How am I supposed to do any of that?"

Zeus spread his hands and grinned wide. "If you thought I was going to set you on some mighty quest you thought wrong. It would defeat the purpose of assigning you a mission if I told you how to win the game. Figure it out."

Esme nodded. "All right. If I can ask a couple questions?"

"Shoot."

"Do you know who sent the hellhound after me?"

Zeus shrugged. "My omniscience loses potency when divine beings are involved. Could be anyone really. Persephone is the likely culprit, but she's too smart to openly attack you like that. Everyone knows about the rivalry between you two."

"Everyone except me. Are you going to help?"

He shrugged again. "Not my concern. I don't interfere in petty god squabbles now. You may be mortal, but now that Hermes, Ares, and Hephaestus have made their claim, that brings you into our divine circle. You're their problem now."

"And that's it?"

"That's it. If you want back in, you need to prove yourself. The boys can help within their capabilities, but that's it."

Esme raised her chin. "All right. One last question."

Zeus glanced down at his watch and tapped it. "Out with it then."

"The guys said you used to be a real hard-ass back in the day. *Why* did you stop doing it all?"

Zeus shrugged and raised his cigar to his lips again. "What's the point? After a while, micromanaging this crap loses its appeal. It's the same shit every day, every year, every century and millennia when you're the king of the gods. I've spent thousands of years of my existence bossing around the mortals and ruling the gods of my pantheon—supreme unchallenged control." He shook his head. "Pointless. None of it has any point. Waiting for you to fail will be the first ounce of honest excitement I've had in decades."

Esme studied Zeus, noticing the way his eyes cut away from her. There was a dull ache in her heart whenever she looked at him too long, like a sore or a bruise, a knot that needed a gentle rub. She didn't question it. "I won't lose. Expect to see me again when I've figured out how to win your game."

"You do that."

Zeus dismissed her by turning his back on her. Esme looked down at the unfinished drink in her hand and raised it to her lips. No way was she going to let that deliciousness go to waste. This time it was as if she ate a summer berry garden with mint sprigs, different but just as wonderful. She set her glass down and returned to the door where Luke was still waiting with his hands in his pockets, a thoughtful look on his face.

Luke didn't speak until they were in the lobby again. "So," he said in a conversational voice, "wanna stop and have some good Greek cuisine before we head back to California?"

"Sure. Why not? How often am I going to have the opportunity to eat authentic Mediterranean food?"

He arched a brow. "Baby, I'm the messenger of the gods. You can have authentic *anything* whenever you want as long as I'm around."

"Seriously?"

"You want sashimi from Tokyo? I can do that. Croissants from Paris, panna cotta from Florence, Swiss chocolate—anything you crave, I can have for you in a snap."

"And you're just telling me this now? That trick would have been nifty when we had that awful Chinese the other week."

"Yeah, well, you didn't *know* then, but you do now, so ask whenever."

"I could use some serious comfort food after that and what Beau put me through at the gym, so let's get some moussaka and baklava, hit the tourist spots, and you can top off my dinner this evening with sashimi. Deal?"

"You got it."

LUKE BROUGHT HER OUT OF THE IN-BETWEEN, LANDING their arrival in the living room of her grandmother's old house. The room was dark, the entire house silent and in shadows. Night had fallen outside, but the porch lamp was on, casting its yellow glow over the porch.

Her belly was full of baba ganoush, hummus, and a dozen other delicious morsels sampled during a dreamy day in Greece touring the Acropolis and its museum. To top it off, Luke had dashed to Tokyo and brought her back two fillets of authentic sashimi. It took him less than five minutes.

Light suddenly spilled into the living room from the connecting hall. Marie charged from it in her T-shirt and panties with Esme's Louisville slugger poised for the swing. She stopped cold when she saw them.

"Oh my God, it's about time you showed up." She

dropped the bat and stalked up to them, oblivious to prancing in front of Luke in her underwear, her face livid red. "Where the fuck did you go for three days?"

"Huh? Three days?"

"Bitch, don't play dumb." Then the tears began gliding down her cheeks. "I didn't know what to do. Your boss called for you Tuesday to ask why you didn't show up, so I lied for you. I've been trying to call and text you."

"Marie, I didn't know."

"You could have left a note if you were going to run off with your boyfriend. You could have returned my calls. Answered my text. You could have said something! But all this time, you've just been off fucking him." As her shrill voice raised another octave, Luke rubbed his ears and grimaced.

Three days? Panic surged inside her, three days of missed shifts from her job, three days of her life missing in the blink of an eye? "What do you mean I've been gone for three days?" Esme asked, straining to control her voice.

"Were you boning that much that you weren't able to keep up with the time? You just disappeared! I've tried texting you since Monday. No responses, no nothing. I didn't know if you were hurt somewhere or missing or... or fucking *dead*."

Esme's gaze darted to Luke's stony features. He stepped forward and sighed. "I... I'm sorry, Marie. It's my fault. I took her away to San Francisco for a couple days and didn't bring a charger for my phone either. I guess we were just having too much fun."

"You both suck." Marie scrubbed her face with one

wrist. "I lied to Mrs. Robinson and said you were down with laryngitis so bad you couldn't speak a word. She brought you tea and honey. It's on the kitchen counter."

"Thanks."

"God, you owe me."

"I'm sorry. Really sorry."

Marie shot them both—Luke mostly—dirty looks then retreated to her room.

Esme dragged Luke to her bedroom and shut the door behind them. Then she punched him in the arm.

"Ow! What was that for?"

"Three days, Luke? Three days? How did you zip to and from Tokyo in five minutes, but we were gone three days?"

"Uh. Shit. Olympus doesn't run parallel to the mortal realm, and I kinda forgot it takes a little more time to pull along a mortal. Like a lot more. Time can pass differently in the In-Between when you're moving slowly, and I had all of my concentration devoted to keeping you in one piece since you're not a god again yet."

"How do you forget something so important?"

"It's not a habit of mine to take mortals into god country." He made a face, wrinkling up his brow. "I'm seriously sorry. At least she covered for you with the job."

"But now she's furious at me, and with good reason." She plugged her cell phone into the charger then shrugged her jacket off, tossing it over a chair. "All of that trouble just to get three really vague tasks to prove I'm worthy to a depressed ancient god. I feel like a comic book character."

"You'll figure out what he wants, Ez. Be glad Zeus

doesn't have the motivation to give you one of the real quests like the ones of old where you have to hike up a mountain into another realm or venture into Purgatory to find a rare piece of fruit. People failed. Frequently."

Esme raked a brush through her hair and fastened it into a simple braid. "I guess. I kind of expected more, I guess."

"That's all there is now. Minimum effort."

She unfastened her belt and jeans, pushing both down while keenly aware of Luke watching her. She glanced up at him. "If you're just going to stand there and stare, I'm kicking you out."

"Um... just so we're both on the same page, are we undressing to go to sleep or...?"

Esme turned her back to remove her bra, granting him nothing more than a view of her naked spine while she tugged on her nightshirt. "It's midnight, dude. We had a long day walking around Athens, not to mention I've apparently been wired on fun for three days after the self-defense lesson from hell. I'm exhausted and ready to sleep." She hesitated to mention her night with Alex.

"Okay."

He undressed to his boxers and set his folded clothes on the chair while she turned down the sheets and blanket.

"There's an extra toothbrush in the top bathroom drawer on the—" She stopped as Luke pulled his vanishing act and reappeared a second later, backpack in hand presumably filled with all the male toiletries that made him smell so damned good. "Or you can do that."

A few minutes later, once they'd finished with the

hallway bathroom she and Marie shared, they both slid under the sheets and Luke dragged her against him with one arm.

"I really am sorry."

"It's all right. Besides... I had a good time with you today."

Silence lapsed between them after that, his palm resting flat against her middle. His breaths were even and rhythmic, the sound of them, and the warmth of him against her more soothing than the heavy winter blanket she'd drawn over them.

"Hey, I have a question," she murmured in the dark, positive Luke hadn't drifted off yet.

"Hm?"

"Hera left him, didn't she?"

"How'd you know?"

"I sensed it. He's hurting, and I guess some part of Aphrodite still exists in me because I felt his heartache."

"Yeah, well, I can't really say I blame her. It was, I dunno, twenty years ago? Thirty? I lose track."

"I don't blame her either, I'm just curious about how. I mean, we always learned in mythology classes that she was the goddess of marriage, women, and family."

"And she is, but being the goddess of family didn't stop her from throwing Hephaestus off Olympus to die, did it?"

Esme quieted.

"The thing about being a god is that we evolve with the times. We change and adopt the views of the world, the people who worship us, and the modern way of life. Women across the world in every civilized country are told if a man isn't a good husband, they can leave. Zeus wasn't a good husband."

"So she left."

"Yup."

"What about you? How did you evolve?"

"You ever hear me spout sonnets?"

"Um, no?"

"That's because they're out of style, but I can kill a rap battle."

"Still, it would be nice to have some romantic poetry with all these flowers you send me."

"Heh. I'll see what I can do." He kissed her head and squeezed her. "Get some sleep now, baby. We can talk more tomorrow."

Tucked in close and warm, Esme closed her eyes and drifted to sleep.

hen Esme awakened the next morning, Marie was already gone. While Luke showered, she drifted into the kitchen to make breakfast and caught up on the three dozen text messages. Between friends and family, she wondered if she'd offended the entire world.

Was it illegal to unplug for a few days?

She cracked eggs into a bowl and whisked heavy cream into them while the speaker broadcasted irritated voice messages.

"Hey, Esme, you coming in to work or not? I've left like five text messages, and you need to pick up the damn phone," said Clover, the girl she worked alongside during high-traffic, busy days in the store. The message was left an hour after their shift began.

"Esme, dear, it isn't like you to fail to report in to work. Are you okay?" asked her boss, the sweetest old lady in the world. She'd left her message for Esme around eleven.

"God, I swear, it's like you get a boyfriend then you drop off the face of the planet," said her coworker Meg. "Why didn't you show up for your shift? They called me in on my day off to cover for you. You better have one foot in the grave."

"Esme, sweetie, I know you're busy, but we'd really like to know if you made up your mind about coming home for Christmas," said her mother on the second day of her disappearance.

"Esme, is everything all right?" asked her father, his message a day later. "Your mother is worried. Anyway, give us a call as soon as you receive this."

"Esme, this is your mother again," she said, as if Esme had somehow forgotten the sound of her voice. "Marie says you've been busy with your boyfriend. You're more than welcome to bring him home too. And it's absolutely okay to say no if you'd rather do your own thing this year with him. Please call soon, we'd love to hear from you."

She grimaced, listened to a few more messages of varying passive-aggression levels from different friends, then started a pot of coffee. Beau liked his lightly sweetened and dark as sin, but Luke wanted his served like lattes with a generous amount of creamy milk, sugar, and a few pumps of flavor.

But how did Alex take his coffee?

Esme cleared the messages from her inbox, returned a few texts that didn't piss her off, phoned her mother with an apology, scrambled eggs, and made french toast with the yummy cinnamon bread Marie always bought.

Luke emerged from the bathroom and stared at the plates on the table.

"The old you couldn't cook worth shit."

"The new me has parents who insisted," she replied, sitting down with her coffee.

Luke settled beside her and chuckled. "Nah, for real, like, if I didn't have an immortal's stomach, I'd be concerned right now."

Esme shot him a dirty look. "Eat your damned eggs."

He did, though a nervous moment of silence passed before he sheepishly added, "You're good in the kitchen."

Smug satisfaction spread her lips into a big grin. She sipped her coffee, choosing class over rubbing it in his face. "Thank you."

Luke cleared his plate then did the cleanup, although she hadn't asked him to help. "No, I got it. I don't mind helping since you made it all."

Leaving the kitchen to his capable hands, Esme showered and dressed for the day. She pulled on insulated leggings and an oversized sweater that reached her midthigh. Luke was waiting in the living room in front of her television, watching an action movie on the digital service.

"Nice to see you can make yourself at home," she teased.

"Home is wherever you are."

"And that was really cheesy."

"But accurate. Who do you think inspired Hallmark? Anyway, got any plans for the day?"

"I dunno..."

"As much as I enjoy having you all to myself, it's been three days to everyone else."

"Yeah... Beau sent me a text. He just asked how I was enjoying Greece." She rubbed her hands against her thighs and watched an explosion ripple across a field of soldiers before a mutant raced in with magical powers to level the playing field. She'd seen the movie a dozen times.

"Figures he'd check in."

"But there's nothing from Alex. I guess I'd hoped he wouldn't be, I dunno, such a loner."

"Nah. I'm telling you, that reclusive billionaire thing isn't an act he puts on. He really likes being alone. Or rather, he's *used* to being alone, if you get my drift."

Esme worried her lower lip and gazed at her phone. Alex had fallen completely off the radar, not even sending a text or a hello. "He seemed lonely before."

"Then if you think he's lonely, maybe you should visit him, babe. Nothing's keeping you from going over there and invading his bachelor haven."

Bachelor haven? The unease stirring in her gut lifted enough for her to laugh. "If it was a bachelor haven, I'd expect to see sixty-inch televisions and video game systems everywhere."

"Nah, he'll jump into a game of *Call of Duty* with us sometimes, but Heph is into the whole roleplaying game thing more than anything. I think he plays *Elder Scrolls* on his computer. Look, we didn't lie about being fully committed to sharing this time around and not being a bunch of assholes to each other, but if you want my advice, Beau can wait a day. He spent centuries with you as Ares. Go see Alex first."

"Okay."

"Want a ride?"

"Yes, please. I hate driving on the ice."

Esme left a note on the fridge whiteboard, stating she'd gone to visit Alex. Then she tossed on her coat and followed Luke outside.

"Luke?"

"Hm?"

"How does Alex like his coffee."

"He doesn't. He drinks tea. Why?"

"Just curious."

Luke glanced over the street and adjacent yards before sweeping her into his arms again. Seconds later, after the whirlwind of divine power settled, the frost-kissed grounds of Alex's estate surrounded them. "Text me when you're ready to go home, unless you have Augustus drive you."

"Okay. Thank you, Luke." She kissed his cheek.

The door opened to reveal Alex's suited manservant before she reached the top step. "Greetings, Madam Esme. How may I be of service?"

"Is Alexander in?"

"He is in the forge. Shall I announce you?"

Esme pursed her lips. "No. I'd like to surprise him."

"Very well then." Augustus gestured her onward as Luke faded away.

Led by her memory of the estate, she made her way from the main building and onto the path to the forge. At first, she stared at the door, but nudging the oversized stone portal slid it with minimum effort.

The sweltering heat provided a welcoming respite from the wintry chill, and the fire cast an orange glow over the adjacent surfaces, shadows pooling over others distant from the immense hearth where an enormous dragon sat back on its hindquarters. One of its claws wrapped around the largest hammer she'd ever seen.

A dragon.

There was a dragon in the forge, the top of its head almost touching the ceiling, though it hunched over and studied its work with the diligence of any master artisan. Light flickered off its molten orange scales. Each one gleamed like amber, and his claws resembled obsidian scythes.

"Holy shit." When her voice echoed against the domed ceiling, the creature jerked its attention toward her and stared through two glossy scarlet eyes divided by narrow slit pupils. She saw her own reflection and shrank back against the door, a shriek torn from her throat.

Instead of surging across the forge to devour her, it dropped the hammer and squirmed back against the adjacent wall like a petrified wild animal seeking a place to hide.

He didn't move, and neither did she. They stared at each other across the distance, one woman and one mythological creature with an eerily familiar face and scars across its scaled body matching the ones she had committed to her memory during a beautiful night of lovemaking.

"Alex?" The terror pounding behind her breast eased, and then there was only concern for *him*.

Fleeing wasn't an option, so she swallowed her panic and moved across the floor.

"Don't look at me." He shrank back on his haunches, forearms raised in front of his face and one wing partially folded in front of him.

Esme crossed the floor to him. He turned his back on her, revealing the other wing. It was stunted, less than half the size of its twin. Still, she raised her fingers to touch the leather surface and feel the warmth of it beneath her fingers. "Why not?" she asked gently.

"I didn't want you to see me this way."'

"In what way?"

"Like *this*. Hideous."

"You aren't hideous, Alex."

He looked down over his shoulder at her and snorted in disgust, releasing twin plumes of black smoke and fire. "Don't lie to me." Although he had no human face, his features remained expressive, as there were ridges above his eyes like brows, and his tooth-filled maw had a distinctive shape that seemed to frown.

"You're not hideous. Nothing about you like this is hideous."

As a dragon, he loomed above her, but she could reach his flanks and touch his lower spine. His skin—or were they scales—was rough in some places and smooth in others like unconditioned leather. Like the interior of her cousin's current restoration of an old Dodge Charger, the seats all beat to hell and worn by time, aged, but not hideous. Touching him reminded her of a snake a zookeeper once allowed her to pet as a child. But so warm. So warm she dared to rest her cheek against his powerful ribs and listen to the mighty thunder of his heartbeat beneath it. One tremendous crash, then silence. Another great roar, then silence. His heart must have beat once every few seconds, if not slower.

"You've never lied to me about my looks before, Esme. Don't do it now."

"Of course I've never lied." She racked her brain to think of any time she'd ever implied he was anything but perfect, and then she knew, without asking. It was like he'd winded her. Assaulted her with a slap in the face.

"You're comparing me to her again."

Alex said nothing.

"I don't know the past things Aphrodite has said to you. I know the hurtful things she's done behind your back, but I am *not* her. If she saw ugliness, then that only proves how different we've become. Because I see beauty, Alex. I see beauty, strength, and power. Yes, there are flaws, but they make you someone unique and different, someone special who is worth being loved. Your mother didn't deserve you. The old Aphrodite didn't deserve you."

He twisted around and lowered closer to her. "You truly do not despise my appearance?"

"No. I..." Realization hit her. She gazed up at him, seeing the image of the flawless bronze dragon with his wings spread open, prepared to take flight. The model from which it had been inspired was no less majestic. "The statue is *you*."

"It was how I wish I could be. Powerful and strong. Not this... this crippled body."

"Then it's no longer my favorite piece of work from you, because I love the person you are *now*."

Alex didn't move. For a moment, he seemed to be struggling to process her words. So was she. They had come out of her on their own, like another person had taken control of her mouth and used her as a puppet.

Something from deep within her soul had surged out and taken the lead, lifting a tremendous and oppressive weight from her chest in the process. Freeing her.

"You... love me?"

"I suppose I must. Saying it felt... *right*." Though the word love also felt inadequate and far too weak to describe the flourishing emotion building in her chest.

"I have always loved you," he rasped out suddenly. "From the moment I first saw you in Olympus, the day I set my mother free from her golden prison, I knew no woman, no goddess, would ever compare. Until now. *You*, Esme, are a true treasure. I never thought I could love as deeply as I do."

Esme placed her palm against his scaled cheek and kissed his warm snout. As a shudder went through him, old memories surged to the surface and danced through her thoughts, some nebulous and almost formless, others more cohesive and solid visions. She saw herself, a different her in the past sitting beside the magnificent creature on the balcony of a golden, celestial palace, and together they had watched the sunset over Olympus. "Will you watch the sunset with me again as we once did?"

"Yes. But first, I have something for you." Hephaestus —it felt right in her mind to think of him as Hephaestus now, seeing him in all his draconic glory as a true god of fire—lowered to all fours and hurried to the distant side of the forge. He claimed something from a shelf and returned.

"What is it?"

The dragon lowered two silver cuffs and a white belt onto her open palms. The latter shone like opal or mother of pearl, and it was softer than conditioned leather but glossy as metal with a rose gold buckle.

Esme traced her thumb over the silhouettes of rose buds and flowers. "These are gorgeous."

"My gift to you. The belt is designed to amplify Aphrodite's talents over love, some of which you seem to retain in small amount. May it help you during this journey in the coming days to regain your immortality."

"And these?" She traced her thumb over the polished silver bracelets.

"They will shield you from danger."

While he watched, she donned the cuffs then slipped the belt around her waist and fastened it, noticing it slimmed by magic to fit into her belt loops. She used his narrow pupil as a makeshift mirror to admire her reflection and grinned. "Thank you."

His ember-bright eyes shone with joy. "I have finished the sword for Ares, but I have two other commissions to complete. Will you stay? Your advice has always been invaluable to me."

"Of course. After all, I've always liked watching you craft, right?"

Without needing him to remind her where to sit, Esme took the seat once occupied by her former incarnation. And there she remained for the afternoon while her metalworking dragon made art from formless ore.

Not now, but soon, she'd have to speak to him about his mother and do whatever she could to mend the broken bond between them.

After all, hadn't he claimed her guidance to be helpful?

AFTER SPENDING HER FRIDAY AFTERNOON AND EVENING with Alex, Esme worked extra hours over the weekend to make up for missed time at Memory Lane, going so far as to take over Meg and Clover's shifts so they could have both days free. Not that it was hard or overwhelming work when all she had to do was sit behind the counter and answer questions. A few customers came in Christmas Eve morning for last-minute gifts, and Esme kept eyeballing the clock, waiting for it to strike three.

During that shift, she borrowed a sheet of floral stationery from the manager's office and wrote a letter to the Underworld.

DEAR PERSEPHONE,

I WANT TO BEGIN THIS LETTER BY APOLOGIZING FOR ANY WRONGS I HAVE COMMITTED AGAINST YOU IN THE PAST DURING MY PREVIOUS LIFE AS APHRODITE. I HAVE FEW MEMORIES OF

THESE TIMES, BUT WHAT I HAVE LEARNED IS TO BECOME A DIFFERENT PERSON IN THIS LIFE. YOU HAVE MY WORD THAT I WON'T PURSUE ADONIS AGAIN, IN THIS LIFE OR ANY OTHER.

I HOPE WE CAN ONE DAY FIND FRIENDSHIP.

After a moment of debating how to sign it, she wrote her mortal name, folded the letter into an envelope, and texted Luke a request to deliver it. He did.

Time dragged after that, but the moment the chimes rang out, she bolted for the door and flipped the sign to closed. Freedom, finally.

Since Christmas held no real meaning to the guys, she had made plans with her friends instead to help make up for disappearing three days. She'd been kissing Marie's ass ever since she returned, even sending Luke away for delicious truffles from Belgium and French wine to share until her friend forgave her.

Jordan picked her up outside and they headed to her home, where Marie and Ashley had already covered every horizontal space in garlands and cheery holiday knickknacks. A modest pile of presents filled in the space beneath their decorated tree.

"Are your dudes not joining us?" Ashley asked once they were all settled in the living room with drinks and a holiday movie playing on the television.

"Nah, they all had, um, other places to be."

"Girl, I still can't believe you have two men," Jordan said.

"Three," Marie corrected. "Alexander Smith is sweet on her too."

They all stared at Esme. "What? He's a great guy."

Marie cackled and clapped her hands before

hurrying to her feet. "Go look at our backyard."

"What's back there?" Ashley asked.

Esme sighed. "Marie—"

"Just go look." Marie grinned at her and led the way to reveal the dragon sculpture arranged beside the garden patio.

Jordan stared out the window for a while before he turned to raise both of his fair brows. "He gave you that piece from the auction?"

"It arrived yesterday. He bought back his own piece that night at the auction because Esme told him she loved it."

Jordan leered at her. "What'd you have to do to get that?"

Ashley sipped her rum-laced eggnog. "How many of them have you boned yet?"

"You people are terrible."

"What? After all the time we spent picking you up after Daniel, we totally deserve to see you happy. And hear your sordid and dirty sexcapades," Jordan said as they migrated back to the living room.

"I've only slept with one of them. Yes, he was hung, no, I won't say which, and yes, it was amazing. The end."

"I stand by my previous assessment: lucky bitch." Jordan raised his beer in toast.

Esme rolled her eyes. "Enough about me. What about you? I thought you were going to ask out that guy in your English class."

Jordan's face fell. "I did. He's got a guy down at UCLA already. He was really sweet about it, but I'm mortified."

"Hey, don't be." She reached out and rubbed his back.

"It just means he's not the guy meant for you, but I know there's one out there and when you meet him, he's gonna be blown away by how amazing you are."

"You're the bomb, Es, you know that?" Jordan put his hand over hers and squeezed.

"I do my best."

"Since when did you get all optimistic about love?" Ashley asked.

"I dunno. I guess when I figured out I that I didn't have to be miserable about Daniel dumping me. Once I realized that, everything sorta fell away and started sorting itself out."

"Plus, three guys," Marie added, to everyone's amusement.

"Speaking of Daniel..." Jordan's eyes lit up. "Word has it that Shelly is banging the middle linebacker behind his back. Talk about sweet justice, right?"

"Actually, I think it's kinda sad."

"All right, who are you and what have you done with my friend?" Marie demanded.

"It's true," Esme said. "Look, I agree, Daniel was a jerk and it hurt when he cheated on me but... but I wouldn't wish that on anyone. Not even him."

"I agree," Ashley said in a soft voice. Esme smiled at her.

Marie sighed. "In the spirit of Christmas, fine, no more smack talk about douche exes and cheating skanks. Agreed?"

They all clinked their drinks together. "Agreed."

15

*T*ime without the guys around gave Esme time to think with a clear head, a mind unclouded by muscles and promises of sex. After a lazy Christmas afternoon with her friends—they'd all slept in—opening presents, watching slasher flicks, and stuffing their faces with sweets from the local bakery, Esme had been ready to go back to work. But while shoppers perused the store displays, her mind wandered.

How could she prove she was the goddess of love and worthy of getting her powers back? Did she even want to become a divine being?

The obvious answer was yes. Who wouldn't want to be a powerful goddess? Especially one who was renowned for her beauty. But something still made her hesitant. She didn't want power to be beautiful. She wanted to be equal with the three men who had turned her world upside down.

So how did she do it?

"Excuse me, miss?"

She snapped out of her thoughts and glanced at the man standing nearby. "Sorry, can I help you?"

"I'm trying to find a gift for my wife. I mean, my ex-wife." He smiled in a sad sort of way.

"A gift for your ex-wife?"

The man chuckled, and his wind-reddened cheeks flushed even darker. "Yeah. I know that has to sound strange, but she used to be my best friend, you know? And she's still the mother of my children. Doesn't seem right to not send a gift for her too."

"Doing a second Christmas?"

"Yeah."

"All right. If you don't mind me asking, what sort of gift are you going for? Just a general 'thinking of you at the holidays' gift or more along the lines of 'I still care for you' gift?

"I miss her," he admitted. "I miss how things used to be."

The ache in his eyes reached out and spoke to her deep down inside. "Tell me a little about her. What do you remember most?"

He stroked his chin and gazed at the items on the counter and adjacent tables. "She has amazing hair. A *lot* of it. It's dark like yours, and she collects fancy pins and clips from around the world since she likes to wear it up while at work. She's a doctor."

"That's a good start. We have some beautiful pieces over here." She led the way to a display further in the room. Heirloom hairpins and clips rested on velvet beds next to several antique brushes and hand mirrors. "What colors does she like?"

"Everything."

When his gaze gravitated to a piece on the end, he sucked in a quiet breath. Esme unlocked the case and carefully took out the jeweled peacock comb. Gemstones in various shades of blue, green, topaz, and purple stood out against silver filigree.

"I'll take it," he said.

"Don't you even want to know how much it costs first?"

The man shook his head. "No. It's perfect. Do you do gift wrapping?"

"Absolutely."

Later on, after she'd sent the man on his way with a beautifully wrapped gift, she sat down at the front counter and texted Luke. Seeing the love in the gentleman's eyes, and hearing his story, had given her the inspiration she needed for what to do next.

We need to go back to Olympus to see Zeus tomorrow, she sent in a message.

Okay?

She chuckled at his confused response and sent another message. *Time to play marriage counselor. Trust me.*

If she was going to prove herself the personification of true love, then what better way to start than by fixing one of the oldest loves in the world?

FREED FROM A LONG WEEK OF KISSING ASS TO HER BOSS AND coworkers, Esme awakened Friday morning to shower and squeeze into jeans. She pulled on a sweater, slipped into a pair of boots, buckled on Aphrodite's girdle, and sat on the edge of her bed to text Luke.

Morning, speedy. Are you busy?

The response came seconds later, *Not at all. What's up?*

I need that ride to Olympus.

A subtle wind stirred her hair. When Esme glanced up to her left, Luke was standing in her room, brows raised. "You sure about this? You're going to lose another day if I take you into Olympus again. It's a long trip."

"That's okay. I told everyone we're heading down to San Diego for the weekend. No one will freak out about me being missing."

"Alrighty then. Ready to go?"

"Let's do it."

As before, Luke took her by the hand and led the way into the In-Between. Everything rushed by in a weird blur that lacked saturated colors or clear sound. Without any way to keep track of the time, she simply let herself drift, pulled along by Luke.

"And here we are."

When they stepped out into the same posh office, the sky beyond the windows were dark and the secretary's desk was empty. Unbothered by her absence, Luke grabbed the key from her desk and then crossed to the stairwell door and held it open.

"After you, Esme."

"Hey, um... You stay down here. I think this is a chat I need to have with Zeus alone."

Luke sucked in a deep breath through his teeth. "You remember which door?"

"I do." She leaned in and kissed his cheek. "Thanks. I'll see ya soon."

Leaving Luke behind, she hurried up the floating steps until she reached the door to Zeus's office. She found it ajar, the room beyond it lit by the pale silver moon. At first, she hesitated to enter, but then she saw Zeus beside the window with his back to her and made her way inside.

He didn't turn to face her. "Why are you back when you haven't completed your quest?"

"I'm back because I've finally figured out what's been bothering me since I came to see you the other day. I felt your pain."

"The ruler of Olympus feels no pain."

"Doesn't he?" she persisted, waiting a breath for lightning to strike her. "You don't rule the skies anymore, and you don't look into the lives of your offspring. You don't leave this office."

"I have a business to run."

Esme stepped up beside him to share the view. "Business hours are over, but you're still standing here. You're certainly not working. Would I be wrong to assume you haven't moved from this spot since Luke and I left?"

"That would be my business."

"Maybe, but I kinda think it's mine too."

He finally turned from the window to face her.

He wasn't as intimidating as she remembered, not the all-powerful and mighty Zeus. Instead of a proud divine being, she saw a weary man, a flawed man. She also didn't need to look through his window to guess at what he'd been gazing at with such longing.

"What is it you want? What is it you think I need?"

Esme nibbled her lower lip. The speech she'd rehearsed along the way had flitted away, every word evaporated like ether. "After the guys rescued me from the hellhound, I was a wreck. I didn't know what to believe, so I spent a couple days reading all the Greek and Roman myths I could find. The stories say you raped Hera—"

"I've never taken *any* woman by force. I haven't *needed* to. Women fucking fall before me and throw open their legs, and that's the way it's always been."

"Uh-huh." Esme felt no such compulsion, which made her wonder if the god had lost his touch, if pride led to exaggeration, or if she alone was immune. "What good has that done you recently? Where has your wife gone?"

His heavy brows furrowed, and fury flushed red across his face. As soon as he began to anger, he also deflated. His shoulders dropped in defeat. "None. I haven't..."

Esme moved closer and perched on the edge of his desk, waiting for him to finish. "You haven't..."

"I haven't lain with a woman in decades. Not since she left."

"Well, that's a start I suppose. A good one."

"Except it's been for nothing!"

"Why do you believe it's been for nothing?"

He growled his response. "She doesn't care. What

good does it do if she doesn't care? I don't understand why she won't return to me. I apologized."

"But what good is an apology when you've already fathered half of Olympus?" Esme asked. "Your wife is the goddess of marriage and family. I'm not saying she's without fault, but you took something that she cherished, something that meant a lot to her, and you spat on it. You did that dozens of times every time you seduced another woman. Every time you fathered another child, you showed her how little her reason for *existing* means to you."

The old man frowned, deepening the creases in his face. "I... I never thought of it that way."

"And that's half the problem. Forgive me for saying so, but you don't think much beyond yourself. None of you gods think of anyone but yourselves until you're inconvenienced."

"You weren't much better," he muttered.

"Maybe I wasn't, but that's not me anymore, and I'm making a new life for myself. *Have* made a new life for myself, for the better I think."

His heavy brow furrowed again. "Why do you care what happens to me? You have a mission to complete, yet you waste valuable time prancing about to Olympus to see me again."

"I know, but I'm here now because it's the right thing to do."

Zeus scoffed. "Well then, what do you suggest? How do we fix this divine fuckup?"

"The humans would call your relationship unhealthy, but honestly, I don't think it's fair to hold immortal beings to the same standard as humans anyway." She nibbled her lower lip. "But you have to want to fix this. I mean, *really* want it."

"Of all my wives, of all the lovers I've taken, goddess and mortal, Hera was the only one to see through my bullshit and call me on it. The only one who treated me as an equal instead of the mighty Zeus." He chuckled. "Even led a revolt against me."

"Didn't you hang her from Olympus by her ankles for it?"

"No. But I wanted to. The mortals told stories of me punishing her and showing mercy the next day, but I loved her. She brought spice to a life that had already begun to dull. Her wit. Her sass. I miss every fucking moment, I would tolerate a dozen more revolts to have her stand beside me again."

"Then why not do something about it?"

"I've tried. She won't listen."

"But what if she would this time?"

He cocked his head and squinted at her. "Go on."

"I'll go and talk to Hera, soften her up a bit, but then *you* need to be ready to step in and do what's right. To set aside your pride and, well, grovel."

"I don't grovel."

"If you want your wife's forgiveness, you'll kiss her ass. If you love her the way you claim you do," Esme said, raising her hand to cup Zeus's cheek, "you'll tell her whatever it takes, and you'll mean every word because she's worth it. Because if she had even a fraction of the love you felt for her, she's hurting too."

His stoic features softened. "Fine."

"And you better bring her a gift. Lilies and nectar," she blurted out, without even understanding why. "And treats for her peacocks."

Zeus raised a brow at her. "All right."

"Okay, good. So, I'm going to go somewhere and celebrate that you didn't smite me for talking to you this way. Goodbye."

Zeus's voice stopped her two steps from the door. "When will I need to be ready to see her?"

"I'm not sure yet," she said, looking back over her shoulder. "I'll send Hermes for you when it's time."

Without waiting to see if he had anything else to say, she pulled open the door and headed down the stairs. She didn't slow or stop until she pushed her way back inside the lobby, right into Luke's waiting arms.

"Esme? Are you okay?"

She sagged against him and turned her face against his throat, overcome by a bout of hysterical laughter. "I can't believe I gave love advice to a god. I'm still waiting to wake up from this and discover I've been in bed asleep and dreamed up one amazing, fantastic story to tell Marie."

"So it worked?"

"In a way. I have to talk to Hera next."

Luke whistled and glanced at his watch. "Well, you won't be able to talk to her now. Trust me, you never wanna interrupt her evening routine. Ever. But we can go first thing tomorrow."

"All right, I'll trust you on that."

"Good. Now, are you up for one more adventure tonight, or did facing down the big guy wear you out?"

"I think I can handle one more adventure. Where to?"

He took her hand. "You trust me?"

"Of course I do."

———

LOUD MUSIC AND BRIGHT LIGHTS DOMINATED THE ROOM Luke brought them into from the In-Between. They moved through a room crowded with people while models walked down an illuminated runway. It was everything she'd seen while binge watching one of her favorite reality shows or Entertainment News.

"Are we at a Victoria's Secret show?" she hissed.

Luke scoffed. "Nah, that's too cliché for Dito."

"What?"

"Dito." Luke flashed a smile up at the muscle-bound guard at the stage door and passed by unchallenged.

"Dito? As in super model, million-dollar business mogul *Dito*?"

"Yeah, I guess that's what you'd know them for."

Backstage was chaos. Men and women in varying states of dress and undress bustled about. Luke didn't seem to mind and led her to a dressing table toward the back.

"Hermes!"

A body threw itself into Luke's arms before Esme had a chance to see who had rushed them. He chuckled and returned the embrace, making Esme seethe in jealousy until the figure pulled back. Her jaw dropped.

In person, they had to be the most beautiful man Esme had ever seen, or the most handsome woman she'd ever encountered. From the flawless, sun-kissed skin to the thick, black curls framing their androgynous face, Dito had become a highly sought-after model for the ability to play both sides of the scene from lingerie to menswear.

Esme held a hand to her chest. For as much as she made fun of screaming fangirls chasing their favorite actors for autographs, she'd never met one of her own idols before. "H-hi."

Dito raised both dark brows and glanced at Luke. He nodded, like some kind of nonverbal conversation was taking place between them she wasn't privileged to hear.

"You look so different," Dito said. They reached out and touched Esme's dark hair. "I like it. I think it suits you better than blonde."

"Blonde?"

"This a bad time for you right now?" Luke asked.

"No, not at all. I was just finishing up and can totally ditch."

"Great. How about that Greek restaurant you took me to last time I visited? We can talk over a meal." Luke smiled and tugged Esme to his side. "Sound good to you?"

"Um, yeah, I guess."

Dito's lips spread into an exuberant grin. They bounced on their toes, kissed first Luke then Esme too. "I'll dress and meet you there."

Dito had kissed her. Stunned, she was barely aware of Luke leading her away again. They went from bright and chaotic to quiet and intimate—the dimmed restaurant filled with candlelit tables and the delicious aroma of roasting lamb. A smiling hostess led them to a secluded table in the back despite sending away another couple without a reservation.

"Luke, are you going to explain what happened? I mean... Dito. That was completely random and just... wow. I mean, wow." She'd been crazy about Dito since reading about the model's eccentric Manhattan penthouse in *Vogue* over two years ago.

He pulled out her chair, settled her, then took the opposite seat. His silence unnerved her. "I figured... you have a lot of kids with Ares, but Dito's our only one. *My* only kid." Luke fidgeted, messing with the napkin and silverware. "I know the myths claim I have a lot of children, but Dito was it for me."

"You mean that Dito is—"

"Ours, yeah. Beautiful kid, don't you think?"

"Holy crap, my kid is a supermodel." Esme cupped her face with both hands.

"Look, if it's too much, I can call and cancel. Dito won't mind."

"No, don't do that."

Luke relaxed in his seat. "Great."

"Does this mean the story about the nymph and the spring is true?"

He nodded. "Yeah. Hermaphroditus was our son first, but he and a river nymph fell in love to such a degree they were joined forever. Now I just kind of consider it's like having the best of both worlds, you know? I got a kickass son *and* a daughter."

Dito joined them before the waiter arrived to take an order. The model slid into an empty seat and smiled. "Thanks so much for letting me join you two."

"Anything for you, sweetheart," Luke said.

A moment passed before Esme regained her voice, and even when she did speak, it was thick with a sudden upwelling of emotion. "I'm glad you were able to join us." Studying Dito, she picked out the subtle traces of Luke in their child's features, and it no longer troubled her at all to consider Dito *theirs*. Their child from another lifetime.

"I couldn't believe it when Dad said he found you again."

Esme sniffled and wiped her cheek with her wrist. "You have his curls."

Dito beamed. "It's blonde usually, but I—"

"You cut and dyed it when you started doing the menswear fashion shows. It's super cute. I love it."

Dito's eyes lit with excitement. "You followed my career?"

"Yeah. Of course, I had no idea who you were. Then again, maybe something deep inside of me did know."

"Do you remember anything now?"

"Only snatches and bits of things. A face, sometimes a voice or even a room from a special place. Fleeting bits of memory come back to me every now and again, like right now when I look at you. At first, it was like reliving a stranger's past, but it's..." Esme bit her lower lip. She didn't know when things had changed. "Sometimes they feel like things I've forgotten for a very long time, and it's only now coming back to me."

Food arrived not long after. She and Dito shared a

love for spanakopita and, because Esme imagined it was what her own mother would do, she split the last piece instead of keeping it for herself.

How the hell was she ever supposed to learn how to be a mother to seven children?

"Hey, we should totally go shopping the next time you can visit," Dito said. "I bet I can find you some amazing outfits. Heck, you might even fit some of the show stuff."

"Do you get to keep those?"

"Oh yeah. I have trunks full of designer clothes."

"Aren't kids supposed to raid their mom's closet and not the other way around?"

When Dito's smile widened, dimples appeared. "Maybe. I bet I'd find cute stuff in yours too."

"Marie would flip her shit if you showed up to swap clothes. Like, I'm pretty sure she'd die on the spot."

"That's her roommate," Luke said. "You'd like her. She's a nosy troublemaker who pokes in everyone's business."

"Then I can't wait to visit. Nosy people are my favorite kind of people."

When Dito hugged her close, Esme's eyes overflowed with the tears she had tried to keep at bay. How was it possible to miss someone she'd never met before?

"Come see me any time, Mom. I would be happy to show you New York City."

"I'll bring her back again soon, sweetheart. I promise."

Esme and Dito exchanged phone numbers while Luke hung back and watched them.

Then they embraced again, and the affection of her

firstborn scorched through Esme with such a profound sense of love she didn't want to leave and resume her quest.

But she had to. For Dito, the other children of Aphrodite, and the three men counting on her to regain the immortality she'd sacrificed. They deserved to have her in their lives again, and she'd do anything to grant their shared desire.

16

*E*sme parted from Luke on the expansive green lawn leading up to Hera's door. A few peacocks trailed behind her along the way, and one even allowed her to brush her thumb against his glossy cheek.

The door opened before she reached it to reveal a tired woman in a fluffy robe over gaudy peacock print leggings and a long shirt. She cradled a pint of ice cream in the crook of her elbow. "What do you want?"

Esme halted shy of reaching the steps. "To talk."

Alex resembled Hera so closely they could have been siblings instead of mother and son, though the goddess lacked his unusual height and stood eye level with Esme. She wore her wavy blonde hair pinned in a messy bun beneath a golden crown.

"Really? I don't think we have much to talk about, but if you insist." She turned and headed back inside, leaving the door open behind her. "Pour yourself a glass of wine."

"A little early for drinking, isn't it?"

"Darling, it's never too early."

Esme followed Hera to a wine-scented living room decorated by a low glass coffee table and an L-shaped sectional. She took a seat and eyed the platter of chocolate chip cookies beside an open box of chocolate truffles.

An image shimmered in a wide bowl of water. A married couple in the middle of a domestic spat.

"Are you helping them?" Esme asked.

"No, no, darling. These are my morning soaps. I wouldn't waste my time." Hera plucked a chocolate from the box. "He lost their savings gambling, and he'll only do it again. They *always* do it again no matter how much they promise to change."

"But aren't you supposed to help out with those sorts of things?"

"We don't interfere as much as the stories would have you believe. Besides, it's not like they've called upon me." She sighed and refilled her glass with a generous pour from a bottle of red. "So few of the mortals remember."

"Times have changed, but so have you. I mean, look at you, a free and single woman now. That never would have happened back then, right?"

"Get to the point. Why are you here?"

"I want to help you and Zeus fix your issues."

Sharp laughter filled the room. "No really, darling. Why are you here?"

"Exactly what I said." She drew in a breath then added, "And I want to help mend the rift between you and your son."

"I have nothing to say about that." Hera took another drink and looked away.

"Zeus may have broken the vow between husband and wife, but you broke the bond between mother and child. He was a newborn. An innocent. He trusted you to love him unconditionally from the moment he came from your womb, but you destroyed that because he didn't meet your expectations of beauty."

"I know," Hera said in a soft voice.

"Then what are you going to do about it? Drink away your days and eat bonbons, or actually try to atone for what you did to him?"

"He doesn't *want* to see me. I've tried to reach out, and I decided to respect his wishes. I could at least do that much for him."

Esme studied the woman's subdued features and nodded. "I'll talk to Alex—Hephaestus, and see what I can do, but in return, you have to do something for me."

Hera poured her wine into her ice cream. "Why do you care?"

"Because I care about *him*."

"You never gave a damn about him before. How many times did you break your vows to my son before he finally caught you in the act?"

"Look, I can't answer for things done in a past I barely remember. That woman, the Aphrodite you all remember, is gone and never coming back. There's only me now, and I care for Alex, just as much as I care for Luke and Beau."

Hera chortled and took another sip of wine. "Ridiculous names if you ask me. So, you've decided to fuck them all? Well, I can't say much against it, I suppose. Times are what they are now, and the definition of marriage has changed. I only care that Ares and Hephaestus have the happiness they deserve, and if... if you're able to give them that, it's no business of mine."

"But you're still unhappy."

"Am I?"

Esme raised both brows then nodded toward wine and double chocolate fudge ice cream. "I never ice cream binge unless I'm upset. You haven't stopped shoveling it in your mouth since I've arrived."

"I like it, and I have nothing better to do."

"So this has nothing at all to do with Zeus?" When Hera didn't reply, Esme persisted. "Well?"

"I miss him," Hera admitted, drying her wet eyes with the back of one wrist. "So much it hurts. There are so many days when I don't want to crawl out of bed. Why should I care about the marriage of humans when even mine failed?"

Esme moved closer, heart thundering in her chest as she lowered a palm to Hera's hand. The other woman was consumed by so much bitterness, the taste of it seemed to fill the very air itself, stale and oppressive. "It failed because Zeus couldn't keep it in his pants, and because instead of confronting him about his philandering, you decided to be a vengeful twat."

"I thought it would make him stop."

"But it didn't. You took your anger out on the women he seduced and the children he fathered, but you never took your grievance to *him.*"

Something changed in the air, and the bitter tang of resentment diminished.

"Because that is not how it was done then." Hera's voice rose with each word, and then the tears coursed down her cheeks too fast to be wiped away, the proverbial and literal floodgates opened. "That isn't how the mortals wanted us."

"That's an *excuse*," Esme spat out, heat flushing under her skin. "You can't blame all of your problems and troubles on the mortals who follow you. You have a will of your own."

"Oh, child. How young you are. Still..." She sighed and set the ice cream aside. "Suppose you do have the right of it. Do you expect me to go crawling back to him when he's the one who wronged me for so many centuries?"

"No. I don't. Because he's here to crawl back to you."

"Excuse me?"

"He's outside, and he's ready to talk, if you're willing to do the same."

"But I'm a mess." Hera leapt up and tore off her robe. She patted her hair and moaned. "I have nothing to wear. For the love of Styx, I don't even know when I last shaved."

Esme bit back a snort. Just barely. "He'll wait."

While Hera vanished into another room to primp and prepare, Esme let herself onto the porch to find Zeus hand-feeding a flock of peacocks.

"Hera will be with you in a moment."

"She'll speak with me?"

"I did promise I'd try, didn't I? It's up to you to do the

rest. Tone down the godly arrogance a little though and remember what I said about who she is."

Zeus nodded.

The urge to collapse in hysterical laughter came over her again. She'd given a pep talk to a divine being like a football coach chatting up the team before the big game.

When the door opened again behind them, Esme and Zeus turned at once to find Hera framed over the threshold in a radiant white, sleeveless gown, a jeweled belt of gold strands around her slender waist and gemstones glittering in her hair.

Zeus gazed at her with naked, unconcealed longing. Upon dropping the sack of bird-feed, he joined her on the porch and bowed before presenting a single lily to his estranged former wife. Once Esme mouthed for him to say something, he cleared his throat.

"You look lovely today, Hera. May we sit and talk?"

"I suppose. Please come in."

Pressure eased off Esme's chest, a weight she hadn't known was there until it raised and the burden was gone. They'd work things out, of that she was certain.

She meandered down the golden road, away from Hera's abode. Every house was different with a facade to match the divine being who dwelled there. She found Luke lounging farther down in a garden with a bevy of nubile nymphs dancing through the yard. The moment he spotted her, he jumped up and excused himself.

"Having fun?" she asked.

"It's always a party with them, and they have the best snacks."

"Are you going to introduce us or not?" someone

demanded, the voice masculine and deep. Esme turned, coming face-to-face with a satyr. He wasn't wearing pants.

"Um." She ripped her attention from below his waist somehow and tried to focus on his bearded face.

Luke snickered quietly into his hand. "Esme, meet Pan. Pan, Aphrodite in her new flesh."

The goatman kissed her knuckles then sniffed her wrist afterward. His furry ears twitched. "I would recognize such unmatched beauty anywhere. Will you two be staying for a while?"

"I'd love to, really, but I have to get back home. I'm not exactly sure how many days have passed since I left the mortal realm."

"It's Sunday," Luke assured her. "I've been keeping track this time."

"Which means we need to head back. Another hour here and a day will pass before we know it. Still, it was nice to meet you, Pan, and I promise to come back another time."

"I'll hold you to that," the horned god said. He winked then trotted back to the party, where he quite shamelessly, and very vigorously, mounted one of the nymphs in front of them.

Esme stared.

"Yeah, time to go." Luke tugged her arm and led her away. "Sorry about that. I forget sometimes because it's a normal thing around here. So where to?"

"Home. If it's Sunday, that means we have a New Year's Eve pool party to catch at the resort, and I need to figure out which swimsuit to wear."

17

*E*sme's spirits had been soaring high since her victory in Olympus. After ringing in the New Year with Luke and her friends, Beau sweet-talked her into spending the end of the week with him on the slopes, promising a spa treatment and a miniature vacation to prepare her for the upcoming semester.

While Esme often doubted her skill in the ice rink, she had absolute confidence on the skis and her ability to leave Beau behind.

Wasn't hubris what began 90 percent of the tales from ancient Greco-Roman mythology? Then again, Beau wanted in her pants and wasn't likely to curse her if she whipped his ass.

Wednesday morning after she did some finagling with the work schedule and promised to step in the next two weekends in a row for Meg, Esme dragged her skis out of the garage and met Beau at the resort with two days of clothes in a backpack.

"You wanna take the amateur slopes?" Beau asked once they were outside in the frosty air, insulated by ski jackets, warm boots, goggles, and gloves.

"Nope. No bunny slopes for me."

Beau grinned. "Great. I hoped you'd say that."

She glanced down at his black, flame-trimmed board and laughed. "I still can't believe the god of war spends his time ice skating *and* skiing."

He grunted. "It's a snowboard. Much cooler than your skis. I'll kick your ass on this thing."

She wondered how much of his big macho persona was an act. "Uh-huh."

They claimed an empty lift destined for one of the resort's advanced trails, a piste she'd only practiced a few times since moving on from the intermediate slopes her sophomore year. She'd been too busy during the last ski season to run them with her friends.

Beau raised the safety bar as they neared the top. "You sure about this?"

"Pffft, yeah. My dad raised me on these slopes."

"But not *this* slope."

"But not this slope."

Esme rose from the seat and glided away from the lift's loading area. Beau followed her.

It had been too long since she'd come up here. The cool breeze ruffled through her hair, carrying the crisp scent of fresh snow. A few other skiers occupied the trails, but not many. Most kept to the beginner and intermediate trails further down the mountain.

"You ready?" Beau asked.

"Ready to kick your ass? Yeah, let's do it."

Beau proved to be skilled with the snowboard. Every dip and ramp became an opportunity for the god of war to demonstrate his prowess as an extreme sportsman, performing jumps and spins that would put Tony Hawk to shame. Esme managed a few small leaps, but never came close to matching his caliber.

Not that she needed to. Racing down the slopes, she breezed past Beau and claimed the lead despite his pomp and flash. She stole the win and glided to a finish, spinning at the bottom to shoot him a smug grin.

"Beat you!"

He challenged her to several rematches, and more times than not, she came out victorious until at last, he surrendered to her greater speed. They spent the entire afternoon on the slopes until they broke for dinner to satisfy Esme's rumbling tummy.

By the time they finished swapping snow jackets for dinner attire, Esme was famished to the point of swooning in Beau's arms. "I am starving and ready for cocoa."

Beau stole a kiss, setting her soul ablaze. He smelled like rum and cinnamon, like danger and fire, reminding her of Alex and that unique scent she associated with him. They were brothers after all, of similar divine spheres.

"I see Luke wasn't exaggerating about your lust for chocolate, but your wish is my command."

Taking her by surprise with his manners, Beau offered an arm and escorted her to the resort's restaurant. She realized two things at that moment—her god turned heads wherever they went, and some, but not all of his bad boy persona was a farce. Every time a female guest stared at him, Esme smiled even wider.

Mine. He's all mine.

While waiting their turn to meet the hostess, she leaned against him and closed her eyes. Then a familiar, masculine voice called her name. "Esme?"

Esme cringed, turning in time to see her ex nearly trip over his own feet as he crossed the lobby to catch up with them. Crap. She'd forgotten Daniel worked there during the winter and summer breaks.

"Want me to send him packing?" Beau asked in a quiet voice.

"No, go on ahead and get our table. Order me a cocoa with extra marshmallows."

Something about Beau's curt nod irritated her, but he stepped forward to meet the hostess as Daniel reached them. Was he jealous of a mortal? Torn between amusement and exasperation, she turned to face her ex. He was dressed in all black and sporting an apron around his waist.

"Something you need, Daniel?"

"Hey there, Essie. You're, uh, you're looking good. Real good."

"Thanks. Now what do you want?"

"Can't a guy say hello to his girl?"

The absurdity of his words struck her silent for a split second, and then she burst out into laughter. "Okay, wow. What happened? Did Shelly finally dump your ass so now you're crawling back to me? Or did you find out about her activities with your football bros? Well, forget it."

"Why the fuck not? Es, I missed you. I was planning to break up with Shelly anyway, but you were with that jackass rich boy." He glanced toward Beau's retreating shape. "Looks like that didn't last either."

"Luke and I are doing just great, not that it's any of your business."

"Essie, babe, think about how long we've been together. Since like, what, end of tenth grade? That's a long time to throw away."

"Too long. Now, if you don't mind, I'm gonna catch up with Beau."

"C'mon, babe. Please? I was an idiot, I know that. Let me make it up to you. Ditch the hippie with the hair and come out with me."

"Daniel, I'm gonna say this once, and once only." Esme bridged the gap between them and placed her hand on his arm. "You're an asshole."

He blinked at her. "What?"

"You need to take a hard look at yourself and the way you treat women, because you're never gonna find love until you make a change. No one wants to put up with your bullshit."

"I..." His mouth opened and closed like a fish. "You're right. I was never very good to you."

"You had your moments, but maybe you should spend some time alone too. Time to think about what you want and how you can improve yourself before the next relationship, so that when you find a good woman for you, you're the kind of man who can keep her."

His dark brows notched together. "Alone, really?"

"Uh-huh. Some alone time without bouncing from

girl to girl. You're more than the people you date. You're an amazing wide receiver, and I think you'll be scouted for sure. You used to volunteer and do nice things, remember? Take some time to figure out you. Go volunteer at the shelter and walk some dogs in your free time. Foster a pit and fall in love with something that doesn't have a vagina."

"Okay. Shit, I guess I never really thought about it that way. I mean, Dad always told me college was about sleeping with as many girls as possible. I just figured..."

Esme pressed her lips together. How far did she dare to test him? "Your dad was wrong then, because college is about more than who you can fuck. Take a dating break without boning everything that moves. Learn to love *yourself.*"

He nodded. "Okay... okay, I will. Thanks, Esme. I guess I better get to work. Best tippers will be coming down to eat soon."

"See ya."

Something shifted, like another layer of rust crumbling away from an old hinge. Something had happened again. The same something she'd awakened when speaking with Zeus and Hera, and this time, she'd consciously used it on Daniel to the same effect.

She hurried inside the restaurant where Beau waited for her with a steaming cup of cocoa loaded with marshmallows beside a plate of fluffy croissants stuffed with chocolate. Nothing beat dessert as an appetizer.

"Everything go okay?" Beau asked.

"I did something to my ex," she whispered to him.

"Yeah? I hope you punched that asshole in his nose."

"No. Not a physical something. We were talking, and I felt this weird compulsion to touch him. And... all I wanted was for him to take a little break from dating. And when I suggested it, he just agreed with me like it was the best idea in the world. I'm not wearing the girdle Hephaestus gave me."

"Sounds like you've tapped into a little of your inner mojo."

"But you guys said I'm mortal. How is this working?"

Beau nodded. "You are, and your body *is* human, but there's something left of the old you deep inside. A little spark you awakened when you helped Mom and Dad out, and I think it gets a little stronger every day. Hell, maybe it started when you helped out my brother. He's always been self-conscious about his looks."

Esme nibbled her croissant. "Thanks for bringing me here today.

"Hey, since the douche is waiting tables tonight, you wanna order up to the room instead?"

"Sure. Let's head up now."

Despite Marie's urging, Esme had packed onesies and flannel, hoping to convey a nonverbal message to Beau not to get his hopes up without putting in some work.

"My everything hurts, and we've only been here one day."

Beau powered on the electric fireplace below the flat

screen television in the bedroom. "I don't plan to take it easy on you tomorrow either, so you better take a long soak in that enormous tub and stretch before you tighten up."

"You better be talking about the slopes tomorrow."

He cocked one dark brow. "Your mind is as filthy as I remember."

"Ha ha." She sprawled across the bed and decided her bath could wait until after food. They expected room service in the next half hour.

"Not a bad thing." He chuckled and kicked back on the nearby sofa.

"Ares?" She tested his true name on her tongue and decided she liked it more than Beau.

"Hmm?"

"I wondered if... you'd tell me what happened between us and Hephaestus. I know his side of the story. I haven't spoken with you about it, and I don't remember."

Beau dragged in a breath. "I kind of hoped you wouldn't care to ask."

"Why?"

"Because it was all my fault. Indirectly mine anyway. You know how all throughout mythology, Aphrodite is considered my consort?"

"Yeah?"

"Because that's how I wanted it. I had a thousand opportunities to make you my wife. I could have married you before Hephaestus even had the chance to win you from Zeus, but I didn't. And that's my fuckup. Because I was afraid of commitment."

"And?"

VIVIENNE SAVAGE

"So I put it off. Then one day, Hera receives a golden throne from Hephaestus and she's delighted, thinks he's forgiven her and extending the olive branch. Fuck, she was so overjoyed, she sat in it right away."

"And was stuck."

"Right. He enchanted it to hold her captive, and *no one*, not even Zeus, could break the spell. So someone gives Dad this bright idea to offer you as a prize to the first god able to convince Hephaestus to release her from the throne. You agreed to get back at me. When I showed up to try to talk him into it, Heph breathed fire on me, melted my armor, and didn't leave until Dionysus got him drunk enough to decide he wanted to be married to you."

"No wonder Alex barely looked me in the eye at first." She bit into her remaining chocolate pastry from the dining room. "So what happened then? I mean, obviously I wasn't very loyal."

Beau sighed. "You were heartbroken, and I was so pissed at Heph, I said to hell with it, let's carry on the way we were before. Then you found out you were pregnant with Harmonia—"

A flash sparked through her memories of a young girl with honey-colored curls. Esme blinked rapidly a few times, eyes stinging. She remembered singing to a warm, ticklish little girl who snuggled against her at night in a palace of rose gold and ivory, the two of them all alone. She'd had Ares's blue eyes in a heart-shaped face and dimpled cheeks.

"The day you told me about her was the day Helios ratted us out. Bro made a trap to catch us in bed the next time I visited, and the rest of the story is as you know. I got exiled by Zeus, you cursed Hephaestus and Helios, and then things were never the same again."

"Answer my next question. If I had you, why did I want Adonis? Persephone and I fought over him."

Beau's expression darkened. "Zeus offered to grant your divorce if I paid your bride price to Hephaestus. I didn't. That's my second fuckup. I hurt you because I was too proud to pay for what I thought was already *mine*."

"Sorry to repeat this again, but the Greek gods sucked. Myself included."

"Yeah, we did. I like to think I'm a better, wiser man now. I learned that day it's possible to win the battle and still lose the war. I could have ended everything right then. One day, Heph granted the divorce on his own and withdrew to his forge. Stopped taking any outside visitors and said he'd see no one but you."

"Did I ever visit?"

"No." He looked away, toward the window and the dimming sky beyond. "Everything sort of fell to shit after that. Hermes and I fought, I killed Adonis, Hephaestus retreated to the mortal realm. You got tired of the fighting in your name. The contests to try and win you. So you left. And our world was so much poorer to have lost you. *This* world was poorer to have lost you."

"Then one day, you guys decided to wait for me to be reborn. Is this the first time you've ever approached me, or the first time I've ever agreed to give you another chance?"

He chuckled. "First time we've approached. Your life —*lives*, I should say... have been loveless. One reincarnation after the next, you push away anyone who might care about you. Then Hephaestus moved to Ashfall a few years ago. One day, he saw you, recognized you, and he contacted Hermes. Hermes found me in Iraq, and we both made lives in America."

"Wow."

"Yeah... I've been shunning my duties for a while, but I figure the twins and Eris have it covered."

"The twins?"

"Our boys. Deimos and Phobos. They were born after Harmonia."

A knock interrupted before she could ask more about their children. Room service wheeled in a cart bearing several dishes and a chilled bottle of moscato. Between the two of them, they'd ordered enough to feed four or five people.

Esme ate until she was stuffed, polishing off a whole steak and several creamy, garlic encrusted scallops. Somehow, she made room for the caramel pecan brownie. "Ugh, I'm so full I could burst."

He looked over and grinned. "You should get ready for bed. The time crept up on us, and if we're gonna hit the slopes again, you'll need your rest."

"Yeah, yeah."

She retreated to the bathroom and soaked away her aches in a steaming bath. Since the resort provided scented salts and fancy soaps, Esme didn't crawl out until her fingers pruned.

"You were right about the bath. I feel so much better."

Beau stared at her purple dragon onesie. "Are you five?"

"Shut up. They're warm."

"You know what else is warm?"

"Don't you—"

He gestured to himself with one thumb and flashed the usual cocksure grin that melted her insides and made her want to slap or kiss him.

She rolled her eyes and sprawled across the king-sized mattress. "I'm claiming this side."

"That's the entire bed."

"Yup."

"Nice to see time hasn't changed you."

"Be nice or you get the couch."

He vanished into the bathroom, and then the steady, rhythmic drum of the pounding shower spray lulled her into a drowse. When she stirred again, a half hour had passed and silence had fallen over the room. Beau wasn't beside her.

"Beau?"

"Hmm?" his voice came from behind and above her.

Esme rolled to the other side to face him, and her breath caught in her throat. Beau stood beside the nightstand with his cell phone in his hand, idly texting. Light from the adjacent lamp cast pale yellow highlights over the sculpted planes of muscle, leaving each chiseled dip in shadow.

Scars of varying size and shape accented his bronzed skin, but none of them detracted from the absolute beauty of his form. He had a physique that belonged in artwork.

"What? Should I have brought unicorn pajamas or something?"

"I'm guessing jammies aren't your thing." Her gaze wandered down his naked body despite her best intentions to keep it above his waist.

"Never saw the purpose in them."

It wasn't fair. She'd wanted to stand firm and strong, to at least put up the appearance of resisting him.

Now she couldn't wait to have him inside her.

Esme eased onto her knees beside him, though he was so tall it only brought her face level with his magnificent chest. He and Alex were alike in that way, both specimens of masculinity, each gorgeous in his own right.

"You fight in every war, don't you?"

"Yes."

She traced her finger over a healed gunshot wound above his heart, imagining the pain he must have experienced. "Where did this come from?"

"World War II. I followed a few Greek immigrants to the UK and joined them in battle. They believed in me, so it was the least I could do."

She kissed a long line below his left pec. "And this one?"

"The Thessaly Revolt."

Esme stroked down the aroused length and circled her thumb over the soft tip. He jerked and thrust his hips forward. She could have marveled over him for the rest of the night as a study in the ideal male anatomy.

"Like what you see?"

Seeing? She'd done more than see, staring at him with unabashed feminine appreciation, touching him with fingers eager to explore every inch her mind already knew. She recognized these scars, she could put battles to them, name fights where they'd been earned.

Leaning forward, she kissed his muscled stomach. The next kiss landed at his navel and followed the dark treasure trail leading to her prize. She placed the third kiss even lower—tenderly delivered to the tip of his cock before she took him between her lips.

Beau hissed, twitching in her mouth. Those same muscles she had admired tensed, and a low groan of appreciation came from him. He unzipped the front of her pajamas and shoved it down her shoulders until the fleece pooled around her hips, her breasts exposed to him, hips clothed by plain cotton panties.

His groan sent a pulse to her core, and when she teased the sensitive spot below the rounded head, his hand fisted in her hair.

"Have mercy on me, babe. I... if you keep that up, this is going to end real fast."

Despite his warning, she continued, nibbling the fat underside with her lips and locking gazes with him. He shuddered.

Esme wanted to taste him, but she also wanted him inside her, wanted him to finish deep within her, trembling in mutual ecstasy. Through a feat of Herculean effort, she dragged her mouth away. "Condom?"

Beau frowned. "Huh?"

"I hope you have a condom. With all the kids we have, I'm not sure if I should take chances with you."

His eyes twinkled in amusement. "I didn't even think about it. Would it be so bad if we did have number seven?"

"I'm still in school another semester."

"You'd graduate before it was born."

"But the others..."

"Would wait their damned turn."

Did she even want a child? Her mind was hazy with bliss and desire, but there was an appeal to the idea of carrying Beau or Luke's child again in this new body—or even bearing Alex's little one and giving him the child their marriage had deserved.

Esme shoved Beau down against the pillows and straddled his hips. "Fuck it. I'm on the pill."

She slid onto him, and the fit was so perfect, so deep, she could have sobbed in relief. Something in her had awakened the night she made love to Alex, and that something wouldn't be contained. *Couldn't* be.

"Yes," hissed between Beau's teeth. He thrust up as she rode him and found their rhythm.

It may have been centuries, but her body remembered him. Beau was branded there on her soul, her god of war and battle, her lord of the arena, her immortal soldier who had followed her across lifetimes.

She kissed him again, flicking her tongue between his lips, savoring every divine taste of him.

His hands traced her body, slid over her ribs, and cupped her breasts, teasing the nipples and plucking them into pebble hard points that ached. His mouth broke away from her lips and found the tender spot below her ear that always sent pleasure trembling through her core.

He knew where to touch, *how* she liked it, locating each of her spots as if she'd labeled them by preference.

When orgasm crashed over her, the false name of his new identity wasn't the cry that fell from her lips. Ares. Ares. *Her* Ares. Just as Alex had been her Hephaestus, Beau's divine name burst from her in a triumphant shout.

Beau thrust his hips up, her name a guttural cry as he found release. The name no longer sounded alien and unusual to her ears. It *was* her name, and she was Aphrodite, his goddess of love, passion, beauty.

Some time passed before Esme moved again, though she was content to remain astride him, listening to the thunder of his pulse. She stroked his chest and kissed his chin while Beau's fingers drew lazy circles over her back.

When she peeked up at him, he kissed her brow. "I missed you."

"I..." Lifetimes of loneliness, of never meeting her other half, of always seeking but never finding flit through her mind in fragments of memory. Now she had Hephaestus, Ares, and Hermes, the three missing pieces of her heart. "I missed you too."

And now that she had found them, she wouldn't let go again.

ROOM SERVICE DELIVERED BREAKFAST FOR THEM. AFTER A day on the slopes and a night of lovemaking—Esme had lost count of how many times Beau had proven his virility to her—she lacked the energy to tread downstairs to the resort's restaurant.

After she donned her gear, she sat on the couch and watched him zip into his snow jacket.

"How long will you be in California until you return to the battlefield?"

"Eh, I'm actually heading down to New Zealand this summer for a while to help with the new *Queen of the Shields* movie. Wanna come? I can get you on set."

"Yes! Will I get to meet the cast?"

"Sure."

By the time they reached the slopes, her breakfast had settled, but her thigh muscles screamed disagreement with her plans to outrace him again.

Beau smirked. "We can head back if you're too tired."

Esme ignored him and stared at a bright spot above them moving rapidly across the serene blue sky. "What's that glow up there?" She shaded her eyes against the sun's glare.

"What glow—oh, shit. It's ambrosia." Awe filled Beau's voice. "There hasn't been a scrap of any new ambrosia going into Olympus in a few years. It's all vanished."

"But it looks like a grape or something." She squinted to focus on the ivory bird flying overhead. It carried a bunch in its beak, all four of the swollen grapes a lustrous and shimmering gold.

"All ambrosia comes from earthen fruit. Berries, grapes, apples... everything. One in every ten-thousand is touched with a divine spark, and the doves carry it up to Olympus."

"I had no idea."

A bright lance, fiery as the sun, pierced the bird

through the breast and engulfed it in flames, consuming both the creature and its golden bounty.

"No!" Ares charged forward across the snow, leaving a melted swath in his wake. Too late to intercept the attack, he skidded to a stop and stared at the few black flecks that drifted down.

Esme hurried to catch up. "What happened? Who did that?"

"I don't understand why he would do this," Beau said.

"Who?"

"Helios. That was one of his lances, but I don't know why he'd do this..." He scooped up the smoldering carcass in the black flecked snow and turned around. Cold fury replaced his smile and warm eyes, expression tight with broiling anger. "I need to go see the others."

18

*L*eaving Esme at the resort hadn't been easy, but Beau made it up to her by booking an entire afternoon pamper session at the spa. Then he took the In-Between to the others and laid the scorched dove on Alex's coffee table, interrupting an online video game lesson between the other two gods.

Luke blinked at the charred carcass. "The hell is that?"

"An ambrosia dove. What's left of it anyway. Esme and I were about to hit the slopes for the day when a sun bolt shot it out of the sky."

Alex shook his head. "Then you saw wrong. At my request, Helios has been watching the skies for the birds to help us locate the ambrosia we need. He wouldn't slay one of the creatures. That is an offense against all of Olympus—against every god."

"Maybe that's what he told you, but it isn't what I saw. A lance from his spear killed it."

Luke rubbed his face with the heel of his palm. "Do you think this is what's happening to all of the birds?"

"He wouldn't do that," Alex insisted. "He knows how much finding the ambrosia means to us."

Luke shook his head. "Aphrodite also hit him with a wicked curse, man. We got off easy. She cursed him to discover ruin in every relationship he enters 'til the end of time. And he knows I told you it was him. He probably hates both of us."

"I know what I saw," Beau growled. "Esme and I were standing right there when the dove went down. It was a solar bolt from his spear. No one else can command the powers of the sun."

Alex ran his fingers through his hair and groaned. "All right. Fine. We'll take it to Zeus. Maybe he'll be in better spirits to deal with divine issues now that... she's there again."

Beau glanced at his brother and sighed. On one hand, he couldn't blame the kid for his resentment. He'd been different already at the time of birth, but Hera's impulsiveness had only crippled him further. "Bro, if she's there, you can leave, all right? I just figured you might want to bring this grievance to Zeus, too, since Esme is involved."

"No. It's fine. If Helios truly did this awful thing, I want to confront him as well. Everyone knows we have searched to find the ambrosia needed to restore her divinity."

"Indeed," Luke said. "Don't you find your discovery of her and the timing of the doves' disappearance to be a little suspect, man? You found her four years ago."

"The ambrosia shortage began a little while after that," Beau mused.

"I just don't understand," Alex said with a heavy sigh. "He swore to me only months ago that he holds no ill will against her, and now it appears he has gone back on his word. Has lied to me."

They reached Olympus sometime later, and after a while of waiting in the lobby, were granted the key to Zeus's office by Iris. The king of the gods sat behind his desk with his wife perched on his lap, both laughing together over a scene from the mortal world playing out on a viewing glass.

His mother was smiling again. He hadn't seen her happy in so long that he hadn't remembered—couldn't remember—how radiant she became when filled with joy. When her gaze darted to Alex, her eyes widened. She scooted from Zeus's lap and into the adjacent seat, though it wasn't golden or anything remarkable.

"Ah, what brings you three here today? I told you, I'm not interfering with your woman's quest, so I hope you didn't come here seeking help."

"This isn't about Esme," Luke told him. "It's about the doves."

"Have you discovered something?" Hera asked. The laughter faded from the room, replaced by a grim intensity that was mirrored on both gods' faces.

"Show them," Luke muttered.

Beau stepped forward and set the charred dove on the desk without a word.

His mother held a hand to her heart. "Who would do something so terrible to one of the doves?"

"It was a sun lance," Beau replied. "I saw it struck down myself. There's no mistaking it for something else."

The clouds beyond the enormous windows turned dark and stormy, mirroring the furious expression on Zeus's face. Lightning flashed in the distance as he slammed his hand down on the intercom button. "Iris, assemble all deities of the divine realm for a trial. Participation is mandatory. Send in Helios last."

It didn't take long. Beau and the others kept back while the room filled with their fellow deities—gods and goddesses he hadn't seen in generations.

"What's going on, brother?" Eris asked from behind him. He glanced over his shoulder and studied her desert fatigues.

"Still in the Middle East?"

"Where else would I be, since when I try to visit you, you never have time for me? Now, are you going to answer the question or not?"

He grunted. "You'll see."

"Fine, be mysterious."

More and more people entered, but the room never seemed to fill. The office widened, elongated, and when it was done shifting, the room had become a grand amphitheater, complete with a roaring fire pit in its center. Zeus's desk vanished, replaced by two golden thrones and a small podium.

"Everyone is here," Hera said.

"Good. Send him in."

Helios entered, as regal as Beau remembered despite the hundreds of years since their last encounter. His purple robe trailed behind him on the polished floor and, for a moment, Beau wished the old fashions hadn't gone out of style in the world below. He easily imagined Esme dressed in a colorful, linen chiton with jeweled pins and silk ribbons.

He'd have to buy her one soon.

"My lord Zeus, how may I be of service?" Helios asked once he reached the golden throne.

"Helios, son of the titans Hyperion and Theia, you stand accused of a most heinous crime, the slaughter of the ambrosia doves."

A low rumble of conversation began around the edges of the amphitheater as the spectating gods whispered among themselves in varying levels of outrage. The loss of the ambrosia affected them all, a crime against every person present.

Helios blinked, visibly taken back. "I did no such thing."

Zeus placed the blackened remnants of the dove on the podium before him and gestured to it. "Was this not done by your spear?"

"I... The damage done is by a solar lance, but I swear upon my honor, I did not do this." His brow furrowed beneath his golden hair.

"Are you in possession of your spear?" Zeus asked.

Helios presented the weapon. It appeared on his outstretched palms as six feet of polished gold. "I am. I have watched for the creatures to aid my friend, but I would never harm them. They are innocents, and as innocents, they are to be protected."

"And yet this one was taken from the sky by your divine gift. If not by you, who could it be?"

Alex stepped forward. "Please, I am the one who asked him to assist with finding the doves. Helios sees all and has always spoken truth, even when that truth hurts. You must know this."

"He's right." Hera laid her hand on Zeus's arm. "We have never known Helios to be anything but honest, a pillar of integrity when other gods would choose dishonesty. He is a good man, and I don't believe he would do this."

Zeus shook his head. "While you make an exceptional character witness, my love, what say you to this proof on my desk?" When she had no answer, his hard gaze returned to Alex. "For some time, we have gone without fresh ambrosia in this realm, and the shortage occurred only after you initiated your plans to restore Aphrodite to godhood."

Helios frowned. "I have no grievance against Aphrodite."

"Don't you?" Beau spat. "Didn't she curse you to never find love?"

The sun god raised his chin and stared back. "She did, but I have accepted her retribution as the cost of my loyalty to Hephaestus. After all, would I have shared your betrayal with her otherwise, slayer of Adonis? Though she had cursed me, I still did what was right."

A low murmur spread throughout the office.

"One could say you shared the news to hurt her. Does misery not enjoy company?" Athena spoke out from the front row.

Helios frowned. "I am sworn to report all I see, whether good or bad. Withholding the truth to let her continue dallying with the one who killed her lover would have been a spiteful retaliation."

Several gods murmured agreement with his logic, but others appeared unconvinced.

"I saw the dove killed with my own eyes. Esme, current incarnation of Aphrodite, witnessed this as well," Beau said.

Alex frowned at him. "You saw the weapon only, not who threw it, brother."

Beau grabbed his arm. "I saw what I saw."

"The fact still remains that this dove was struck down by your spear. The crime must be punished." Zeus rose from his throne. "Once again we have learned the titans are not to be trusted. You will be sent to Tartarus to join the rest of your kind in eternal damnation."

Alex pulled away from Beau's restraining grip and stepped forward. "Great Zeus, please, I beg you to give me time to find the true killer."

Demeter rose, elegant and poised. "I agree. You do a great disservice to Helios by damning him to Tartarus under such flimsy evidence. Was he seen perpetrating the crime? No. Ares speaks of nothing more than seeing the figurative gun, but not of who pulled the trigger. I know Helios and the kindness in him, for he is a man who has always spoke with candor and more integrity than many gods within this room." She raised her chin and stared across the amphitheater at Zeus. "Give Hephaestus his chance to clear our friend."

Hekate was the next to stand. "I, too, wish to see more time given."

Persephone joined them. "Do you do this in the name

of justice, or do you judge him so harshly for being the one to uncover your crime in gifting me to Hades, Father?"

A low hum of agreement spread throughout the chamber until most of the gods were standing, nodding their heads and offering their own tales of Helios's endless benevolence.

Hera placed her hand on Zeus's shoulder. "Please grant them time. What harm is there in giving them the chance to prove his innocence? You swore to me you are a changed man, my husband. Show me today that you are in actions, not in promises."

Zeus grunted. "One moon cycle. I grant only this to uncover the true villain behind these acts. Until then, Helios must remain under close watch. This court is adjourned."

19

Despite mending Zeus and Hera's relationship, the king of Olympus claimed Esme hadn't yet fulfilled all three stipulations of her quest. Zeus wanted her to prove herself capable in war, but that seemed a tall order when she wasn't a member of the armed forces and didn't have a chance of surviving any branch's basic training.

Marie popped into the living room and pinned her under an exaggerated stare. Her jaw dropped, then she feigned clutching a pearl necklace, raising one hand to her bosom. "Oh, wow, look who's actually home for once. Not off boning one of the boys?"

Esme sighed. "No. I'm exhausted, and I need a vacation from my winter break." She also wanted some time with her friends, for as much as she adored her men, she also missed Marie's jokes, Ashley's compassion, and Jordan's perverted sense of humor. Christmas and New Year's Eve seemed so long ago.

"Hey. Is everything okay? I was just joking, but you looked really sad just now. Everything's still good with the guys, right?"

"Everything is still fine."

"So what's wrong?"

"Everything else."

"Worried about how you'll balance school and three dudes?"

"That barely scratches the surface of my problems."

Marie's flashed an encouraging smile then veered into the kitchen. "Well, if you need an ear, I have two. I'm going to start the chili now for dinner. You want some?"

"Sure."

Esme thought about Marie's offer. Since the hellhound attack had turned her life upside down, she'd confided all thoughts, worries, and fears in Luke or Alex, finding they were the most empathetic and the best listeners.

Love you. Hope your day is good. Is it okay for humans to know about Olympus? Esme sent in a text to Alex.

A few minutes passed before his reply. *There was once a time when all humans knew of Olympus and the gods. Now we are tall tales, a myth told in fantasy novels and romantic movies.*

That doesn't answer my question. 😂

Sorry. If you refer to your friend, the trustworthy are always permitted to know.

Esme tapped out her response on the iPhone. *Thank you, Alex. I'm going to go for it then.*

Let us know if you need anything. Or any proof.

I may need Beau or Luke. We don't have room to unleash a

dragon here.

Ha ha. She imagined it in his laugh and replied with a kissy face emoticon before setting down the phone.

When Esme stepped into the kitchen, Marie stood in front of the pantry while consulting her phone. "Beans or no beans?"

"Beans, duh. I don't plan to see Luke until Sunday. He's busy doing a few things." Like running errands for Zeus to every corner of the world. All of Olympus was in a rage over what happened, to such a degree the big guy had beseeched help from gods of other pantheons, wanting to know what they saw.

Marie fetched ground beef, chuck steak, and minced Italian sausage from the fridge. "What about Beau and Alex?"

"Beau has some work to do outside of Ashfall, and Alex is behind on some of his commissions. He wanted my opinion on a few though, so I might check him out Monday once he's cleared some of his plate."

"I can't believe the billionaire artist wants your opinion on his art."

Esme retrieved the tomato paste and canned beans from the cabinet. "I can't believe a lot of things about him. Um, which is kind of why I came in here. Can we talk for a minute?"

"Sure. I'm listening."

Esme watched Marie slice the round steaks into meaty pieces to offset the ground meat. Her active imagination told her knives and shocking information weren't a good combination. "Um, maybe put the knife down first."

Marie glanced at her, amused expression sliding off her face. "Are you pregnant?"

"What? No! It's... bigger than that."

"Did one of them ask you to marry him?"

"No, well yes, technically I guess—"

"Oh shit, oh shit, that's awesome. Which one? What will you do? Is it—"

Esme held up a hand. Her pulse drowned out all other noise, and she was so dizzy she wanted to puke. Being pregnant would have been easier than confessing godhood to her best friend. "No. Hold on, okay. Just let me try to explain."

Marie's excitement didn't dim. "Okay."

"I know this is going to sound crazy impossible, but just keep an open mind." Esme wiped her sweaty palms against her flannel bottoms. "Beau, Luke, and Alex are Greek gods."

Marie's face fell. "You put me through all that suspense for *that*? I know they're sexy as Greek gods. I saw Luke with my own eyes in his swimsuit at the resort."

"Don't remind me." Esme had been so tipsy by the end of the night, Luke refused her advances. She sighed. Another opportunity to get him in bed spent cuddling instead. "But I don't mean in the figurative sense. I mean they're actually the Greek gods Ares, Hermes, and Hephaestus."

A quiet moment passed between them, Marie's face frozen with her brows raised. Then she laughed. "You're ridiculous. Is that the dream you had last night?"

"No dream. Real. They're really gods, supernatural divine creatures who have lived thousands of years."

"Okay. I'll bite. So, if they're gods, what do they want with you?"

Esme decided to try Luke's method of breaking news, ripping the Band-Aid off all at once. "I'm the reincarnation of Aphrodite, their lover, and I've been in and out of Ashfall so much because Luke had to take me to Olympus for a quest to regain my immortality. I met Zeus, Hera, a horned god, and Hermaphroditus too, because they're the kid I had with Luke."

Pursing her lips, Marie moved to the pot on the stove and added seasoning to the water. "Uh-huh. Did Luke get you on drugs? Whatever it is, it sounds like some good shit."

Esme groaned and ducked into the living room to fetch her phone. She texted a quick request to Luke then returned, phone in hand. "If you don't believe me, I'll just have to prove it to you."

"Esme, short of presenting a god to me, there isn't—"

Dressed in his white tunic and golden sandals, a winged helmet covering his dark curls, Luke stepped out of the In-Between, arriving in the kitchen.

Marie shrieked and dropped the can of Guinness she was pouring into the chili. Beer splattered everywhere as she leapt into the counter and banged her hip on the edge.

Luke crossed his arms. "Sup, ladies. You needed me?"

"How did you do that?"

"I told you, he's the messenger of the gods."

"Zeus's personal messenger." He tossed Esme his

phone. "Mind charging this for me? It's almost dead. I'll pop in again later for it."

"Sure."

"You're lucky you caught me in the mortal realm. I'm about to head west to pay a visit to Amaterasu for Zeus."

"You're gonna meet with the Shinto goddess of the sun? I'm so jealous I can't come with you."

"I'll bring mochi back for you both. Nice seeing you, Marie." He stepped over the veil again and disappeared.

Marie appeared frozen, still standing beside a puddle of beer on the floor. Most of the can had landed in the pot at least. "He just... he disappeared."

"He does that because he kind of runs between time and space."

"Esme, he *vanished*."

Taking Marie by the arm, Esme guided her friend to a seat at the kitchen table. She mopped up the beer on the floor with a paper towel, wiped the stove, and waited.

"It's real. He really, really is a god. I thought you were... I was sure you were having a joke. That you were going to spring something else on me." Marie sagged in the chair and pressed her palm against her face. "If that's real, then does that mean you're really...?"

"Aphrodite. Yeah. Remember when I sat on the couch for days after my date with Beau went all wrong? That's what I found out."

From start to finish, she shared every experience from the hellhound attack to the end of her most recent journey of visiting Hera in Olympus. At the end, Marie stared at her in disbelief.

"I can't believe it. I just... I don't believe you."

"Seriously? You just saw Luke—"

"No! You've known all this time and *now* you tell me? I thought we were friends. Girl, I thought we were best friends. I thought we shared everything with each other. I mean, I know I talk a lot and spread shit, but something like this..." After a few ragged, tearful breaths, she continued. "I would have kept something like this secret."

Esme blinked. "I'm sorry. And I'm telling you now because I *do* trust you."

Marie nodded and wiped her face. "Does this mean you're going to leave me now after you get your god stuff back?"

"Leave? You'll have to beat me away. I guess a lot of gods live in this world like a normal human."

"Oh good." She sagged against the cushions. "Wow, that sounded really underwhelmed. I mean, it would suck to lose my bestie, but... this is really awesome. I'm still trying to decide if I'm dreaming or not."

Esme reached over and pinched her. Marie grunted and swatted her hand away.

"Not dreaming, see?" Esme grinned. "It's a relief to finally be able to tell you."

"Seriously. So... what are you bummed about then?"

"The trials. I have no idea how to finish the last one."

"So, you need to win a war, right? Maybe it isn't a literal war. That'd be too easy, because Beau could just take you over to Africa or the Middle East. Maybe the war you need to win is in the symbolic sense. If you think about it, you completed the love trial by mending a marriage and finding closure with Daniel. Beauty must have been convincing Alex to see his own inner beauty...

and I will never forgive you if I don't get to see him as a dragon."

"He offered to show you."

"Seriously? Forget chili, let's go eat at his place!"

Marie's hug squeezed all the air from Esme's lungs. Laughing, she squeezed back. "All right. Throw that stuff in the fridge, and I'll make arrangements for Augustus to pick us up. Besides, he's given me free rein to redecorate, so we have some work to do."

Her friend's eyes glittered. "We get to redecorate a billionaire's crib?"

"Oh yes. You game?"

"Totally."

"You're taking this surprisingly well. Like it took me three days to even start to come to terms with it."

Marie shrugged. "I dunno. I guess it's like believing in aliens and finally seeing a spaceship. You always knew the shit is out there, and now that it's confirmed, why be anything but happy? Maybe the shock will hit me later and you'll find me rocking in my room, but right now, I feel oddly vindicated."

Esme leaned into her for another hug, laughing against her cheek and ignoring the happy tears trailing down her face. "You're the best friend."

"Damn right. Now let's go spend your man's money."

IT WAS A RELIEF HAVING MARIE IN ON HER SECRET. SHE needed that. Needed her oldest and closest friend to talk to without lying and holding back. It lifted a weight from her heart and made the world a little brighter.

They had spent the previous night over at Alex's estate, eating an exorbitant meal prepared by Augustus then touring the beautiful home. Nothing had raised her spirits like seeing Alex come out of his shell to entertain Marie.

Now she had a shift at Memory Lane and needed a tall cup of coffee before she could pull her eight hours.

Cold wind whipped against her cheeks as she hurried across the street with more than enough time to stop for a hot drink on her way into work.

"Hey, Esme, the usual?" the barista asked.

"Yeah, thanks, Carly."

"Mind if I ask you a question?" the girl asked while she started prepping the drink.

"Sure, go for it."

"I've sorta been expecting Patrick from Architectural Graphics to ask me out, but he hasn't yet. I'm not sure what to do. I mean, you've seen the way he flirts with me, right? Or am I totally seeing something that isn't there?"

She'd expected a question about an assignment, since they weren't exactly friends. After a brief hesitation, she shook off the surprise, smiled, and thought back on the cute, freckled ginger in their class. He always managed to get grouped with Carly. "No, I'm pretty sure he's into you, but I also know he's kinda shy. Maybe you should ask him out instead. It's the twentieth century, you know?"

"You think?"

"Go for it."

Carly smiled and added extra whipped cream into the

cup. "Thanks. Here ya go."

"Anytime."

As she headed back out onto Main Street, a euphoric sense of accomplishment filled her with a warm glow. Was this what being the goddess of love meant? Helping people out, giving them a little nudge when they needed it?

"Hey pretty lady, what's your hurry?"

The stranger's voice pulled her from her thoughts. A quick glance to the side revealed a dark-haired man pushing away from the wall of an adjacent building. Esme ignored him and continued down the sidewalk.

"Hey, baby. Hey. Hey, baby." The stranger's hastening steps crunched over the snow behind her. "Didn't you hear me talking to you?"

Esme never acknowledged catcallers, but something about the venom in his words, the sheer arrogance in his voice, snuck under her skin and infuriated her. She whirled. "I'm not your baby. Can you take that tired BS somewhere else, man?"

"What, you think you're too good for me?"

"I think it doesn't matter why I'm disinterested. You should turn and leave me alone."

He reached into his coat. "You're ugly anyway, bitch." The knife flashed in the dim streetlight as he drew it.

Esme's eyes widened. When he thrust forward toward her ribs, she spun to the side and dropped her cup. His stab brushed past her into the empty space occupied by her body a mere second ago.

The rest happened in a blur fueled by fight-or-flight

instinct and smoldering confidence. She gripped his wrist and arm, brought her knee up, and crashed both together. The snapping bone made an audible crack accompanied by a roar of pain.

Her assailant's knife clattered to the snow-flecked sidewalk. Esme kicked it away, twisted, and drove her elbow back and up into his face. Her foot dropped next, bearing down on the top of his with her heavy and hard-soled snow boot. A second later, she crashed her knuckles into his nose and sent him sprawling.

A siren signaled the arrival of the police. She stumbled back from the groaning man on the ground and backed into the wall with her heart racing. Carly ran over and caught her before she hit the ground. Esme hadn't even realized she was sliding down the wall.

"Oh my God, Esme, are you okay?" Carly asked.

"Ma'am, are you all right?"

She blinked up at Officer Frank, aware of him standing over her while his partner attended her bloody-faced assailant. They snapped cuffs onto him and hauled him up. She didn't warn them that his arm was broken, and she didn't pity him for the rough handling they delivered.

"I think so. My hand hurts a little."

Officer Frank raised his brows. "That was some punch you dealt to him there."

"Yeah, seriously," Carly said. "How did you learn to do all of that?"

Her pulse still raced. She blurted out, "Self-defense lessons."

Now that it was over, she wanted to puke all over the

snow. Tears sprang to her eyes, and she hated them, because they made her feel weak in the wake of what she'd somehow accomplished when her life was threatened. Carly passed her a tissue and rubbed her back without pressing for any talk. After a few moments, the nausea passed, but the trembles didn't vanish.

"How did you even see...?"

Carly held up Esme's debit card. "You dropped this on your way out, and since I know you work down the street, I figured I could catch you. Then I saw that creep chasing after you, so I called the cops."

"Thank you."

"Miss, we're gonna need you to come down and make a statement. Is there someone you can call?"

"Yeah..."

She made a call to Mrs. Robinson first, barely managing to keep from bursting into tears again. Then she called Luke. If she was going to be stuck at the police station, she didn't want to be there alone.

———

It didn't take long at the police station. There had been more than enough witnesses to corroborate her story since the man attacked her out in the open. In less than an hour, Luke had her back at his place.

"Thanks for this," she said. "Marie's gonna freak."

"Yeah, well, she's not the only one. I'm half tempted to grab the other two and give that asshole a little midnight visit."

"No, you can't do that. And you can't tell the others."

"Why not?"

"Beau will *kill* him."

Luke snorted. "Alex would kill him too. Not sure yet if *I* won't, to be honest."

"Don't. Something wasn't right there. I don't know what yet, but something wasn't right."

He nodded. "All right. Whatever you want."

Luke ran her a bath and washed her back while she soaked with her knees drawn up to her chest.

It was quiet and intimate, his humming the only noise aside from the fizz of an Arabian Nights inspired bath bomb filling the steamy air with sandalwood, saffron, and spice. He had a great voice, one worthy of musicals, jazz festivals, or even R&B concerts. If the circumstances had been different, she would have melted and dragged him into bed.

"I'm sorry." Her quiet words broke the silence.

"Sorry for what?"

"For this. It's like every time we get a moment alone something's always in the way. I feel like... like you aren't getting a fair chance."

His brows raised. "A fair chance at what?"

"Intimacy. Affection. I dunno." She dragged her hand through the water and stirred up the suds.

"All right. I'm going to break the bro code for a second here and reveal how much we three share with each other by repeating what Alex told you. There's more to intimacy than sex. Spending New Year's Eve with you, taking you into our world, introducing our child to you—

that is my fair share of your time. I don't need to get my dick wet to feel like you care."

"But I've, you know, slept with the others."

"Right. I know. Alex is different now, and it's good to see him smiling. And I always figured you and Beau would get physical early on, because that's just the kind of relationship you had. I'm not upset about it. None of us are going to keep tally of how much we bone you."

"I keep waiting for the jealousy. I guess the part of me that remembers the past isn't ready to let it go."

His quiet laugh snaked around her heart, warming her from the inside. "Would I like to make love to you? I would love to have you beneath me, above me, *any* way you fucking please, but I'm not in any rush to put my wants before your welfare."

She nodded. The tension in her stomach unknotted.

"If everything goes the way it should, we have the rest of forever together." He paused a moment, then leaned close, a wicked smile on his face. "Besides, you went down on me first, remember? I'm not ashamed to admit I took pleasure in tossing that at Beau. We do tease each other a little, but I like to think it's all fun now."

The last of her uneasiness vanished with her laughter. If it had been anyone else, some mortal guy bragging to his buddies, she would have taken offense with his candor, but with her guys it was natural. She splashed a few bubbles at Luke's face.

"I don't deserve you."

"Sure you do. Now, you finish soaking, and I'll order takeout. Sound good?"

"Sounds perfect."

---

20

*E*sme enjoyed nothing more than the warmth of Luke's hand around hers, except perhaps their forays into different realms. He led her down a starlit path in a forest alive with fireflies of a dozen different colors.

Following her traumatizing experience of the previous evening, she'd crawled into bed beside him and slept warm in his arms. His morning treat had been to sweep her away from the mortal realm into a magical place of eternal night.

"What is this? Where are we going?"

He grinned at her. "It's a surprise."

"Olympus again?"

"Nope, but we're almost there. Almost to where you really belong. In fact..." He leaned in, nose skimming against her ear before his lips found the ticklish spot on her neck. "Close your eyes."

Her heart leapt with elation. She shut her eyes and

listened to the serene chirp of crickets. Luke's fingers drifted away.

"Now what?"

He didn't answer.

"Luke? Don't keep me in suspense. What's going on?"

When the silence continued, Esme opened her eyes to find the starlit path had dimmed and the twinkling lights were gone. In their place, only dank and foulness remained, a dark marsh with skeletal trees looming above her, their branches swaying in the rotten winds.

"Luke!" she called.

Silence.

"Luke!" she called again, expecting him to appear at any moment, to laugh and apologize.

Hadn't he said traveling in the In-Between could be tricky with mortals?

There was darkness all around, despair and grasping hands tipped with venomous claws reaching from beneath trees with molding leaves, and all the terrifying crawling, stinging, and biting things Esme ever feared were there with her in the impenetrable gloom. No matter how she ran, where she turned, or how she clawed at the bleak, heavy curtain of night, there was no sunlight here.

There was no Beau, no Luke, and no Alex to guide her way, no shining light of love or divine powers to save her.

When she took another path, the way before her stretched infinitely into shadow, but she still ran, petrified not of what she could see, but what was hidden from her sight.

Because something out there was coming for her.

Esme jerked upright in bed, screaming. Her pulse pounded in her temples with a ferocious migraine unlike anything she'd ever experienced before, and her frenzied heart beat against her ribs, a caged bird desperate to break free.

"Esme, baby, breath."

Luke's hands cupped her face, warm against her clammy skin. She focused on his voice, but her throat only tightened further. Each breath wheezed in and out of her lungs. Crushing pain compressed her chest.

"Hold on, baby, I'm right here." Luke barked out an order for his phone to dial Beau. She wanted to tell him not to bother, that it would pass in time—that there was no need to worry anyone—but words were beyond her.

Nothing existed but all encompassing, crippling terror.

"Beau, I need you and Alex over here right now. I dunno. She woke up screaming, and I don't know what to do."

Luke set the phone down and returned to her. He held her in his arms, rocked with her, stroked her hair and murmured in his low, melodic voice, sounding more like a god than ever in those moments. But nothing alleviated the tenacious, soul-deep fear clinging to her psyche.

Nothing lifted it.

The others arrived after an indeterminable time. Her throat was raw and hoarse by then, and she was furious with herself for the loss of her control.

"Esme?" Alex's deep, calming voice penetrated the

dark haze. Then his warmth surrounded her and the placid thump of his heart beat beneath her ear. "Esme, listen to my heart. Listen to it and try to breathe."

"We're all here, Esme. You're safe," Beau said.

Surrounded by the three men she loved, the fear and panic began to subside. Beau rubbed her back and Luke stroked her hand, and little by little her tight muscles loosened. She dragged in a deep breath and released it on a sob.

"I'm sorry."

"There's nothing to be sorry about." Alex kissed her brow and continued to rock her. Eventually her sobs subsided, but she stayed where she was, spent and exhausted.

"I'll go make some tea. That's what mortals do, right?"

Until that moment, Esme hadn't realized someone else was there. She looked up from Alex's chest and blinked at the woman standing in the bedroom doorway. "Eris, right?"

"Yeah. Sorry, I was hanging with Ares when they called."

Esme swiped at her cheeks. "It's okay, but no tea. Luke keeps a vodka bottle in the freezer."

"Sure thing."

Eris stepped out of sight.

"You wanna talk about it?" Luke asked.

"I dunno. It was a dream."

"Baby, it was more than a dream. You woke up screaming."

She swiped her face again with her wrists, prompting Beau to pass her a tissue. "You left me, and I was alone in the dark. And... and something was there. Something wanted me. And... and I know it was all a dream, I know it was, but it's like it won't let go."

Beau and Alex exchanged glances. Luke stiffened.

"What does that sound like to you?" Beau asked.

Alex growled. "Interference."

Luke stepped into his jeans and shrugged into a shirt. "I thought I felt something, but I figured it was my imagination. That no one would be so fucking stupid—"

"What?" she asked.

"Something did this to you," Beau said in a measured, controlled voice, though he clenched his fists. "Or should I say, someones."

"That sounds extreme, even for them," Alex said

"For who?" Esme asked.

"A couple of troublemakers. C'mon, Luke, we'll go have a chat with them."

"Beau," Alex said in a warning voice. "Don't do anything drastic."

Beau's stare could have curdled milk. "They'll be fortunate if I stop at kicking their asses back to Olympus instead of dropping them in the deepest, darkest pit in the Stygian Marsh until they're old enough to shave." He crossed the veil, and Luke followed.

A moment of silence passed before Eris spoke up. "You should probably go after them, Heph. You know how those boys of his get him riled up."

"Wait, Beau's kids? You mean mine? Ours?"

Alex sighed. "The twins cause havoc and panic, and they're real good at getting under Beau's skin, even though they don't mean to."

"He won't hurt them, will he?"

"Probably not."

Esme pushed at his chest. "You should go make sure."

"I don't want to leave you here alone."

"I'll stay with her," Eris said.

Alex looked between them, his brows drawn together.

"Go on," Esme urged in a quiet voice. "If it was my kids, I'm sure they didn't mean it. Don't let Beau be hard on them. Please."

"All right." He kissed her brow again then stood. "I'll be back as soon as I can."

Alex stepped through the veil and vanished. Remnants of her dream flashed through her mind, making her pulse spike for a moment. She closed her eyes and willed the darkness away, knowing they'd be back.

"Ready for that vodka?"

Esme opened her eyes and looked at Eris. She had the vodka bottle in one hand and two shot glasses in the other.

"Yeah. We can watch a show or something." She left the bed but paused halfway to the door, then hurried back to grab the cuffs Alex had made for her off the bedside table. Their warm, solid weight around her wrists comforted her. Only then did she follow Eris into the living room. "Where were you hanging with Beau?"

Eris's eyes twinkled with mirth. "Ares and I were taking a little break together in the south. Fun with a couple rival gangs in Los Angeles. They're always embroiled in some kind of war, and it's a nice change of pace from the hopeless slaughter in the east. It has a different taste."

"I'm sorry your fun together was interrupted."

The goddess waved off her concern. "It happens. Here, drink, you'll feel better."

Esme accepted a shot and tipped it all back in one go, the spicy bite of horseradish burning down her throat. Her eyes watered.

"Better?"

"Yeah, thanks." She held out her glass for a refill. It went down smoother than the first.

"You know, I see her in you. Aphrodite could drink too. She didn't like spicy though, so that's new." Eris sniffed the bottle before pouring her own drink.

"Not sure if the drinking thing is a compliment or not."

Chuckling a low and seductive noise, Eris leaned back against the sofa cushions while crossing her legs. "No insult intended, promise. Drinking and feasting was the way of life in Olympus a long time ago. Some handled it better than others. I mean, Dionysus was a sloppy drunk. Still is, actually, but I consider him to be an operative drunk. I wouldn't let him drive me in a car anywhere unless I wanted to spend a couple days laid up in bed though."

They shared a laugh and another drink, clinking their glasses together.

"Thanks, Eris, I needed this."

"That's what family is for. You want another?"

"Not just yet. I'm gonna go wash my face first. My eyes feel all puffy."

"Okay."

Esme made her way to the bathroom and closed the door behind her. One look in the mirror showed her what she already knew—red eyes and streaky cheeks. Had it really been her kids to blame? She and Ares hadn't spoken much about the children they shared, and she'd only met Dito so far.

That would have to change. She'd wanted to adjust to becoming a divine being before she undertook becoming a mother.

The handles on the faucet squeaked when she turned them on and cold water flowed into the porcelain sink. She gave herself one last glance in the mirror before leaning down to splash her face.

A crash outside the door startled her. She spun around, face dripping. "Eris? You okay?"

Silence. A dark sense of foreboding made the hairs on her nape stand on end. She reached for the door, but before her fingers brushed the knob, a dark shape from the In-Between grabbed her hair and dragged her into darkness.

———

BEAU TIMED HIS LANDING FROM THE IN-BETWEEN TO PLACE him in the precise spot to bump into the two juvenile gods sneaking around Ashfall. Deimos bounced off his father's chest and landed on his ass. Upon seeing that, Phobos tried to run for it, but Beau caught him by the sweatshirt hood and held him in place before he could abandon his twin.

"You two have a lot to explain. Why the fuck are you harassing your mother?"

Deimos blinked up at him. "Harassing?"

Phobos wiggled. Beau tightened his grip enough for the shirt collar to squeeze his neck. "Dad, I can't breathe."

"If you're talking, you're breathing. Why are you harassing your mother?"

Deimos stood and brushed the snow off his jeans. For a moment he looked ready to bolt, but Luke stepped out of the In-Between and blocked his escape. The boy swore under his breath. "We haven't done anything, dude."

Beau stood taller, looming above them. "*Dude?*"

Deimos shrank back. "Sir, I mean! We did as you ordered and stayed away from her. I mean, we've popped in once or twice to look at her, but that's it."

"Yeah. It's not fair that you get to take her on motorcycle rides, when we don't even get to see what the hell she looks like, Dad. Come on."

Apprehension twisted in Beau's gut. He released Phobos and stood back, arms crossed against his chest. "Then you weren't the ones who petrified her?"

Phobos shook his head. "We don't wanna scare her, Dad. It was just a couple looks. I swear. Eros and Anteros wanted photos of her, so we snuck over to Ashfall and took a couple candids for them."

"Boys, something real bad scared her tonight. Are you sure you had nothing to do with it?" Luke asked. "Even accidentally? We can understand an accident. Maybe you were curious. Wanted to see your mother, and you couldn't control yourselves. I felt something flickering around the edge of the In-Between, and I know how it is when you use your gifts."

The boys quieted and shuffled their feet.

"Boys?" Beau said, striving for patience.

Deimos dropped his shoulders. "We've been hungry with you being away from battle so long. There's enough natural fear and terror in the Middle East without us, but it's tasteless and hollow. Since you don't take us anywhere anymore, we came here to snack. Maybe our powers kind of got away from us. You know it's hard to control the range sometimes."

"But we never tried to hurt Mom. Never. That's why we haven't operated in Old Ashfall. We stay here in the city."

Deimos puffed out is chest. "Yeah. It's diffused here and spread over thousands of people. Makes it easier to control it."

When Alex stepped into view, both boys turned to him with pleading eyes. "C'mon, Uncle Hephaestus, we didn't mean anything by it."

"Were you two peeking in tonight?" he asked.

"No, we swear. We just got here, right before Dad showed up," Phobos said.

"Yeah. We got a message saying to meet," added Deimos.

"A message from who?"

Phobos toyed with the edge of his sweatshirt. "Um... well, I thought it was you, Dad."

Beau frowned. "I didn't send a message."

"Figures." Phobos hunched his shoulders and stared

down at his feet. "Should have known it was too good to be true, you wanting to see us."

Deimos sighed. "Or have anything to do with us."

Phobos nodded, agreeing with his brother. "Now that Mom is back."

"What?" he barked, startled by the fury their words riled in him. "What the hell put that nonsense in your heads?"

"You did," the twins answered.

Beau kneaded his temples with one hand. How long had it been since he'd brought them onto a battlefield or spent quality time with them in Olympus?

Too long. So long it shamed him, and he was the one who couldn't meet their gazes anymore, because in all his effort to reconnect with their mother, he'd forgotten how much he loved the children they'd made together.

"Boys, I'm sorry. I know that's not even going to scratch the surface of what I owe you, but I'll make this up. I was so caught up in getting your mother back for us —for all of us—that I forgot you guys need me."

Phobos didn't look up. "We miss her too."

"I know."

"Aunt Eris said it would be okay."

Deimos elbowed his brother. "Shh. Idiot, we weren't supposed to say anything."

Phobos grunted. "Too late now."

"What did I tell you both about keeping secrets from me?"

"Not to do it," Phobos said, sighing. He licked his lips then glanced around the dimmed alley. "Aunt Eris brought us over the first couple times and taught us the way. Now we've been doing it on our own."

"Told you we can navigate the mortal realm on our own."

"How long have you two been doing this with your aunt?"

Deimos shrugged. "I dunno. Since November I guess?"

Beau looked to Luke and Alex, seeing the same realization come to them at the same moment.

"Do you really think...?" Luke asked.

"I dunno, but we need to get back to Esme." Beau turned to his sons. "Boys, you head home right now. I promise, when this is done, I'll bring your mother over to meet you."

The twins studied him for a moment. Deimos nodded first. Then he dropped his chin to his chest. "Are you upset at us?"

"No. I'm sorry it came to you guys sneaking around. I haven't been a good father to you lately, but I swear, we'll work on it, okay? Now go home."

Phobos crossed the veil first. His brother followed. Once the twins were gone, Beau, Luke, and Alex returned to the apartment, unable to find any other conspicuous signs of divine essence within the city.

A war zone greeted them.

Luke stared at his home. "What the hell?" The apartment stank of filth and bird droppings. Deep gouges scored the overturned couch and a large crack split the flat-screen television.

"Esme! Eris!" Beau called out.

Luke zipped past them and reappeared. "She's not in the bedroom."

"There's blood in the bathroom." Alex said.

Beau drove his fist into the wall. "Dammit!"

Luke grabbed his arm and stopped him from making a second hole. "This isn't gonna help Esme."

"We have no idea where to find her."

"Stop and use your brain." He stuck a dirty feather in Beau's face. "This is what took Esme."

"Harpies," Alex growled.

Which meant there was only one place Esme could be. Harpies only spawned from the Underworld.

21

Darkness surrounded Esme, pressing in from everywhere and nowhere at once.

Luke had once mentioned the amount of care it took to travel with a mortal through the In-Between, and with each second she was there, she understood why.

Something was tearing her apart, pulling and stretching her limbs, pounding her skull and squeezing her flat. Pressure compressed her chest with an unyielding iron band and tore the breath from her lungs before they burst through to the other side. She gasped for air, desperate to survive.

Like her dream, it seemed to stretch forever. But unlike her dream, there was no silence. Beyond the rush of beating wings, low moans and tortured cries filled the air. The sound was muted at first, but the farther they flew the louder the din became, until the cries of the damned drowned out the harpy's flight.

Esme struggled. Sharp talons dug into both

shoulders, introducing her to a world of burning agony. Then she fell. Pain lanced up her right ankle and her leg crumpled, taking her to the rough floor. Tumbling to the ground saved her from a harpy dive-bombing her with its outstretched claws. She rolled and came face-to-face with a skeleton. Esme managed to bite back a scream, but when she scrambled away, she ran into more brittle remains.

As her eyes adjusted to the dim gloom, she saw the ground littered with molted feathers and the corpses of the long dead. A small clutch of eggs sat among piles of straw, shredded clothes, and filthy down. She must have landed in one of their breeding grounds.

The harpy dived again, leaving her no time to contemplate or to even be afraid. The instinct to survive kicked in. She grabbed a rusted blade from the closest corpse and brandished it, but the harpy laughed and struck it from her grip. Claws from another attacker scraped against her back, leaving lines of burning fire.

And then, a shining lance tore through the air and struck the filthy creature from the sky. The body fell at Esme's feet, and then its flock-mates dispersed in a panic. Stunned, she looked up and saw Eris standing on a low ridge clad in crimson and black armor with a dark spear in her grasp. Esme had never been so relieved.

"Eris, thank you." Esme held her hand against the deepest scratch on her side. The blood had already begun to clot.

"Thank you for what?"

"For saving me."

Eris's laugh raised every hair on Esme's body. The

cold, sharp sound echoed off the dark rocks around them. "Oh, you naive fool. I'm not here to save you."

"What?"

Eris leapt down and stalked toward her. "You just had to come back, didn't you? You had to ruin everything."

"I don't understand."

"Ares," Eris hissed. "With you gone, he and I reveled in the chaos this world seems to enjoy so much. We had our pick of battles. We drowned in blood and victory. But if you come back, if love reigns again in Olympus, all that will be gone. My brother barely notices I exist these days because of you."

Esme blinked. "You want me dead because you have a lady boner for your brother?"

Eris hissed again and rushed forward with her spear. Esme twisted, avoiding the weapon by a hair's breadth.

"We were happy with you gone! This world doesn't need love. It needs to be conquered. Only Ares and I can do that. You make him *weak*."

Eris charged again. The spear in her hands morphed, living metal shaping itself to her will from a spear to a sword. She came in with a fury, her face contorted with rage. Weaponless, Esme stumbled back and threw her left arm up in front of her.

The sword glanced off the rose gold cuff with a tremendous clang, sending reverberations of power vibrating through the air around them in sonic ripples.

"That fucking cripple," Eris growled.

"Don't call him that."

"What? Cripple? What about abomination? Hera was right to throw him from the golden city. Too bad he didn't die that day. We only kept him around to make things for us."

Screaming, Esme threw a punch at Eris. The war goddess of strife batted it away. Undeterred, Esme rotated her stance and kicked out, but Eris grabbed her foot, twisted, and brought her to the ground.

"Pathetic. What Ares sees in you, I'll never know."

Everything hurt, but she pushed the pain aside and got back on her feet.

"You're as useful as that hideous creature you and Mother claim to love." She laughed, cold and bitter, all false warmth gone from her voice. "He's such a—"

Esme feigned another kick with her rear leg, anticipating Eris would see through the move and block it. At the last second, she dove forward into a hard left cross and delivered the same punch that had caught Ares unaware in the gym. Her fist met Eris's face, all of her weight and power behind the blow, a punch worthy of the god of war himself. Her opponent cried out, startled, and spun out to the ground. She didn't remain down for long and flipped back to her feet. She spit to the side.

"Luck."

"I don't need luck to kick your ass. Who's the one who can't even kill an unarmed opponent?" Esme taunted.

Eris's eyes narrowed. "As I said, pathetic. You cannot goad me, mortal. I am Eris, goddess of strife. Mistress of discord. I know every trick and every deception."

"Your bloody nose says you didn't see that trick."

Eris ignored her. "I sow the seeds of war, and your death will reap the finest battle yet."

It clicked, understanding dawning over Esme at once.

"You want war with the Underworld..." she whispered. It was the only thing that made sense, explaining the hellhound and the harpy.

"If I can't have what I want, I will take what I can get. With your death, Zeus and Ares will have no choice but to suspect Persephone's involvement."

"And the doves? Would you really deny all of Olympus ambrosia just to get at me?"

"Enough talk!" Eris slashed forward with her blade.

Esme bounced back on her feet, defended again with the same cuff. It flashed again, Eris's sword rebounded off the shield conjured by the magical bracelet, but a second, hidden blade slid past the defense and into her skin.

Agony. The blade burned like fire, sending acid through her veins. A sound echoed through the dark chamber and, at first, Esme didn't recognize it as her own scream.

The blade slid free. There were shouts. Rapid steps thumping against the ground. The dismal atmosphere spun around Esme and the uneven, rocky ground rushed up to catch her.

Luke appeared at her side and knelt, applying pressure to her wound. Bright, bright blood flooded up beneath his hands. "She needs healing."

"I tried to fight her."

"I know, baby."

Tears swam in her eyes, blurring the arrival of Alex and Beau. The latter swore a stream of words in ancient Greek, familiarity of them skimming the edge of her awareness.

Alex crouched beside her. "We need to get her to the river."

"She's too weak to make it to the River Styx even if I carry her," Luke said. "It might kill her."

Beau took Luke's place, putting his strong hands over her wound. "She's already dying! Find someone who can heal her, fool!"

"N-no. Don't go. Don't go," Esme pleaded.

Everything hurt. The pain was excruciating, like fire in her gut spreading throughout her body and consuming her. She grasped at Luke with one bloody hand.

"Please stay. I'm scared."

The threat of spending her final moments without any of them terrified her more than dying. Luke dropped to his knees again at her side, and Alex took her other hand, big tears shining against his brown eyes. She hated that. Eyes that pretty, already so sad when she'd first met him, shouldn't have been filled with tears.

"I l-love all of you. Love you so much. Promise you'll... you'll find me again."

Luke squeezed her hand. "We will, baby. I promise. We'll wait as long as we have to. I'll find you myself if I have to."

"Am I too late?" asked a melodic, feminine voice.

The slap of sandals against concrete echoed as Esme drifted on a cloudy haze of perception in a dimming world slowly losing its colors. Of the three men kneeling over her, Luke was the only one to remain in focus.

"Where did you get this?" Luke asked.

"Later. She's fading fast," the woman said. "I felt her leaving and raced here as fast as I could."

One of the men, she thought it was Alex, pressed something soft and fragrant against her lips, coaxing them to part. A sweet explosion of the juiciest citrus practically melted in her mouth.

Beau's hand lifted from her midsection. "Her wound is closing. Give her the rest of the fruit."

Alex fed her another exquisite slice of orange. It was heaven in her mouth, the single most delicious thing she'd ever tasted in all her life, a sweet and tangy piece of paradise. The darkness faded, giving way to concerned eyes watching her face.

Groaning, Esme tried to sit up, but Luke placed a hand against her chest. "Take it easy."

Piece by piece, they fed her the ambrosia, until it seemed as if her entire body floated, filled with energy and warmth like she'd never experienced. It surged through her and took all the pain away.

Esme opened her eyes to a changed view. The once darkened world around them shone with color, opalescent hues shimmering against the rock. But the beauty paled in comparison to the faces looking down at her.

Beau, Luke, and Alex all seemed to glow from within, as radiant as she remembered.

She remembered. Memories too numerous to count flooded her in an overwhelming rush, but she viewed them from a distance, like watching a documentary rather than feeling them herself. She witnessed every tender moment, every fight, and every petty squabble.

And she watched countless mortal years of self-inflicted loneliness.

"Esme?" Alex cupped her cheek. "How do you feel?"

"Different... The same..." She sat up and cradled her head in both hands. "What happened?"

"Eris stabbed you." Beau bowed his head, both fists clenched against the floor.

"Hey, no, none of that." She reached out and tipped his face back up again. "You can't blame yourself for your sister's actions."

"I should have seen it sooner. Esme, we almost lost you."

"But you didn't. I'm here. I'm back."

"And immortal once more," said the female stranger.

Esme turned. While she'd never laid eyes on the woman during her mortal lifetime, she recognized Persephone. The goddess hadn't changed, not since the last time she saw her so many centuries ago.

"You did this? Why?"

"Because it was the right thing to do. I've had this last piece of ambrosia saved away. Of course, I never thought I'd be using it to bring you back."

"Thank you, Persephone."

The queen of the underworld bowed her head. "Think nothing of it. After all, wouldn't this new you do the same for me? Now, I believe it is time we went to Zeus. Helios will need his name cleared and the search for Eris must begin. She will need to answer for her crimes."

Zeus listened to their tale from his throne. Hera was absent from his side, but the warmth of their love filled the executive office. "And where is Eris now, Ares?"

"I don't know, Father. I would have given chase if Esme hadn't been dying, but remaining at her side took precedence."

"Understandable." The ancient god turned his gaze to Esme, eyes shining with mirth. "Do you understand now?"

"Yes. The power of Aphrodite was inside me all along. I only had to find it."

"Indeed. Now that the ambrosia has restored your immortality, you are as you once were. Love. Beauty. War. You are these traits and much, much more, and perhaps all the better from the years of life spent among the humans. Living as one has taught you the empathy you once lacked. The empathy I would try to learn in my own time." A moment of silence passed before Zeus murmured, "You will be a good goddess of love to this modern world."

Esme dipped her head. "Thank you for the valuable lesson."

Zeus grunted. "A good thing how passed, since the decision to restore your immortality was taken from my hands."

Persephone turned from the nearby window and chuckled. "I did what needed to be done at the time, Father. As it was my domain, the choice was mine to make."

"So it was," Zeus agreed in a rare display of humility, raising the brows of everyone around him.

"Thank you again, Persephone. I'm a little attached to my mortal life's friends and family, even though I hope to have made new ones during this ordeal." She and the floral goddess of the dead exchanged a warm smile before Esme returned her attention to Zeus. "What will happen to Eris?"

His eyes saddened. "We must find her and bring her to justice, as her crimes are many. For now, she is banished from Olympus."

Hades appeared beside Zeus in a blaze of ebony flame. He was a tall man with a kind face, gentler than Esme expected. "As well as my realm. Persephone will never forgive what she did to our pup. Will you, my love?"

She shook her head. "By using Philos, it can only mean she intended I should take the fall. She must suffer for her attempt to tarnish the Underworld with her machinations."

"And Helios?" Alex asked.

"Forgiven. Though I still await an answer as to how Eris used his spear. He should be with us shortly."

"Yeah, about that..." Beau tipped his head toward the open balcony

Fire scorched across the sky in a bloom of light, then a white-gold chariot appeared on the balcony outside of Zeus's office. The four pegasuses leading it stamped their hooves and neighed.

"Helios, I am glad to see you return. What answers do you have for us?" Zeus asked.

"At first, I didn't understand how my spear had been used without my knowledge. Now I see. Eris has been... she and I were close for quite some time. She must have used my solar lance at some point when I closed my eyes to rest," Helios said.

"She deceived us all."

"She did not work alone. Abducting Aphrodite this night made Eris careless. Without her present to distract my gaze from the sins of her children, I noticed two godlings stalking a dove bound for Olympus." He nodded over his shoulder to the chariot. Two young men were lashed to it by golden rope. "I intervened before the Phonoi could kill it."

Beau stared at them. "Eris's sons. The personifications of murder."

"This explains why some random dude in Ashfall tried to gut her," Luke said. "I bet some of the other strifes are responsible for the other evils that have befallen her too. Like her night terror."

At that, Beau drew his sword and lurched toward them. "I should slaughter these two assholes now."

Helios stepped before him. "But you will not. I've brought them to Zeus for a proper punishment."

"And their punishment will be fitting," Zeus said. "Pass them to Hades."

A wide smile spread across Persephone's face. "Will they be mine?"

Hades glanced at the murderous twins. "Of course, my dear. I can think of no greater vengeance for Philos than to see two of his abusers clasped in Stygian iron."

The queen of the dead clapped her hands. "An eternity in the kennels shoveling hellhound shit."

Esme cringed.

"But first, I would like to question them both

quite deeply about their mother and her whereabouts." Zeus turned his gaze to Esme, Beau, Alex, and Luke. "You're dismissed. I will take it from here."

"Thank you." Esme bowed her head and then turned away with the others. She walked between Alex and Luke, with Beau only an arm's length away.

Before they traveled far, Persephone moved to intercept them on the landing outside Zeus's office door. "Aphrodite, a moment please."

"We'll wait downstairs," Alex said. He took the lead and brought the other two with him while Esme turned to face her peer, though it was strange to think of a goddess as her equal at all.

Once they were gone, Persephone cleared her throat. "How does it feel to be one of us again?"

"I don't know. It's difficult to describe. I still feel like me, but I also feel different. Improved and unchanged at the same time."

"And the memories?"

"Some are more intense than others, while a few are like... just there at the edge of my thoughts. If I think really hard, some of them clarify, but others are like trying to remember a birthday party my parents threw for me when I was five."

The spring goddess nodded and toyed with one of the black steel and diamond chains dangling from her waist. The gemstones were arranged in patterns of flowers and skulls. "I received your letter."

"Oh... Good. I know I probably should have brought it in person, but..."

"I understand. The Underworld isn't the most hospitable of places, after all."

Esme ducked her head. "Yeah. Well, I meant what I wrote, but I'll say it again. I know I wasn't a very good person back then and there's really nothing I can do to fix that. It was a different time. A different life. All I can do now is use this new chance to make amends."

"It's quite admirable of you. And appreciated." Persephone glanced toward the lower landing where the men had assembled to wait. "When I heard you were gathering together a harem, I thought you would come for Adonis again."

Esme shook her head. "Pursuing Adonis caused all of us enough pain. It was time to let go. What I liked about him most was his beauty, but it's funny, because I don't recall anything else about why I wanted him."

Persephone's brows rose. "Truly?"

"Yeah. He hasn't crossed my thoughts at all, not that way. I suppose I was in love with what he represented. Not him, the actual man, and certainly not the way you love him. So if he makes you happy, I wish you both the best. I really do, Persephone."

The other goddess gave a small bow. "You *are* different. I suppose time will tell if you remain that way. But I've kept you long enough. Goodbye... Esme."

"Goodbye, Persephone, and thank you again. I don't think I can ever say it enough."

Esme descended the floating marble stairs, less disturbed by the lethal drop to the ground now. The guys were in a football huddle and speaking in low voices, but they broke apart when she neared them.

"What are you three up to?"

"Nothing," Luke said.

"Uh huh."

Beau chuckled. "Guess we can't pull anything over on you. We were discussing a gift we've put together. A surprise we planned to reveal before that shit jumped off in the mortal realm."

"Yeah?"

"Since we're already in Olympus, how do you feel about heading over to Aphrodite's palace for a special surprise?" he asked.

"I don't know if I should. Time passes different in this realm, and Marie will lose her shit if I vanish on her again."

Luke smirked. "I already zipped to Marie and told her you're safe with us. I, uh, even sweet-talked your boss a little and told her the attack shook you up. She gave you the week off."

Esme bit her lip. She'd been attacked by a stranger, cursed in her sleep by a divine strife, and had nearly died. Luke hadn't lied. "Okay."

Alex passed her a golden key and directed her to a door in the stairwell. "This will work in any lock, no matter where you are, whether you are at home in Ashfall, at your university, or in my estate. Whenever you need to escape, this place is yours."

Esme slid the key inside and turned it. A low hum vibrated between her fingers, and then the door opened to reveal an impossible scene, a stone courtyard trimmed by fluffy white clouds.

Beyond the courtyard and elaborate steps flanked by

sculptures of beautiful women and cherubs, an extravagant palace of pink marble and gold stretched before her. It floated on the clouds of Olympus and shone with incredible radiance.

When they stepped through and shut the door behind them, all signs of it vanished and left only uninterrupted skyline, clouds, and distant ground far below them. Beau moved ahead of them and disappeared inside.

"This is my palace?"

"Yes. I have made some changes over the years to adopt some modern standards," Alex said. His arm snaked around her waist and drew her close. She stared at every remarkable inch and let the guys guide her up the stairs and inside into an expansive entrance hall with lush carpets, Renaissance style paintings, and tapestries of glorious doves in flight.

"Mom?" The voice echoed before she traced its source.

Across from her, Beau stood between identical, dark-haired twin boys.

"I think Hermes had the right idea about introducing you to Dito alone, so I've decided to bring our kids to you in pairs. This way is better for them and you. Less fighting."

Esme imagined all six divine children vying for her attention, each one pushing to the forefront with desperation to meet her. She stepped forward to meet her sons. They had her eyes. Her old eyes, a deep and serene blue-green like the Mediterranean Sea, framed by thick lashes. "Yes. You're right."

"We didn't mean to scare you," one whispered.

She cupped his cheek. "Phobos?"

He nodded.

Esme kissed his brow and hugged him tight. "I know you didn't."

"We only wanted to see you again," the other boy said.

They were tall now, as tall as her and on the cusp of manhood with hints of masculinity she didn't remember from her previous life. Broader shoulders, a ghost of dark hair above their lips. She hugged Deimos next and squeezed him tight.

"I missed you both so much, but I'm even sorrier that I ever left you behind at all. I can't make up for lost time, for my foolishness but... I *can* promise to never leave you again."

Balancing a mortal life with her divine responsibilities wouldn't be easy, but this time she wouldn't be alone. Wouldn't be torn to choose between three amazing gods. She looked back at her three loves and took strength in their shared bond.

If—no, *when*—Eris came for her again, Esme would be ready.

ABOUT THE AUTHOR

Vivienne Savage is the pen name of two best friends who write everything together. One works as a nurse in a rural healthcare home in Texas and the other is a U.S. Navy veteran. Both are mothers to two darling boys and two amazing girls.

All of their work varies in steam level, so pop by the VS website for details on which series is right for you!

For more information
www.viviennesavage.com
vivi@viviennesavage.com

CPSIA information can be obtained
at www.ICGtesting.com
Printed in the USA
LVHW042348030523
746072LV00014B/228